Don't go to work

The world is ending

Paul Dalton

First published in Great Britain in 2025
by Indie Novella Ltd.

INDIE NOVELLA www.indienovella.co.uk
Hackney, London

Editorial: Kate Pasola; Damien Mosley;

A CIP catalogue record for this title is available from the
British Library
Paperback ISBN 978 1 738 44217 1

Printed and bound by in the United Kingdom.
Indie Novella is committed to a sustainable future for our readers and the world
in which we live. All paper used are natural, renewable and sustainable products.

Indie Novella is grateful that our work is supported using public funding by
Arts Council England.

For Emma

ONE

BENEATH THE PAVEMENT, THE BEECH

Cities aren't buildings, people or culture as most of us think, they're decisions. A place where millions of choices get made every second. The outcomes are infinite, anything can happen, space bends under the weight of decisions being, or not being, made. It's why cities are big.

Jack found himself with a decision that could change everything. But he didn't know any of this at the time and just ordered a katsu curry with a side of steamed dumplings.

The waiter placed the food in front of Jack with a smile. 'Can I get you anything else?' Beads of sweat ran down the waiter's temples. He was wearing a fisherman's beanie despite the blistering spring heat and being miles from the nearest trawler.

'Ketchup?' Jack said.

The waiter did that head tilt that everyone in customer service does when they want to laugh at someone but can't. 'I'll see what I can find.'

Jack was left alone with his curry and dumplings and ate while looking out at London's South Bank. He didn't normally venture into town for dinner but it was Friday night and next week was half term.

This was his tenth year as a teacher at St George's School for Boys. It had started as an evening job, teaching some of the slower pupils physics while he worked on his thesis. The thesis had withered on the vine and he now taught full-time. But, just that morning, he had received word he was to be appointed Acting Head of Physics and thought it important to mark the occasion.

The food was exactly what he needed – an inoffensive sauce covering soft chicken and softer rice. He was back in the womb and safe.

Balancing a dumpling on his chopsticks, he popped the minced vegetable and steamed dough parcel into his mouth. He expected more womb but got something hard and uncompromising instead. Moving the unexpected object around his mouth to gain as much information as he could before deciding how to act, he discovered it was cold, round and tasteless. Resting it on his tongue, he reached for the napkin and spat the object out.

'Here's your ketchup,' the waiter said, making Jack jump. 'Everything OK with your food?'

'Lovely thanks,' Jack replied, pocketing the napkin. Anything that could be fixed with a mouthful of beer wasn't worth complaining about.

The waiter guided a woman to the table next to Jack's. She wore a brown suit two sizes too big with an enamel pin of a duck stuck to the lapel. Jack recognised the suit straight away, any teacher would, it was from Marks and Spencer and sat in that sweet spot of being cheap, not completely ugly and machine washable. Jack wore an older model in grey.

The woman with the duck pin ordered. The waiter congratulated her on her choice and was gone.

Their eyes met. Jack offered a smile to the woman. 'I like your pin.'

She shook her head and started typing a message on her phone.

The rest of the meal passed without incident except, as Jack finished paying, an argument in the kitchen erupted and threatened to spill over onto the restaurant floor.

Jack made his way back to Charing Cross Station. He crossed the river and avoided the young and the drunk on the bridge as best he could. It hadn't rained in months and London was dry. The city and its inhabitants cried out for rain. When it did not come, they drank. They drank to summon the rain gods and keep thoughts of the coming storm at bay. Medieval peasants had whipped themselves into a frenzy at the thought of the end of the world but their descendants chose liver damage and dancing. Jack didn't blame them; he had a bottle of white waiting for him at home and not a lot else.

Like most people who moved to London from elsewhere, Jack lived as far out as he could manage. Close enough that you could still tell people, and convince yourself, that you lived in London but somewhere quiet enough that you could still get a good night's sleep. For Jack, this meant a one-bed in Catford. He had tried housemates but finding good ones was like capturing lightning in a bottle. His attempts had always ended with migraines in jam jars.

· · ·

Jack walked along the Charing Cross concourse and saw Theo, a biology teacher from St George's. Jack looked for an escape amongst the greeting card shops and Cornish Pasty stalls. It wasn't that Jack didn't like Theo, it was just that Theo knew more than one way to tie a tie, he could say witty things in Latin and had opinions on different types of ski bindings. Whereas Jack fell into teaching, Theo was thrown in gagged and bound and spent most of the time climbing the walls desperate to get out. He wasn't the type of person you wanted to bump into after a meal for one on a Friday night.

Jack squeezed past an 'out of order' sign and headed into the gent's loos. Surely they couldn't all be broken?

The toilets of Charing Cross are accessed by going down a set of stairs and have no natural light or ventilation. This gives the space a timeless quality, which is to say, a hopeless, never-ending present quality. Train announcements drifted down from the platform and skimmed off the porcelain tiles as Jack washed his hands. He checked his watch, his train was due in one minute which meant he had at least six. People complained about British trains but you don't need them to be on time, just consistent, and the train to Catford was consistently five minutes late. Jack finished up, and another man who had thrown caution to the wind approached the sinks. Growing up where London meets Essex Jack had developed a sixth, seventh and eighth sense for spotting trouble. This man was trouble.

'Enjoy your dinner?' the man asked.

Jack fixed a smile and nodded. If you don't say anything they generally stop talking to you.

The man turned and faced Jack. Jack glanced around the room; it was just the two of them.

'Where is it?' the man asked.

'Sorry?'

The man took a step towards Jack. His breath smelt of katsu and dumplings.

Two things happened at once. The man reached for Jack's pocket and Jack bolted for the exit. This was followed by a third thing: Jack tripping over a hole in the floor that he could've sworn wasn't there before, but would explain the out-of-order sign. Jack rolled onto his back. His head pounded and he blinked hard to focus his vision. The man stood over him and passed a chunk of fused cement and floor tile from his right hand to his left and back again. 'Where is it?'

Jack wished he had it, whatever it was. Cautious footsteps echoed on the stairs leading down to the toilets. Jack emptied his pockets onto the floor as a plea for mercy. His phone, work pass and keys, even the restaurant napkin.

The man smiled. 'That wasn't so hard now was it.' 'He reached down to take his loot and his hand disappeared. There was no noise, no flash of light. The hand simply vanished. The man yelled more in surprise than pain and stumbled backwards. A figure ran over to Jack and tossed a detached hand at him while simultaneously pocketing the napkin. The woman with the duck pin.

'Look after that would you,' she said.

Jack crawled backwards along brown tiles damp with condensation and hopefully not much else. Cowering in the corner he gripped the severed hand tight while Duck Pin went toe-to-toe with the now one-handed man. The only exit was behind the brawl and may as well have been a million miles away.

Great sweeping blows from the man's good hand — now a fist — kept Duck Pin dodging and unable to hit back. The man turned to keep up with Duck Pin and slipped on Jack's work pass. A lapse in concentration followed by a jab from Duck Pin and he collapsed on the floor, out cold. Duck Pin caught her breath before walking towards Jack with an unsettlingly friendly smile. A shadow on the stairs. A woman in a garish yellow paisley suit crept behind Duck Pin with a knife gleaming in the dark.

Adrenaline became reckless bravery, Jack dropped the severed hand and tackled the newcomer to the ground, she was strong and twisted out of his grip. They locked eyes and Jack knew how the first one-celled organism felt when it came face to face with a two-cell organism. Duck Pin grabbed Jack by the arm and pulled him up the stairs.

Life continued on the concourse with workers going home and drinkers going out.

Duck Pin turned to Jack. 'Run.'

Jack pounded up Charing Cross Road trying to keep up with Duck Pin. He dared a look back and saw The Woman in The Paisley Suit tracking them through the crowds. It was too busy to run so instead they pushed and squeezed their way north into Soho.

'What are you doing?' Duck Pin called out.

Jack stepped into the road to avoid a hen party mocking a man's choice to pair salmon pink trousers with a navy blue shirt. 'Following you.'

'Why?'

'You told me to.'

'No, I didn't.'

The Woman in The Paisley Suit was catching up fast. Jack

replayed the events at the train station. 'Where are we going?' he said, hoping to change the subject.

Jack and Duck Pin stood in the doorway on a deserted side street somewhere in Soho. The Woman in The Paisley Suit stood at the end of the road. She had lost them when a theatre had kicked out for half time and caused an impregnable wall of people to swarm into the street buying them just enough time to hide. The sounds of revellers summoning rain filled the air.

'I'm Jack by the way.'

'Muriel,' Duck Pin said.

'Who's chasing us? And what did you do to his hand?'

Muriel kept her eyes on the end of the road as The Woman in The Paisley Suit moved out of sight. 'Not sure, elves will work for anyone and you wouldn't't believe me.'

Jack laughed. 'Elves?'

'Didn't you spot her ears?' Muriel mimed points coming from the top of her own ears.

'I had other things on my mind, to be honest.'

Muriel decided The Elf in The Paisley Suit was gone and stepped out.

Jack followed. 'And the hand?'

'Magic.'

'If you don't want to tell me you don't have to.' Jack said. 'Where are you going?'

'To hide, you coming?'

Theo knew it wasn't going to be a normal job interview. Meeting at night was fine. The bag over the head was fine. Being thrown in a van and driven halfway across London was borderline but acceptable. Theo was used to high jinks from his schooldays at St George's but being dragged backwards up two flights of stairs without much care was a bit much. Even Big Seb and his gang knew there was a line.

Unseen hands removed the bag and Theo found himself sitting alone in front of a desk. Wood panelling covered the walls of the room and a green carpet spread out beneath his feet. Hammering and the other noises that come with building work drifted up through the floor. *Builders at night*, his cousin must be doing something right to afford that. He dared a look over his shoulder and found a shell of a room; the carpet didn't extend much further than his chair and most of the wood panelling had been removed. The desk was old. The top carved from a single piece of wood and covered in handwritten notes.

His phone felt heavy in his trouser pocket. He caressed it through the faded material. Pulling out the phone, he scrolled until he found his banking app. The app connected. He needed this to go well. A very small number flashed onto the screen and caused Theo's lungs to deflate. He needed this to go very well.

A door behind Theo flew open and he shoved the phone back into his pocket. Mimi, dressed immaculately in red, glided into the room. He knew class when he saw it because he had it, and she did too. They hadn't seen each other since they were young, perhaps four or five, before being sent off to their respective boarding schools. And once their parents had an agreement to alternate summers at the chalet, childhood became adulthood very quickly and they were strangers in all but blood.

'Sorry to keep you waiting,' Mimi said without a hint of sincerity.

He offered a hand that went un-shook. The impression of her gliding grew as she floated behind the desk and sat. Her chair did not creak. Seated, she somehow seemed taller than when she was standing. Her eyes locked on Theo and he swayed in the breeze.

'Tell me,' she said, 'this seems an unusual job for a failed banker turned teacher. Why do you want it?'

He was failing as a teacher too. He was too much of a free thinker for management. They preferred teachers who nodded along and said nothing. They had even given a promotion to that idiot in physics who Theo had once found hiding from students in the stationary cupboard.

'I wouldn't say I failed as a banker, the markets crashed. Science was always my first love and when Uncle Harry told me about your little project, I asked him to put in a word.'

She smirked at his version of events. 'What did he tell you?'

'Not a lot, you had a new venture you were struggling with and needed a scientist you could trust.'

'So you're here out of family loyalty?'

'No, just the chance to get into research,' he paused, 'and the pay of course.'

She considered this. 'Honest at least, this could work. Now a thought experiment for you-'

'-oh fun.'

'Don't interrupt. Arthur C. Clarke said, "Any sufficiently advanced technology is indistinguishable from magic." Do you agree?' she asked.

He crossed his legs. 'Yes, I suppose so. A washing machine or television would be beyond the comprehension of someone born thousands of years ago and would appear to be magical.'

'Would knowledge of the concept mean the concept no longer applies?'

His mouth opened but he had nothing. 'What do you mean?'

She grew impatient and tapped her perfect fingernails on the desk. 'You agree that an advanced technology could appear magical to primitive people, yes?'

'Yes.'

'Good.' She stood and walked to the far end of the room. Theo twisted left and right in his seat to try and maintain eye contact. 'You can stand up,' she said. Theo didn't see but could almost hear the eye roll. He had to do better, this wasn't his job yet. 'So,' she said opening the door, 'if you came across an item that could do things far beyond our understanding of what is possible, would you believe it to be magic and unknowable or, because of Arthur's famous line, something that could be studied and learnt from?' The door opened onto a set of stairs heading down into a poorly lit hallway.

Theo stood and took quick strides to catch up. 'I see what you mean, yes. You could approach it more rationally than someone who had never considered that technology and magic are the same.'

She led the way and they emerged onto a landing bright with the glare of builder's work lamps. They continued down another flight of stairs and Theo peered into the rooms as they went and saw a mass of workmen stripping the building of every socket, skirting board and light switch. They ripped wallpaper off the walls and smashed furniture. 'Do you think the same applies to biology?' she asked.

'Biology?'

Builders stood flat against the wall as they, or rather she, walked past.

'Forget ray guns and wormholes. What if you came across a creature that broke all the rules of what you know a creature to be? Would it be magical or just something else that could be studied rationally?'

They passed the ground floor and headed through a locked door and into the basement. Sheets of plasterboard rested against bare walls. A clinical light from a single halogen lamp and the smell of damp filled the space. Theo wrinkled his nose.

'I would do something about that but I don't want the builders down here for reasons that will soon become apparent, but back to my question.'

Sense began to creep back into Theo's brain. Whatever was going on here was likely to end badly but history was full of brave men doing foolish things and bringing prosperity for generations to come. His family had had one such man and now it needed another. 'Yes, but living creatures are already pretty strange if you think about it: Dinosaurs, chameleons, anglerfish. Biologists are dealing with a far stranger data set than physicists or engineers. We're pretty open-minded to begin with, nature is already supernatural.'

'I'm glad to hear it.' She slid back a sheet of plasterboard. A tunnel had been dug deep into the soft London clay.

Nisha was an artist. A year at college before university, three years on her undergraduate degree and another year doing a master's. Nisha was an artist so she waited tables in a restaurant. She had grand plans to write an opera based on the music of Jona Lewie. She was going to try and kill a tardigrade with kindness, the only thing no one had tried. But right now she could barely afford paper so made do with the back of old order slips. Closing her eyes, she tried to draw the sounds of the kitchen on the back of an order for two prawn dhansaks and a bottle of rose. If you listened, the room had a rhythm, endless onions being tapped off endless wooden spoons, the whirl of fans, both oven and extractor, and the constant yelling added a top note. She went to put pen to paper when someone shouted her name.

'I can give this to someone else if you want, clearly you don't need the tips,' Chef said, looming over her in his whites. Speckled with food from a thousand dinners his jacket looked like an edible Jackson Pollock. Nisha was never sure if she should frame it or report it to the council.

She looked at the ceiling. 'No.'

'Pardon?'

'No, Chef.'

'Good, take these.'

Nisha fixed her smile in the mirror before entering the private dining room. The room, and the rest of the restaurant for that matter, was filled with paraphernalia intended to soothe customers with a history that didn't exist. Smiling sepoys, moustachioed white saviours delivering civilisation from the back of elephants, photos of English ladies in crisp linen teaching the gospel to willing ears.

The only table in the room could fit twenty but tonight only two seats were filled: A woman, facing the kitchen and wearing a bright red suit, and a man sat opposite in a faded two-piece suit. It was rare for people to book the private dining room for dates but not unheard of. Judging by the man's clothes he needed all the help he could get.

'And then what happened?' the man asked. A few years ago Nisha would have described him as old but now she would say early middle age. She was becoming all too aware that twenty-nine is a lot closer to forty than twenty-one in all the ways that mattered.

'I went down as far as his knuckle and he passed out from

the pain.' The woman's voice was slate, the result of a thousand years of breeding, designed to strike fear and respect into the population. The man's laugh said she was buying dinner so maybe not a date.

'It's strange, the different paths we've taken, you with your little business and me with my science,' the man said.

The woman offered a brusque smile in response to this statement.

'I mean,' the man continued, 'it's not a normal line of work for someone in our family to go into but you seemed to have made a go at it.'

'I disagree, my side of the family has always been ambitious. You remember that great-great-uncle or whatever, Francis I think, gave the Spanish a lot of trouble and got in with the queen because of it. Some called him a pirate but you're only a pirate until you get a Royal Warrant — then you're in import-export.'

'That's a way of looking at it.'

Passive aggression, bragging and tension. Nisha knew a family reunion when she saw one.

Crisp poppadoms, fresh from the fryer, were placed between the diners and Nisha poured them each a glass of wine. Nisha chanced a smile at the woman who didn't so much ignore her as fail to comprehend her existence. *So much for the tips.*

'Even if the food isn't great, at least you don't have to worry about being overheard in a place like this,' the man said as Nisha turned to leave.

A bag of potatoes was dropped in Nisha's arms and Chef turned without waiting for a reply.

'Yes, Chef.'

She contemplated carving the potatoes into different appendages so when Mrs Goodwin — down from Boston Spa for a slice of London life — looked down at her Chana Aloo she'd get an eyeful of stiffened starch.

The woman in red ran her finger around the rim of her glass while the man spoke: 'If it does what it seems to do at face value...'

Nisha approached with two platters of chicken tikka and a bowl of rice to share. The woman flicked her wrist and the man continued. 'Then it will just be a case of finding what triggers it in the body, stomach enzymes for example, and distilling it. Then you could use it as needed.'

He could be an inventor, it would explain the faded clothes and not being able to afford dinner. The woman had the cheek-bones of someone who took other people's ideas and made money from them. Maybe they were working on some new health gimmick for the rich and old: *Is the slow march of time getting you down? Live forever for only two hundred pounds a month.*

Nisha topped up their glasses with more wine.

'I'm glad you're confident,' the woman in red said. 'We have a lot of tissue but I would hate to waste any.'

'Oh no, I think this will be quite simple really.'

Nisha spooned some of the steaming rice onto their waiting plates and turned to leave with the leftover. A hand grabbed her wrist, the woman leaned in and stared. 'Leave the rice.' Nisha feigned confusion, gave a deep nod and placed the rice on the table with a smile. An old waitressing trick: let the customer think they are teaching you how to do your job. If you're lucky they take on the role of a mentor. If not, they pity you and anything you get right is considered a boon.

Nisha returned to her pile of old order slips and wrote down 'source stomach enzymes'. She could place one of her old paintings from university in a vat of the stuff and call it: *The artist consumes their work in lieu of payment.*

'Nisha! I swear to God do some work.'

'Yes, Chef.'

She re-read her idea and underlined it. It was a keeper.

Plates hot from the heat lamp burned Nisha's hands as she passed into the dining room for the final course. She placed their fig strudels on the table and rubbed the heat from her hand onto her skirt while she poured the last of the wine.

The man cracked the pastry on his dessert with the back of his spoon. 'What will you do once you have all that power?'

Nisha waited until they had ignored her for the correct amount of time to show there was nothing else they needed before backing away — another old waitressing trick.

'Change people's minds. For anything to change, people need to be open to different ways of living. Humans are infinitely adaptable and have invented so many ways of existing yet we seem stuck in the same endless cycles of stupidity. There's no one out there saying: "Let's try something new". I want to try something new,' the woman said.

'And bring everyone along with you, very clever,' the man said.

Nisha stood by the kitchen doors and listened.

Jack had never been to war, in fact, he came from a long line of cowards and cheats but ordering two pints in a Soho pub during a heatwave must count for something. Bodies surged towards the bar as those at the back pushed their countrymen onwards. They hadn't seen what those at the front had seen but their time would come. *Their time would come.* Two wide-eyed boys stood behind the bar, barely old enough to serve, holding back the horde as best they could. There was no blame exchanged across the divide. It was Soho in a heatwave; no one wanted to be here.

Jack returned from active service and placed two pints on the table pushing their empties to one side. 'Giants?'

'No,' Muriel said, clinking Jack's glass.

'Goblins.'

'Yes, they look almost human but have big ridges on their head, anyone wearing a beanie in the summer is probably a goblin, or going bald. You probably see one every day.'

He knew about Elves. 'Do I see Elves every day?'

'Maybe, depends on the pubs you go into.'

'Witches?'

'How many of these have you got? And depends on what you mean. Women who can do magic? Obviously. Devil worshippers? Also yes but they aren't mutually exclusive.'

'Only a few more and Devils are real?' Jack said, looking around the pub trying to spot an elf.

'Yes, but they aren't evil as such, they're like cats. Cats knock stuff over and kill mice but they aren't evil, they're just being cats. It's the same with devils except it's burning churches and eating children.' She put her glass down and glanced at the door. 'Why did you get involved back there?'

He shrugged. 'You seemed like you might need some help.'

She repressed something under a smile. 'Thanks, but you've got yourself messed up in something complicated. They'll think you're involved now.'

'Involved in what?'

Her hand went to her jacket pocket.

'What is that?' Jack asked.

'I don't know, but we've heard rumours of something big starting.' She moved her hand back. Her eyes tracked a man too old to be wearing double denim stumbling past their table on his way to the loo.

'Who's we?'

'The people I work for, they're a group. Well, they're two people, but I work for them and they try and stop bad things from happening. They might be able to help you, put the word out that you were a bystander and just did something silly. Keep you safe and out of all this.'

Jack picked up his pint. 'Was it silly or brave?'

'Silly,' she said. 'But you can help me get this to their place tomorrow.'

'Like Frodo,' Jack said, wide-eyed.

'What?'

'Frodo? From Lord of the Rings? Taking the ring to Rivendell, you've not read it?' He was speaking louder than he intended. 'You've not read Lord of the Rings and you're a magic policeman?'

'I'm not a policeman on two accounts and I tried to read it but I don't read books about rich people.'

'Sorry?'

She took a sip of beer. 'Bilbo left him that big house in the country, stocked larder, all those waistcoats. Classic trust fund kid. It wasn't for me. Besides, those kinds of books are a bit of a busman's holiday for me,' she said. 'What do you do?'

'I teach physics at St George's.'

'Ok. So I bet you don't watch documentaries about Isaac Newton on your day off.'

'Well yeah, but he's trash, got lucky that one time. Frodo's a badass.'

She turned to face him. 'Issac Newton could beat Frodo one on one.'

'Frodo's got the ring, Newton wouldn't see him coming.'

'It's not about magic it's about reach, Frodo couldn't land a punch, besides at least Issac Newton is real.'

'Is Frodo not real?' Jack asked.

Her glass stopped on its way to her mouth. 'Are you asking if Lord of the Rings is real because you've just seen an elf?'

He paused. 'No.'

The door to the pub was bolted shut behind Jack and Muriel. The panic and fear of a few hours ago had dissolved into a distant memory and belonged to a different time. A drunken debate about the inherent classism in a beloved fantasy novel is a great way to forget your worries. Jack, adamant he was standing perfectly still, checked his watch, everywhere would be shutting or ringing last orders.

'So,' Muriel said, standing perfectly still. 'What I'm about to say I say as a professional. I may have had six pints.'

'Seven.'

'Seven pints.'

'And that retro cocktail thing.'

'Old Fashioned and let me finish. I may have had seven pints and an Old Fashioned but you should come back to mine and sleep on my sofa. That Elf in The Paisley Suit is out there somewhere and she might still be looking for us. We can go straight to The Shed in the morning and get you on your way. Back to your life.'

Jack was in no rush to get back to his life. 'Only if we get a kebab first.'

Muriel pointed Jack towards the purgatory of Piccadilly Circus at night and the bus stop.

Two

The butter, reading the room, sunk into Jack's slice of toast. Jack clasped a cup of tea in Muriel's kitchen and wondered what the other Jack was doing. The one that went for pizza last night instead of Japanese. You can't hide anything in pizza, something he would remember for next time. Maybe the hangover was dulling his capacity to panic but he seemed to be coping with the existence of magic and elves and such quite well. If he was being honest with himself it made as much sense as quarks, photons, and plektons. If he could trust in Pentaquarks then why not Pentagrams?

Truth be told, he was more disturbed by the knitted duck tea cosy staring at him across the gallery kitchen. It stood between him and the living room and it was a close call if he could get past it in his current state unscathed. Not that the living room was any better — mallards, geese and possibly moorhens guarded that room as well. Paintings, photos, cushions, and even the lampshades were printed with waterfowl.

He took a deep breath. Holding the tea and toast as a sword and shield he stepped forward.

'Morning.'

The tea went up and the toast down but he breathed easy when it turned out to be Muriel.

'Morning,' he said, picking up the toast and popping it back onto the plate. 'I helped myself, hope you don't mind.'

'No worries. How was the sofa?' she asked stepping past him on the way to the kettle.

Jack thought back to night — the moonlight reflecting on the duck bookends would haunt him forever. 'Fine. Thanks for suggesting I stay, I'm too old for the night bus anyway.'

She filled the kettle. 'And too drunk, god knows where you would have ended up or who would have found you.'

Chislehurst. It had happened before and the ducks were preferable.

Jack sat on the mallard green sofa while Muriel made herself some cereal; he scanned the room for somewhere to look that wouldn't look back. It had been a long time since Jack had been in someone else's home and he had forgotten how much life people can accumulate. Four copies of the same book from four different flat shares, a bottle of strange liqueur on the side that didn't taste the same after you got back from holiday and a kitchen appliance still in the box tucked under a chair, no doubt a gift from a well-meaning relative that had no idea how small London flats could be.

'How are you feeling after last night?' Muriel asked, taking a seat on the opposite sofa.

'Couple of paracetamols and I'll be fine.'

'No, I mean about being a wanted man.'

'Am I though? I'm just some guy. I don't even have the thing anymore.'

Muriel made a noise that said she disagreed. 'Yes, but distinctions like that aren't often made in the criminal underworld. It's more slash and burn.'

Jack ate his toast instead of saying anything. The words slash and burn had penetrated his hangover and were running amok. Things like this didn't happen to Jack, he had a routine, he had a system: work home work home. He tried not to break this routine unless he had to. He didn't move to London for the theatre, he moved here for the public transport after that incident on his driving test with the police van. Jack had his world and things like this weren't meant to happen in it. But it was half term and he could afford a day or two out of his normal routine in order to not be slashed or burned.

'Don't worry,' Muriel said. 'We'll have this sorted by the end of the day. My bosses are very well-connected and very respected. You'll be in the clear in time for dinner.'

Jack offered her a smile. 'Great.'

They ate the rest of breakfast in silence, their hangovers lounging over them, muffling thoughts and conversation.

Muriel put her empty bowl on the floor. 'I'm going to shower unless you need it first?' Jack shook his head and took a bite of his toast.

He glanced at her jacket hanging on the door, its pocket still containing the napkin and whatever he had nearly eaten from last night. He took another bite of toast. The sound of teeth crushing burnt bread filled his head. If his life was in danger he might as well know what was in the napkin. He glanced again. A duck gave him a look. A moorhen told him it wouldn't hurt to have a peek. He'd just make some more toast. Bread bin, plastic bag, toaster down, gentle steps to the jacket before it's too late. The shower sang through the bathroom door. Swallowing his heart, Jack pried open the napkin. Inside, a small pebble, polished to a high sheen, reflected a blurred version of Jack back at himself.

He gave it a rub and the image became clearer. The pebble version of Jack stood in a white void and jumped when he saw he was being observed. Pebble Jack walked backwards and away from the real Jack. Pebble Jack then broke into a run until he became a smudge of a man in the distance and disappeared completely. Jack peered to the left and the right to see if there was more. There wasn't. He frowned, he hoped it might be a sparkling ruby that granted wishes or a god trapped in a chuck of amber. Not a small man running away from himself.

The pebble turned a deep orange. Moving on strange currents, flecks of gold danced beneath the surface. In the centre sat a tiny figure on a throne of carved ivory. His flowing robes and glorious beard suspended in time.

The shower stopped.

Jack folded the pebble back into the napkin and ran as quietly as he could back to the toaster.

'Shower's all yours,' Muriel said on the way to her bedroom.

'Thanks,' Jack said, buttering another slice of toast.

The Elf in The Paisley Suit turned right out of Chigwell Tube station and headed north. It was that quiet spot when the weekend workers had finished their rush hour and the leisure classes weren't heading out for brunch yet. The carnations she brought from the supermarket smelled of false spring. She knew Frank wouldn't care, retirement gifts were never well received. The motorway hummed in the distance giving the sensation that the peaceful suburb could take off at any moment. She checked her A to Z before turning down a few streets of Victorian terraces, trackable GPS wasn't for a job like this.

The house looked the same as any other on the street, murky bricks and a front garden turned into a driveway. Someone had painted the door a grown-up blue and attempted some window boxes. She checked the house number and rang the bell. She jogged on the spot releasing some nervous energy, it never got easier but then it never got harder either. The lock clicked open and her game face slid into place. It was a reflex, she was no longer herself. She was the work version of herself, this version didn't have nervous energy or concerns beyond the moment. This version got paid very well which both versions of her enjoyed.

A figure silhouetted by the hallway light stood in the doorway. The stump where a hand should be told her who it was.

'Hello Frank, is the family in?'

For a moment it appeared rigor mortis had already set in but then his shoulders slumped and he was alive again. 'Is this business or pleasure as I'm retired now.' He held up the stump where his hand should be.

'A bit of both, but it's worth your time. I promise.'

He turned without a word and walked into the living room.

She knew the living room was on the left as she had grown up in an identical house a few miles south. Everyone had the living room on the left, the toilet backed onto the kitchen in the converted coal shed with Mum and Dad in the big bedroom at the front. She closed the door and flicked the latch. The hallway was bog roll pink.

'Lovely shade of pink in the hallway, very brave.'

Frank sat in a faded armchair which took up most of the

tiny room and said nothing. As a sign of respect, he had muted the TV.

'May I?' she gestured to the sofa but didn't wait for a reply. 'How long has it been since you joined the other firm?'

'Coming on five years,' he said. 'You were just a fledging when I left. How's Collapsing Cliff Cartwright?'

'Dead,' The Paisley Elf replied.

'Oh?'

'He had a job down near Dover,' she said. 'Perry Winkle had been talking to police about the Cambridge Job and been moved to the coast for his own protection.'

'Right.'

'So Cliff finds out where Perry's hiding and it's this big house, middle of nowhere, right up on the cliffs.'

Frank nodded along.

'Perry spots Cliff and runs off, as you would. Cliff is chasing him across the actual White Cliffs of Dover. The wind is howling, driving rain, the lot.'

Frank whistled. 'It's why you get into the job, isn't it? Days like that. What happened next?'

She shrugged. 'He catches up with Perry so Perry climbs over the fence and is running along the very edge of the cliff now. God knows what he's thinking.'

Frank nodded along, eyes wide.

'Then there's a big gust of wind.'

'Yeah?'

'And Perry falls over the edge into the sea.'

Frank looked confused. 'But how did Cliff die?'

'Oh, hit by a bus on the way back.'

Frank burst into laughter. 'Good. Never liked the guy.'

She crossed her legs. 'You've probably guessed why I'm here.'

He nodded and the small talk was over.

'Mimi wants you to know there's no hard feelings about you switching sides all those years ago, it was just business. But I've got some questions about last night. In exchange for some answers, your family will get one of these,' she pulled out a small bar of gold and threw it into his lap. 'Every Christmas until your youngest turns eighteen.'

Frank held the gold bar up to the light as if it were a totem or a gift from the gods. In some ways it was, pensions were rare in this line of work.

'But you also need to retire. Permanently.'

His head tilted to one side. 'Seems harsh.'

'Mimi wants this shut down. Most of your former colleagues are having eventful mornings as we speak. Anyone with even a whiff of it is to be taken out of the game, with or without answering questions.' She scratched at what was probably dried blood on her suit while he mulled the decision over. It was an easy choice but not everyone took it. Some of her colleagues had spent their whole lives fighting the world and having it fight back. Most didn't throw the first punch but they wanted to try to throw the last.

'Ok,' he said, something in him deflated. 'But I need a favour before I answer any questions.'

'Go on.'

He stood, walked to the chimney breast and pointed to a brick with his good hand. "Can you pull that out?"

Without getting up from the sofa, she held out her hand and the brick appeared in her palm. A small alcove had appeared in the brickwork, space for a few things that it would be useful to forget about when the inheritance tax had to be paid. He placed the gold bar in the alcove and nodded.

The Paisley Elf walked across the room and slid the brick

back into place. It fit perfectly, barring a chisel the only way to move it would be magic. Something Frank could no longer do but presumably his wife could.

'Let's start with what I know and then move on to what you know,' she said, returning to the sofa. 'I know some of Mimi's property had been stolen and was being exchanged at the restaurant. I turn up and spot you having some dinner which I know is not a coincidence. Am I right so far?'

He nodded.

'So let's start there. What was the job?'

'It was meant to be simple. Go to the restaurant and order a katsu curry with a side of dumplings and take whatever was inside back to the boss.'

'Inside?'

'In the dumplings, there was meant to be a package of some kind. Seemed a bit dramatic for my tastes but you know how management can be.'

She smiled and he continued: 'That's it, I don't know what the package was, where it's from or where it is now.'

'That's good, so what went wrong?'

'My dumplings were uneventful but I noticed some guy struggling to chew and slip something into his napkin and then his pocket, so I followed him back to Charing Cross.'

This tallies with what she saw, she had waited outside and didn't give the napkin guy a second look as he seemed like a civilian but that must have been who she chased through Soho.

'I give him a scare and go to grab the damn thing when some woman swoops in and does this.' He held up his arm. 'And takes me out the game.'

'Did you get a good look at them?'

'She wasn't young, about your age. Gangly with red hair.'

She would ignore that. 'And the guy?'

'Looked like an elder tree in a cheap suit. Either very good at playing dumb or just plain dumb. I could probably point him out if you wanted some help,' he said scratching his stump with a hopeful look in his eyes.

These must have been the same people she chased. She stood, took off her jacket and folded it neatly before placing it on the sofa. 'You know that's not how this works but I'll be sure to tell Mimi you were very cooperative.'

Frank pulled himself out of the chair, and he winced as he put weight on his wound without thinking. 'What will you do now?'

'I'll start with the Gods, I'd rather not deal with Foresight unless I have to.'

Trying not to get blood on the sink, The Elf in The Paisley Suit picked up the bar of soap with the tips of her fingers. The soap mixing with the blood had turned her hands bright pink. She gave them a sniff, sandalwood and expensive at that, *you always were full of surprises, Frank*. She washed the soapy blood away and rinsed her hands again to make sure. Killing never bothered her. The job isn't to be good at killing people — which is surprisingly easy — what's hard is forgetting about it afterwards. That's what she was good at, forgetting. Once she was done here she would step outside and forget what happened, she would forget Frank, she would forget his blood and his crying. When she first started the job she tried to repress it, bury it deep but keep it somewhere so she could learn from it and get better but after a while, she realised there wasn't much to learn.

She chose the dirtier of the two tea towels to dry her hands, the last thing Frank's wife needed was two dirty tea towels. She picked up the carnations and searched for a pair of scissors before giving up and holding out her palm, the bottom few inches of the flower stems fell away and dropped into her hand. Magic never got old, not really. She threw the bottom of the stems in the bin, spotted an empty milk carton, gave it a rinse and arranged the flowers in the makeshift vase. The room looked tidy but she gave it one last pass, straightening the tea towels and wiping crumbs onto the floor. She worked her way around to the sink and her eyes lingered on the bar of expensive soap.

Jack and Muriel got the train from Waterloo to the far reaches of South West London. It was the land of magnolias and parakeets. Victorian mansions besieged by postwar sprawl. It reminded Jack of Essex, except no one knew how to have any fun.

'Your boss is all the way out here?' Jack said as they approached a rusted chainlink gate leading to an allotment. They'd got off the train at a small suburban station about half an hour from town. Still London, but far enough out that you could live your whole life without ever needing to go into the middle. Jack liked it. He bet no one here accidentally ate magic pebbles and got chased through Central London by gangsters.

'Bosses, there's two of them. They like to be near trees and this part of London has the most, it's good for their chi apparently.' Muriel's look implied that she wouldn't be answering any more questions on that. She opened the lock on the gate and waved Jack in.

'And these guys are the police?'

'Not really, no one's in charge enough to call themselves the police but they, we, try to keep a lid on anything too loud. The Laurels — that's what they call themselves — never venture out but there's a group of us, myself included, who try to keep things in order,' she said with pride. She shut the padlock with a click behind them and tested it with a shake.

The last time Jack had set foot on an allotment, he had fled at the first opportunity. One sunny weekend he had put his name down on the waiting list for his local site. The website estimated the waiting time to be over twenty years and implied only a fool would add to it. Jack had added his name anyway as waiting twenty years to start a hobby gave you carte blanche to spend the next two decades scrolling aimlessly on your phone and pretending you would go outside if only you had something to do. To Jack's surprise, a spot opened up after a few months. It turned out that most of the people on the list had died, presumably while scrolling aimlessly on their phones. He had turned up on the first day to be met with treacle-thick enthusiasm from the other plot holders. Invites to AGMs, beekeeping courses, and even a birthday party. It was all too much and Jack had never returned. 'So what do The Laurels do?' He said.

'Listen mostly.'

Jack nodded as if he knew what that meant. 'How do you do this? You must have rent to pay.'

'One of the things they listen to is the stock market.'

They exchanged a smile with a woman laden with courgettes heading for the exit.

'That doesn't seem very magical,' Jack said.

'Making money out of thin air is about the most magical thing you can do.'

Jack conceded the point. The allotment site was like any other: plots in various states of use, each an expression of the owner's soul. Union Jacks, wind chimes and bug hotels all stood side by side. Neatly trimmed verges fought wildlife havens and old tyres.

About halfway down, taking up most of a plot, sat an ancient apple tree. its trunk thick and draped in moss, its upper branches casting shade onto the nearby houses. Under the tree sat a small shed painted blue with yellowing net curtains hung in a Perspex window.

Muriel turned down a gnome-lined path towards the shed.

'Here?'

'Why, what were you expecting?' she said, watching the uneven ground.

'I don't know, a stone circle or something.'

'Would be a bit obvious, wouldn't it?'

Muriel's knock on the shed door was answered by an elderly man in a pink cardigan.

'Muriel my love, how are you? Come in come in,' he said, not waiting for, or expecting, an answer to his question.

'Who is it, Nigel?' a voice asked.

'It's Muriel, Denise.'

'Well let her in, don't leave her standing out there for goodness sake.' Denise appeared at the door matching Nigel in outfit and age. 'Sorry about him.' Her face brightened when she saw Jack. 'And who's your gentleman friend?'

'I'm Jack.'

'Enchanté.' Her hand reached out for a kiss.

Not a single atom on Muriel's face moved. He was on his own. Jack leant in before thinking twice and gave it a gentle shake instead. Denise's smile dropped for a moment before she recovered and invited them in.

The shed was full of rusted tools, the smell of turps and

faded plastic garden furniture, of which, two chairs were offered to Jack and Muriel.

'Cup of tea?' Nigel said, he pulled a bone-white mug of tea out of nowhere and placed it in Jack's hand. Nigel and Denise fussed over Muriel for a moment and Jack took in the shed. It was a perfectly normal shed and not what he imagined the headquarters of a secret group of vigilantes who protect the country from magical threats to look like. The only nod to a workplace, or at least workplace humour, was a faded Keep Calm and Carry On poster on the wall.

'What do you do, Jack?' Denise asked, jolting Jack back into the room.

'I'm a teacher at St George's,' he said.

Denise hit Nigel on the arm. 'No? St George's? Very nice. Did you hear that, Nigel?'

'Doesn't the Prime Minister's son go there?' Nigel said, equally impressed.

As did the Prime Minister and his dad. 'We're not really meant to talk about it,' Jack replied.

Nigel tapped the side of his nose and gave Jack a wink that implied they shared a secret about the education of prime ministers and their sons.

'Anyway,' Muriel said.

'Yes. Tell us about last night,' Denise said with a subtle nod in Jack's direction. 'Seems eventful.'

'It was mixed,' Muriel said with a sigh. 'I got this.' Muriel pulled out the napkin from her pocket and passed it to them. The Laurels looked inside the napkin and then looked at each other with barely contained excitement.

'What do you know about The Dragon?' Nigel said. He held the pebble up to the light. The bearded man and tiny Jack were both gone. Instead, the pebble's reflective surface took on a rosy hue.

The question seemed to throw Muriel for a moment. 'They're big and scary. Breathe fire if the stories are to be believed.'

'Yes and no. It is big, scary and can definitely breathe fire but it's also singular, there is only one dragon and this is one of its scales. Was only one dragon, I should say. And it's somewhere under London,' Denise said taking the scale from Nigel and placing it on a shelf next to an old lawnmower blade and jar of nails.

'A dragon?' Jack said.

'This feels like the middle of a story,' Muriel said.

'I guess it was the end until you brought that in here. Somewhere under London is the corpse of The Dragon,' Denise said.

'The beginning was 1666 when it attacked London,' Nigel said.

'The fire?' Muriel asked.

'A dragon?' Jack tried again.

The Laurels nodded.

Denise suddenly had a plate of custard creams in her hand and placed them under Muriel's face; she performed a patient smile and took one.

'But that was a baker,' Jack said, feeling like he should say something else.

Nigel took a biscuit. 'No, it was The Dragon but we chose to pretend it wasn't.'

'Sorry?' Jack said.

Denise offered the plate to Jack's nose and his hand accepted.

Nigel shifted and crossed his arms, his biscuit uneaten. 'PTSD, repressed memories. These things aren't new, we just

33

have words for them now. You have to remember this was the 1600s, witch hunts were still in living memory and standing up and saying you saw a dragon could be a quick way to the end of a rope.' He took a bite of the custard cream.

'It would disappear for years, centuries at a time before returning and razing a city to the ground. Rome, Moscow, Stockholm to name a few,' Denise said.

Jack leant forward and pointed at the plate of biscuits. His hangover needed feeding.

'What use is a dead dragon?' Muriel said sitting up to see over Jack's crouched form.

Denise bent low and offered the plate to Jack.

'Plenty, have you ever wondered how we conquered half the world?' Nigel stood on tiptoe to see Muriel over the biscuit exchange.

'Coal, the oldest son getting all the land leaving the youngest with nothing to do, the Inclosures Act, and my God sit down.' Muriel snatched the plate from Denise and gave it to Jack.

'Yes, but other countries had things going for them too, Spain had a literal mountain of silver, Portugal had the best sailors, China could command millions of men.' ' Nigel's chest swelled. 'No, it was glorious England and her plucky redcoats and factories that seemed to come out of nowhere, and they did. When The Dragon died it started to decay, not just its flesh but its life force—'

'—magic life force,' Denise added.

'Yes, it seeped magic into London and the rest of the country, slowly at first but soon vast amounts was embedding itself in the buildings, institutions and people. We were suddenly capable of great things, we no longer needed the weather to keep Spanish ships from invading, we discovered new trade routes and whole continents without guns. We dreamed things and made them real,' Nigel said.

'We're getting off-topic,' Denise said. 'What matters isn't what it did, it's that someone has a scale.' She nodded to the shelf where the scale had been placed. 'Which means someone has found it. The Dragon can change everything, Muriel.' Denise's eyes grew serious. 'Its life force brought about the modern world and if one person had all that power there is no telling what they could do. They could do terrible things with that power if they wished.'

'Or great things,' Nigel added.

'Yes or great things,' Denise replied with a nod. 'But until we know more let's presume terrible. Muriel, see what you can find out.'

'I think I know someone who can help. Which brings us to the other matter,' Muriel said.

Jack put down the empty plate.

'Would you be able to put the word out that Jack isn't anything important? He's just a bystander in all this. Let him go on his way?' asked Muriel.

'Of course,' Nigel said.

'It will take some time to get the word out though.'

'Will it?' Nigel looked at Denise.

'Yes, it will, Denise said, bringing decades of marriage to bear with a look.

Nigel caught on. 'Oh yes, ages.'

'I'll tell you what Muriel, why doesn't he stick with you for now?' Denise said, directing them to the door. 'You can be his knight in shining armour.' She laughed at the idea; Denise seemed like the type of person who thought Germaine Greer was a type of apple.

'You can teach him a thing or two, a bit of self-defence,' Nigel said with a wink.

Muriel opened the door and ushered Jack out without saying goodbye.

Jack and Muriel stood outside the shed in silence. 'I thought it would be a quick fix. They would contact a few people and I'd be fine,' Jack said once he had processed what had happened.

'Me too,' Muriel said. 'It's ok, they know what they're doing.' She took a deep breath and looked Jack up and down with so much pity it almost became wonder. 'I know you can run, which is good — ninety per cent of this job is running. The other ten is the spell. You should learn the spell.'

Empty tin cans had been lined up on a garden bench outside the shed. Muriel gave the cans one last tweak and joined Jack under the tree and away from the hot sun. 'Ok, the first and only rule of magic, here it comes, are you ready?'

Jack jumped on the spot like a boxer. 'Hit me.'

'Any adult can do magic. The only thing stopping them is that it never occurs to them to try.'

He stopped and stood. 'That can't be true.'

'Yep, watch.' She held out her hand and a baked bean can fell through the bench, as if the space under the bench had disappeared, and landed in her palm. It was the greatest thing Jack had ever seen and in no way exciting.

'You said adults, can children not do magic?'

'No, their brains aren't developed enough so forget about getting a job at a magic school. Kids need geometry and crafts.' She walked to the bench and placed the can back with the others.

He stood side-on and took a deep breath.

'Now, you aren't trying to move the can, you're trying to will the can into your hand. It was always there,' she said, moving to stand next to him.

'Why will it appear in my hand? It wasn't there before, why would pretending make it move?' he asked.

'The convenient lie you can tell yourself is you're rearranging atoms so the ones above your hands turn into a can and the ones that make up the can become air. The actual answer is: it's magic,' Muriel said, an empty custard tin falling into her hand. Jack took a deep breath and turned back to the bench, his eyes narrowed. *Don't move the can. Move the atoms.* He reached out. *Don't move the can. It was always there.* Nothing. He breathed out.

'It's tricky at first, but you'll get it,' Muriel said with a kind smile.

'Is there an easier spell I could try?'

'Nope.'

'So I have to learn this first?'

'There isn't anything else, there's one spell.' She looked at the cans making them disappear one by one and form a stack on her open palm.

'What about dragons and goblins, this thing,' Jack said waving his hands at a very mundane looking shed.

'Goblins aren't magical, they're people. Are you magical?'

'But there's got to be more to it than moving things around, you can't just be a really efficient lorry driver.'

She let the cans fall. 'Well, you need to see both points at once so in some ways lorry drivers are better as they can move things to places they can't see.'

He knocked the last few cans to the ground and sat on the bench. 'Very funny.'

'Look, there is powerful magic out there. It's just not for the likes of you and me. Those two in there aren't what they seem I can tell you and it sounds like The Dragon was capable of a lot more than us.'

Jack folded his arms and stared at the ground near Muriel's feet. The hangover was wearing off and it was all becoming real. Being real, it was all slightly disappointing but still scary and a bit overwhelming.

She patted him on the knee and headed towards the gate. 'Come on, we've got to speak to a ghost about a dragon.'

THREE

Every great artist had a studio: Botticelli, a villa outside of Florence, gifted to him by the Medici. Barbara Hepworth managed to grab a small piece of Cornwall before she was priced out by people who moved there to be around creative people while simultaneously driving out the creative people. For Nisha, London was her studio, inspiration would strike by simply existing in the capital. This was helpful as the cost of an actual artist studio in London was well beyond her reach.

After graduating, she and some of her fellow course mates had found a warehouse to rent on the cheap. No running water, no heating and the power came from not asking what the cables hooked up to the lamppost outside were for. A haven for arty types. They would change the world and it would all start there. One by one they had drifted away: an internship their mother had sorted for them, an uncle's friend had an empty apartment in Rome, acting — one just decided to be an actor one day and headed back to school for a few more years. Soon, it was just Nisha in an old warehouse with no running water, no heating and questionable power but plenty of rent due. She moved home and made the city her studio. This included the restaurant. She had her best ideas when she wasn't meant to be thinking.

Somebody was yelling her name.

'Yes, Chef,' she said without looking up from adding tiny mint leaves to the top of a tray of pistachio baklava. Baklava was Chef's newest whim after yesterday's fig strudel hadn't gone down well. Last week it was cardamom panna cotta, the week before cashew fudge. The man was all about the sugar and fat.

Her face sat inches from the desserts, close enough to make a food inspector blush.

Chef came and bent over next to her so they were face to face. 'What are you doing?'

'Adding tiny mint leaves to these cakes for some reason.' Nisha stood up and clicked her back.

Chef stood, following her lead. 'Baklava.'

'More of a leg woman myself,' she said.

Chef's lips moved but no sound came out. Nisha and Chef often danced like this. She had the upper hand before they opened, when the restaurant was still relatively calm. Once the first few orders were in and Chef's heart rate got going it could go either way.

'How can I help, Chef? What do you need?' she asked, putting him out of his misery.

Chef shook his head as if trying to forget the last few seconds. 'They've mucked up the delivery again. I need you to go buy onions.'

'How many?'

'All of them,' he said, walking away to prepare for round two.

· · ·

There is no greater joy than being outside on a sunny day when you should be working. The restaurant was in the warren of streets just north of Covent Garden and the converted houses — both ware and work — hid the worst of the sun and made Nisha's walk almost pleasant. Central London still had useful shops you didn't expect to survive amongst the tourist traps and offices because, despite no one living for a mile in any direction, life still went on here. Life was generally boring but that meant you could find haberdashers, ironmongers and greengrocers if you knew where to look.

'Hello Nish, you're not still working at that restaurant, are you?' Reggie Chapman, fifth generation greengrocer and one of Nisha's favourite people, asked as she entered his lock-up that served as the shop floor. The room was dark, cool and stank of ten generations of cabbage. Every conceivable vegetable was piled high. He didn't do fruit though, apparently it unbalanced your humours, and he didn't want that on his conscience. Nisha had once turned up eating an apple and he wouldn't sell her anything until she promised to lay off the stuff.

'Morning, and I'm afraid so,' Nisha said, picking up a bulb of garlic and giving it a sniff.

'Don't let them grind you down, you're better than that place.' Reggie snatched the bulb and put it back on display.

'You know me Reggie, I'm a diamond, even if they grind me down, I still sparkle.'

'Me too Nish, me too,' he said, 'but what are you here for? I've had some lovely pak choi in if you're interested. Only a few boxes left and if you don't take it someone else will.'

'Just onions for now, as many as I can carry.'

Reggie scratched his chin. 'Might be tricky, we had that dry spell last year which is bad for them. They're in short supply. Let me see what I can find.'

41

'You know, I'm not sure the dry spell ever ended,' she said picking up the garlic again and giving it a second sniff.

Left alone while Reggie checked out back out (out back being his van), Nisha inspected a photo of all five generations of the Chapman family standing in front of the lock-up. The baldness gene seemed to have adopted a scorched earth policy with the Chapmans as they all wore hats.

'Blimey,' Reggie said when he returned, his lip cut but carrying onions. 'That was mental.'

'What happened? You're bleeding.' Nisha took a tissue from her pocket and gave Reggie's lip a dab.

'Some tourists were getting to know each other up against my van.' He dropped two bags of onions at Nisha's feet. 'I said this is neither the time nor the place and they didn't take it well. What is the world coming to?'

'It's this dry spell,' Nisha said. 'It's bad for us too.'

Saddled with onions, Nisha made her way back to the restaurant taking the odd detour to eke out her trip. She passed an art gallery, the intimidating kind where you could take out all the art and replace it with sports cars and it would give off the same vibe and attract the same clientele. Art for people with more money than sense and more sense than confidence in knowing what they wanted on their walls. Nisha didn't want her art to end up in that kind of place but she didn't judge the people that did. All she wanted was the chance they had. *The artist blows everyone away and affords a studio in the process.*

The bus kicked Jack and Muriel off somewhere south of Ladywell, so Ladyknees? Muriel didn't find it funny either.

'Should I expect Poltergeist or Casper?' Jack asked.

'Neither, she's not dead, she's very, *very* alive.'

'But ghosts are dead.'

They walked around the back of the bus and crossed the street. 'Not really,' Muriel said, 'the defining trait of a ghost is they have unfinished business and can't leave until it's done, unlike a zombie that just won't leave. She has unfinished business so hasn't died. Some people need to die before they realise what they want to do with their lives, and some figure it out when they're still alive. Either way, you've got a ghost.'

'Are you saying anyone with ambition is a ghost? Am I a ghost?'

Muriel stopped walking as the question weighed on her. 'It's not any old ambition, like a nice house, it needs to be something you really need, and I do mean need, to do. Your life can't go on without it, it fills your waking day and your dreams, it scratches at your brain and gnaws at your concentration. A real passion.'

Jack was not a ghost.

They passed a parade of shops, a few useful but mostly the type of places hedge fund managers set up when they stopped being hedge fund managers: Nordic florists, single-origin furniture collections and artisan beehives. The owners get interviewed for the Sunday supplements and tell you that it's important to follow your dreams but neglect to mention that although they've stopped being a finance guy they still have half a million in stocks and keep in touch with the old firm to pick up the odd tip.

The shops became a street of old workers' terraces built for the bottom rung but now occupied by the middle. Tastefully painted front doors and 4X4s on credit couldn't hide the fact that they were spending a lot more than their parents did at their age to sink slower than everyone else. Nestled amongst the Farrow and Ball sat a house of peeling paint and unwashed windows. Muriel held the gate open for Jack who nearly tripped over a recycling bin full of empty flour bags, egg boxes and beer bottles.

'So why can't she die?' Jack asked. 'What's her unfinished business?'

Muriel closed the gate behind her. 'For a while, it was popular for people to record things and give them Latin names. Plants, animals, anything. Suze decided she was going to do cake. She was going to categorise every cake, tart and pastry by genus all the way back to the Ur Cake.'

'And that means she can't leave?'

Muriel rang the bell. 'There's a lot of cake.'

The door ripped open and a dozen still-warm caraway and poppy seed muffins flew past. 'Flimflam!'

Stood in the doorway was a woman, no older than Jack but with more confidence than he had mustered in his whole life. She wore a faded maroon dress embroidered with roses under a canvas apron tied at the front. The knot looked fused shut. Two gormless rabbits sat at the front of her slippers; centuries of spilt flour and egg had imprisoned the rabbits in a batter cage and their eyes screamed for the sweet release of death. Jack wouldn't have noticed a few days ago but her ears, poking out of her long black hair, were shaped like arrowheads. She was an elf.

'Muriel! Come in,' Suze said.

'Thank you, how have you been?'

'What? I'm quite deaf you know.'

'I said, how have you been?' Muriel repeated louder.

Jack grabbed Muriel's arm, stopping her on the threshold. 'Why are we here?'

'She was there.'

'Come in, come in, have a seat,' Suze said, leading them into the kitchen.

As far as Jack could tell all the seats were piles of cookbooks — in fact, the kitchen table was a pile of cookbooks with a piece of plywood resting on top. Every piece of furniture in the kitchen seemed to be cookbooks. He contemplated a Gordon Ramsay but thought better of it and settled on eighteenth-century shortbreads while Muriel made do with Flans of the Adriatic.

'What can I do for you, young girl?' Suze placed some unmarked bottles of beer on the table along with a Victoria sponge cake. 'Are you ok with *Victoriam Autosurgens*? I've got *Pinguis Malefactorem* if not?'

'Do you have any tea? It's still early,' Muriel asked, giving the beer a sniff.

'What? Nonsense. You know I don't go in for fads. Get that down you,' Suze said.

Muriel shrugged and mimed a cheers to Jack. 'I'm afraid this isn't a social visit.'

'It never is anymore, but what can I do for you?' Suze said, cutting the cake into slices and piling them onto side plates: thick slabs of the most beautiful cake Jack had ever seen.

'Do know anything about The Dragon?' Muriel asked, her eyes transfixed by the cake as well.

The cake was handed out. Icing sat like fresh snow on inches of rich sponge. The smell of pure joy crept over Jack.

Suze pulled up a well-used Delia and joined them. 'Not anymore. Bottles are much easier to store than flagons. Just put them in the recycling when you're done.'

'Dragon,' Muriel repeated.

Jack felt useless so mumbled something about needing the loo and left them to it. The book-furniture continued in the living room with piles of cookbooks pushed against every wall; plates of stale cake littered the room which had been forgotten once they had been assessed, categorised and logged. The wallpaper should have been rich mustard but had faded to a grey-white; strawberries that punctuated at regular intervals had become pink smudges. In the far corner sat a desk, a real one. Rolls of paper were piled high on top. He checked no one was watching and tried to slice a roll of paper into his hand. *Slice the Space. Don't move the can, it was always there.* Nothing.

Raised in suburban Essex, Jack knew little about faith. The Church didn't seem to have a hold on places that didn't exist seventy years ago. It wasn't that he was raised an atheist, religion and faith were just treated the same way other people treat The Battle of Hastings: something you learnt about when you're a kid but didn't really need to worry about as an adult. In fact, if anyone did bring up the Battle of Hastings you quickly made an excuse and left.

He had entered adulthood with very little experience of trusting in things bigger than himself. Faith meant believing things would work out and things hadn't worked out for Jack. He had very little faith to begin with and had even less as time had gone on. Not faith in a higher power or a grand plan but faith in himself, the world and the idea that things would work out. Maybe this was why he couldn't do magic? Magic seemed to require a belief that the world was malleable and could change. Jack's world hadn't changed in years.

Consigned to his fate, he walked across the room and unrolled the paper. A family tree of baked goods had been drawn on the paper. Lines of ink danced up the page, converging to a single grandfather cake. He traced his figure over the names: *Pluvia Citrus, Clamor Atrox, Ricardus Pistorum*. Each was accompanied by an intricate drawing shaded with watercolours.

He let go and the paper re-coiled and returned to its former position. Jack circled the room, a map of London hung above the fireplace, or London as it was four hundred years ago. Fleet Street and Cheapside were recognisable along with the tell-tell parade of trees towards Buckingham Palace. Hand drawn, it seemed to only list the places important to the owner, the Tower wasn't shown or any churches, just pubs and shops. Even the river seemed an afterthought with it cutting straight above Greenwich instead of looping down and around the Isle of Dogs.

'Dragon? Why didn't you say so?'

Jack took this as a cue to return to the kitchen.

'Remember it like it was yesterday. Bloody scary I can tell you,' Suze said. 'Came out of nowhere. Circled for hours over the city. Roaring, before it... you know...' Suze's hand swooped low over the table.

'Do you know where it went?' Muriel asked.

Suze paused. 'I was busy loading up my collection.' She tilted her head towards the books. 'But I remember its roar. It wasn't a proud or threatening roar, almost sad. If you can imagine such a thing.' She stared into the middle distance. 'So we went out. The help and I, this was back when I could afford help, and watched it fly right overhead. Low. You could *feel* it. Then it disappeared behind some houses.' Her hand took another pass over the city. 'There was a mighty crash as it hit the water.'

'So it's in the Thames?' Jack asked.

Suze flashed back to the kitchen. 'That was quick. Did you wash your hands?'

The first god came into being in 1637 when Descartes had his thought about thinking. Real gods don't control the weather or care about the affairs of mortals, or even having affairs with mortals. They don't care about anything except judging others for their choices. It wasn't Descartes' one-liner that caused the first god to pop into existence but the smug sense of satisfaction that Descartes had after writing it down that did it. Gods spring into being all over the place, there are gods of the country who think they're better than town gods and town gods that are slightly scared of city gods but judge them anyway. There are milk-in-last gods and only-freshly-ground coffee gods, triple-ply-toilet paper gods and all-inclusive-holiday gods. Every time someone has a self-important thought or passes judgment over someone the thought takes on a life of its own; once enough have congealed in the same spot a new god is formed.

This means on any given Saturday thousands of new gods are wandering around London after Clive had the audacity to wear salmon-coloured trousers with a navy shirt on a night out. This was perfect for someone like The Elf in the Paisley Suit trying to retrace someone's steps. A judgmental god sees all.

She had lost the two that had run off with the napkin on Wardour Street, so it seemed like the logical place to start. It was nearly lunchtime and Soho bustled with street cleaners, white vans dropping off restaurant supplies and people having a morning after the night before. She walked down the narrow pavement, keeping an eye out for a god. Once you spotted one, the rest would follow.

A man in his early twenties stood outside a coffee shop wearing a handwoven poncho and texting on a phone old enough to protest the invasion of Iraq. A god if ever she saw one. Another telltale sign was the fact he floated half an inch off the ground.

She approached with a smile. 'Hello, were you here last night?' She found her voice creeping up as if talking to a cat or small child.

The god looked her up and down and disapproved. 'Where else would I be?'

If only you could stab the immaterial. 'Did you see a gangly redhead and a man run past here at about half ten?'

He pulled back his poncho and placed his phone in a fluorescent pink bumbag. 'No, and please leave. I can't be seen with someone who would voluntarily wear a Paisley suit.'

'I saw them,' a voice said.

The Paisley Elf turned to find a woman wearing a sun hat the size of a small Italian car. 'Where did they go?'

The hat kept flopping down over the god's face as she gestured in three different directions. 'That way I think, I'm not sure but I would guess they were heading to Firth Street, they seemed like jazz club people if you catch my drift,' the woman said as if they shared a secret about jazz clubs and the people that frequent them.

Not even stab, just wrestle to the ground and shake.

'Nope, they went towards the river.'

She turned again, a man dressed for a summer on the Riviera sipped a glass of white wine at a small table that didn't seem to belong to any of the cafes or restaurants on the street.

'The river?'

'Oh yes, they looked like paper-travel-card sorts if you ask me. Probably got scared and ran back to one of those ghastly chain restaurants on the South Bank.' *Maybe stab after all.*

More gods joined the conversation, each pointing in a different direction and offering a different critique of why the gangly redhead and her companion were terrible people.

'Ok,' The Paisley Elf said. 'Ok stop. Stop!' One by one the gods caught on and fell silent. 'Thank you all for your help. But can anyone tell me for certain which way the gangly redhead and the man went?'

The gods thought about this.

'I'll tell you where they haven't been. A decent hairdresser's.' A goth god, with admittedly beautiful hair, said. The gods erupted at this contentious point and she pushed herself out of the crowd and set off to see about getting an appointment with Foresight.

Jack had decided it didn't matter if his life was in danger or he couldn't go home because he was a dragon hunter. A dragon hunter on a dragon hunt. The criminal underworld that Jack had fallen into seemed to be filled with gardeners and bakers. In this world, Jack could hunt a dragon. And the fact that this involved a stroll along the River Thames on a sunny day with zero danger was to be ignored.

Jack and Muriel started at Battersea Bridge and walked along the river heading east. They found a riverside cafe and decided to pick up a late lunch. Jack reminded Muriel that he had got the last round at the pub the night before and sheltered from the early afternoon sun under an awning while she ordered and paid.

Muriel approached the counter and the queue seemed to part for her. There was no subtle cough or disregard for personal space. She didn't loom. The people just knew that they had to move. A thousand years ago Muriel would have led the charge against the Romans. She didn't give off a threat of violence although clearly, that wasn't an issue for her. It was something else. It was as if she knew what was going to happen next and was ready for it. She didn't move through the world, the world moved around her.

Muriel gave Jack the choice of chicken mayo or a BLT. He took the former and they continued on their search for dragon clues.

'Do you ever feel guilty?' Jack asked.

'About what? Bacon?'

'No, using violence, taking people's hands off and stuff.'

She took a guilt-free bite of her sandwich. 'Not really, they're bad people and it generally stops them doing it to me first.'

'How do you decide who's bad and who isn't? Aren't we all just victims of circumstance, aren't they just paying the bills like everyone else?' Jack asked.

The pained expression of an expert talking to a layman flashed across Muriel's face. 'I didn't know that guy last night or why he does what he does but I do know the type and he's paid very nicely to do terrible things for worse people. The people I deal with aren't scraping by on the poverty line, they've got everything and want more.'

Jack nodded, he saw the difference between necessity and greed. 'But how can you claim to be the good guys if you go around slicing hands off people?'

'Because the bad guys kill people.'

Jack said nothing. He didn't agree but he wasn't sure why. There didn't seem to be much in it. He had always thought he was against all forms of violence. There were no shades of grey when it came to it. Don't get him wrong, he was glad she turned up last night at Charing Cross when she did.

'How do you feel about letter bombs?' Muriel asked.

'Not great.'

'Agreed, but the Suffragettes didn't mind and I get to vote because they invented them and didn't have any qualms about using them.'

'So you're saying what you do is the same as the Suffragettes?'

'No, but I don't need to be a Suffragette because someone sent the prime minister a letter bomb on my behalf, and you don't need to concern yourself with the moral implications of slicing people's hands off because I've done it for you.'

Was this how it had always been? People with different moral codes coming together to make everything work. Jack could never kill a chicken yet he was eating one. He would never lock someone in a tiny room against their will yet he had no issue with the police doing it on his behalf. If everyone was like Jack there wouldn't be any sandwiches.

They talked of lighter things until the sun became too much and they slumped into a silent march across the city. Jack had never seen the river so low, it had shrunk at its edges revealing centuries of city life. Discarded shopping trollies acted as lobster cages catching detritus in the passing tides, lumps of long-forgotten dock life had rusted and turned dysentery red. 'What are we even looking for?' Jack said, finishing his third packet of crisps.

Muriel walked ahead and didn't reply. She stopped every few minutes to lean over the wall separating the river from the city and searched for a sign of The Dragon.

They entered a spit of park, the sort that property developers create to get a thirty-storey block of flats built nearby. It was a city planner's idea of rural living in the city. Jack knew what had been said at the council meeting: trees and bushes to invoke Arcadia and a bench to encourage a sense of community. Instead, you got a weird park everyone thought they would get stabbed in.

'Seriously, you're not going to see a wing pop out of the water. It's been four hundred years, it's either gone or was never there in the first place,' Jack said, throwing the crisp packet into a bin and sitting on the bench. He slipped off his sweat-soaked shoes.

'I'm not looking for a wing,' Muriel said. 'I'm looking for a scar on the landscape or something out of place. A dragon doesn't crash in the middle of a city without leaving a sign.' She leant over the wall until her feet were off the ground.

'I won't go in after you.' He pulled off his right sock and tried to wring the sweat out, a single drop landed on the hot concrete and evaporated. 'Maybe we built on top of it.'

'What?' she said, turning back to face him.

'You know how Southwark Cathedral is in that dip? Well, that's because people kept building on top of the buildings around it and slowly they got higher and higher while the cathedral stayed at the same original level.'

'Why are you talking about Southwark Cathedral?'

Jack pulled his sock back on. 'I'm saying maybe the same thing happened to The Dragon. It crashed, caused a big hole and, with London house prices being what they are, people built on top of it.'

She ran her tongue along her teeth and leaned against the wall. 'Where are we anyway?' Her hair was wild in the heat.

'Woolwich, I think.'

She pulled a face at his answer. 'Fancy some food?'

'Always, but let me do the other sock first.' He slid his left sock off and began the whole ordeal again.

Muriel gave him a look that cats give dogs and turned to face the river.

'Jack.'

He finished tying his laces and stood. He looked both ways down the path. She had vanished. 'Muriel?' He shouted her name. Something rustled in the hedge behind him. 'Very funny.' Jack stepped towards the noise and heard a low growl. The rustling continued. A snout emerged from the bushes, brown and slick with mud. It stepped into the open. It was a hog, as tall as Jack and twice as long. Mud covered its body and oozed down its flanks in waves. Sludge dripped onto the yellow grass. *The ocean become pig.* Perched on its head was a threadbare flat cap that seemed to scan the path for its owner as the creature sniffed left and right. A wave of putrid air washed over Jack as it came close. A sharp, hot pain filled his throat. Jack swallowed vomit. He skirted towards the bin. The beast looked directly at him and paused. They both paused.

Jack's hand crept into the bin: crisp packet, newspaper, hopefully a banana skin. He clasped a beer bottle. It clattered against the path sending the hog pursuing new prey.

Powered by fear, Jack bounded towards a shrub and snapped off a branch, dry and weak from the heat. 'Muriel?'

The pig turned at the noise and ran towards Jack, quickening its pace into a charge. Jack raised the branch ready to strike. The beast lowered its head, iron black fangs exposed. The branch struck a flank and was consumed by the mud. Jack was on the ground. His hands grasped for escape but found only mud. The beast's jaws snapped inches from Jack's face, drool rained down into his mouth and nose. *Keys*. He shifted to allow his left forearm to take the weight while his right searched his pockets. The drool flooded over his face and chest. Clenching his keys in his fist he pulled back ready to strike the beast's neck.

A hand crossed his vision and whipped the flat cap from the monster. It reared and let out a squeal as it turned to chase after the hat. Muriel stood over him, dripping cool water onto his face. Jack scrambled to his feet wiping himself as clean as he could. The beast charged again with the hat in its mouth; Jack grabbed Muriel by her sopping wet sleeve to run but she didn't move. The pig slid to a stop and bowed. She picked the hat up with a flourish and threw it back along the path.

'Everyone's a suffragette when they need to be,' Muriel said. Her eyes watched the creature intently.

'What is that thing?' Jack asked, putting some space between himself and it.

'Mudlark,' Muriel said. 'Made of nothing but mud, they live in the sewers eating our,' she paused, 'leftovers. Rare to see them above ground.'

The Mudlark returned with the hat and no desire for the game to end.

'It tried to kill me!'

Muriel rolled her eyes. 'No, it didn't.' She stroked the mudlark's chin. 'You wanted to play, didn't you?'

The mudlark stared at Jack and almost nodded. Muriel threw the hat and the creature scrambled after its prey.

'You can't go around thinking something is out to get you just because it looks odd. Mudlarks have lived here for hundreds of years, they're perfectly normal.'

The Mudlark returned and dropped the hat on the floor, ready for another round of fetch. She pretended to throw the hat causing the mudlark to trip over its feet unsure of where to go. Laughing, Muriel threw the hat in the river and they watched it leap into the air and disappear behind the wall with a splash.

'Odd? It's a wild pig in the middle of London!'

'The correct term is semi-domesticated, like swans or deer,' Muriel said.

'I've never been attacked by a swan.'

'Count yourself lucky, my aunt had a run in with one at Hampton Court. Nasty business.'

'I'm being serious, it's a monster,' Jack said.

'A bruised coccyx is serious.'

Something at the back of Jack's mind came to the fore. 'Where did you go? And why are you wet?'

She reached into her pocket as if protecting it from Jack's eyes. 'I thought I saw something.'

'In the river? What was it? Was it something to do with The Dragon?'

Muriel hesitated then took something out of her pocket and it hit the ground with a clang. A crushed drinks can. 'It looked a bit like the scale at a distance.'

She's as mad as the rest of them, Jack thought. The Dragon hunt was over, it was time to go home. Jack wanted wise old sages and majestic fire breathing creatures, not agoraphobic shed dwellers and semi-domesticated pigs. Like many, Jack had come to terms with his fears but never had the opportunity to face them. Now that he had, he knew what kind of person he was. 'I'm going home.'

'I'm not sure that is wise,' Muriel said. 'You're meant to stick with me. The Laurels said and they know how these things work. Let's get a drink.'

He turned and headed to find the nearest bus stop. He would take his chances with The Elf in The Paisley Suit if she ever turned up. Going by what he had seen so far she would be just as incompetent as everyone else and he could foil her with a banana skin or two. *A bloody drinks can.* He didn't mind incompetent people, he was incompetent, but he was humble in his incompetency and stayed out of other people's way.

'Jack! Where are you going?' Muriel called out.

'Home!' he shouted without turning around. *Where it's safe and I know what will happen next.*

FOUR

Other than the smell it seemed like a perfectly ordinary piece of meat. Theo couldn't get enough of the odour and took a long breath as he placed the meat on the scales. The Oxfordshire countryside distilled into a perfume. The meat would define him, change his lot and return him to his rightful place, or at least the money Mimi was paying would. If he could find out what made it tick he could cash the cheque and live off the interest like he was always meant to do. Why his father had put all their money in stocks to help poor people get mortgages he'd never know. No good came from handouts.

Theo had just started his final year of university when the markets crashed. His father had phoned one afternoon and tried to explain that there was no money. Theo didn't panic at first. Money was always a small thing growing up. No one spoke of it, he rarely saw anyone handle it or worry about its absence. It was invisible, beyond his grasp, like a whale unable to comprehend the edge of the ocean until it washed up on the beach. The family had sold the estate and been made to shack up in their holiday cottage. Banished to Cornwall and forced to seek employment. Like the whale, Theo had been stranded on the beach for too long. It was time to swim again and if that meant doing menial science for a cousin who, by rights, should be working for him, then so be it.

That Mimi had got messed up in crime was no surprise to Theo. Uncle Harry had always been broad church when it came to his choice of friends and business partners. Perhaps the apple hadn't fallen far from the tree and Mimi had been misled by the wrong sort as well. She wouldn't be the first from their set to let naivety get the better of them and be led astray.

Theo jotted down the weight of the meat and dropped it in a vat of stomach enzymes, being careful not to get any on his fingers. An image of where Mimi had found so much bile at such short notice started to creep up on him. He shook it off and tried to picture the boat he would buy when this was over.

The meat fizzed as the enzymes got to work. Waiting for something to happen, his eyes wandered around the lab. Although lab was a stretch for a storage container in Bermondsey that had a long and storied history as an abattoir, prison cell and toilet — possibly all at the same time. The equipment wasn't much better: scratched and chipped beakers, a fridge so old it had turned yellow, and he had seen better measuring equipment on a market stall. But at least he wasn't teaching anymore.

The meat did nothing. Theo checked his watch; when Mimi had given him a demonstration it was instant.

She had taken him down into the tunnel and shown him the creature, that ungodly thing — far bigger than it had any right to be. They had walked for hours and it had slowly dawned on Theo what he had got himself into. Mimi's operation didn't quite match her ambitions — but it would. The crew working underground was minimal but she had plans to expand as soon as Theo made some progress. She had told him about the years of research to find the creature, what it had done to the country and how it had changed it all for the better. She had hunted for evidence of The Dragon everywhere — archaeological anomalies, folk stories and children's rhymes. She had even stolen Pepys' diary, not the one on display at Cambridge, but the real one kept locked away in the university's vaults. The diary contains what appear to be the ramblings of a madman overcome with smoke who thought he saw a dragon, but what is really an accurate account of the day London was attacked by one.

Pepys didn't know much of what happened that night but he saw the creature crash south of The City with such force it had practically buried itself, sinking into the boggy mess that used to be South London. Over a few days, it sunk further and further into the mud. Returning to hell, Pepys said. The clergy would go out and exorcise it with holy water and prayer. By the end, only the very tip of a wing still stood above ground, children would climb on it and play games until one morning it was gone. A few brave souls dug down to see if it was still there. It wasn't.

Mimi had taken Theo to her base camp underground. There, she had taken a chunk of muscle, a fist-sized piece of meat, peeled fresh from The Dragon and devoured it. She picked up a stone from the ground and a blinding light had filled Theo's vision for a moment. The stone was gold, real gold.

'Quite useless I think you'll agree,' she had said, dropping the miracle. The piece of gold became an unremarkable stone again before it hit the ground. 'It seems to do different things for different people, it allows some people to fly, others to shoot lightning, all manner of unimaginative things. The change only ever lasts a minute at most and there doesn't seem to be any logic to who gets what. What I need from you is a way to make it do what I want, when I want, and for as long as I want. I want to channel all of it.'

'To what end,' Theo had asked.

'To bring about a bright new future, one of peace and order. Something I think we can all agree is much needed.'

Mimi had gone on and on about the memories of the nation, and of people, how they are one and the same. 'To change the nation you must change the people and vice versa,' she had said. An associate of hers, sadly no longer with us, had tried the meat and it had wiped his mind completely. He no longer knew who he was or where he was, to the point he didn't seem to understand he was even human. In hindsight, it was a mistake to have him sample the wares on top of a multi-storey car park: he imprinted on a pigeon and although he had the will, he didn't have the wings. 'Imagine the potential,' she had said, her eyes far away in thought.

Other than that, everything was very "need to know" which Theo could appreciate to a degree. He understood the workers and the thugs not needing to know but he was a man of science, family, and the right sort. If he wanted to stay a mindless cog he would have carried on teaching. But, then, the amount she was paying would sort Theo out for life so maybe he could forget his place for a few weeks. After that, he'd buy his boat and leave. Mimi's world of peace and order sounded awful, he had wasted the best years of his life teaching and he wasn't going to spend the rest somewhere where nothing happened. His family were full of men of action and he would be too. Kenya, South Africa, Bengal — his family had gone to them all and shaken them into the modern era. He had no plans to go to such places. Instead, he would sail off and find adventure — but somewhere sensible like the south of France or Italy.

Back in the lab, the stomach enzymes failed to do anything. Theo's watch told him he was late for lunch at the club with the boys. He would come back to this tomorrow with a fresh head. He gave the meat a half-hearted wash under the tap before placing it on the counter. Theo shut the lab door just as the meat began to chirp.

The toaster in Jack's kitchen fizzed and hissed as it cooked the frozen potato waffles. Jack stared into the orange heat of the toaster element and tried not to scream. It was just hunger, it would all be ok. No wonder humanity had spent so much effort trying to eradicate famine, it really put a downer on things.

The toaster popped and Jack grabbed a waffle as it flew out of the slot. Regretting it when the still-cooking waffle burnt his fingers; he threw it onto a waiting plate and grabbed a fork to pry the other waffle out of its slot.

It had only been a few hours since he had stormed off and left Muriel by the Thames. Going home was the right choice. He would go back to his life, put the last twenty-four hours behind him and see where this temporary promotion led. Second waffle retrieved with all but the lightest of shocks. He waved a hand over the saucepan of lukewarm baked beans that sat on his decrepit electric hob. Still cold. One day, when Jack had his own place, he'd buy a brand new cooker with gas burners and have beans at the drop of the hat. Today wasn't that day and he gave up, took the beans off the "heat" and headed for the bedroom with its bed and duvet and safety.

Some people would call the walls of Jack's flat magnolia but he knew them as off-brown. The carpet and sofa were off-white, the kitchen and his bedroom were a pale corn colour that you could call off-yellow. He took a sip of tea from one of the mugs on his bedside table, even the milk was off.

He climbed into bed still wearing his mudlark-stained suit. The sheets needed changing anyway.

Nothing on TV could take his mind off everything that had happened. He cycled through the channels anyway and caught the end of the news while he ate his waffles. Police were warning the public to be vigilant for a new drug that seemed to allow for superhuman acts of endurance after a spate of robberies across the capital that couldn't be explained.

The TV turned into a black square. Jack's alarm clock was off. He sighed. The third power cut this week. The energy companies blamed people running air conditioning units all day and increasing demand. Which, for a group of people who burnt oil for a living, seemed bold.

Jack stared at the blank walls of his flat as he ate. The day he got the keys was exciting. A one-bed, a sanctuary, to exist in without sharing. He had moved in just after leaving his PhD, when he needed some space to be alone. The trouble was all Jack seemed to do was exist. He had always meant to put up pictures and mirrors and bits of art, knick-knacks and ornaments — the type of thing you're meant to do when you get your own place but he never had. He had searched charity shops, vintage furniture warehouses and high-end department stores for anything that summed up who he was as a person or who he wanted to be. He had found nothing. Instead, he had left the walls blank. The same was true of the rest of the flat: white bed sheets, flat-pack furniture, even his view was of nothing — a patch of blank turf, as devoid and lifeless as the sun. *But safe.*

A low drone filled the room. The bed vibrated. Someone was calling. *Muriel.* Jack burrowed into the bedding to find his phone. He reached it on the tenth ring. *It wasn't Muriel.* The caller ID read: Work. 'Hello?' Jack said.

It was the Deputy Head.

'Yes, not bad, thanks. You?'

The Deputy Head was also not bad.

'Oh I see, no I didn't know that.'

The Deputy Head was explaining that now Jack was Acting Head of Physics he would need to attend meetings during the holidays. There was a half-hearted apology for not mentioning this at the time he offered Jack the job.

'Every holiday or just this one?'

Every holiday it seemed.

'Even the summer holidays?'

Two, in fact, one at the beginning and one at the end.

'And this is on top of my lesson planning and teaching?'

It was. That's why he was being paid more. Jack wasn't sure if the extra money was worth meetings during the holidays but then, he didn't do much in the holidays so maybe it was ok.

'Tuesday?' Jack checked his watch without really knowing why. 'Yes, I can make it.' He hung up and rolled onto his back. It was Saturday, he had almost three days to fill until his meeting. Three days in a blank flat with empty time. He tried to picture his life when school started again. The lessons, the marking, the yearly trip to the Science Museum and now more paperwork and the more serious detentions with the scarier pupils. Having to come up with plans to make things better, reading government papers and staying up to date on the newest teaching techniques. He would have to listen to the complaints of other teachers. All of it was laid out so clearly before him and he didn't care. Not one bit. He always thought that one day he would care, it would just happen. Some threshold would be reached and suddenly it would click into place and he'd stay late and talk at great length when people asked him about his job, like he used to when he was doing his PhD. But it never happened with work.

He had felt fear and then anger when Muriel had left him alone with the mudlark. Anger at The Laurels for not being what he imagined. Maybe anger meant he cared? Fear meant he was trying? It had been a while since he felt anything as strong as anger. He couldn't remember the last time he was scared but that didn't mean he was brave, it just meant he played it safe. Three days. He should find Muriel and apologise — another sign he cared — and then fill the days with things that mattered, things he cared about that made him scared and angry. Before, he was playing as a hero, but he didn't have the anger and fear needed to stand up and do things. It was why he had run from the Mudlark. Finding a dragon and stopping someone from doing something serious with it, he cared about that. But first, he would eat more waffles in case this was all just hunger.

As Jack bounded up the steps of Tottenham Court Road tube station, potato waffle filled his stomach and purpose his bones.

He tried not to have an opinion on local planning decisions as it was a slippery slope to neighbourhood watch duty and letters to the editor but they had ruined this bit of the city when they allowed the station to be knocked down and rebuilt as a stupid person's idea of what the future should look like.

He headed into Soho without much of a plan. He hadn't caught the name of the pub Muriel had taken him to last night but if he retraced his steps he might be able to find it. Closing his eyes, he tried to remember where they had gone after they left Charing Cross. Trafalgar Square, Charing Cross Road then a theatre kicked out. Which one? He pushed his way through the crowds and tiny streets until it all started to become familiar. At the end of the street sat a building too grand for Soho. It had pillars and art deco windows, it even had an awning. *Theatre*. It was coming back to him now, the crowds had flocked out into the street when Jack and Muriel had passed, giving them time to hide from The Elf in The Paisley Suit. But where? Jack spun trying to remember which way they had gone. It was no good. Every street in Soho looked the same and unless you kept up to date with the ever-changing restaurants and shops it was impossible. You can't step into the same river twice and you can't retrace your steps in Soho.

He walked through the courts, yards and roads that made up this part of London at random. Soho seemed calmer than normal. Heat flooded down its narrow streets and dulled the noise. People stood outside the pubs and bars and spoke in small groups. The rain god had ignored their pleas and now they worried.

Jack found nothing that led him to the pub or Muriel.

Taking refuge on a kerb opposite a record shop, Jack sat and tried to think of his next move. He thought about moving on in case someone from work walked past and wanted to talk. The millions of faceless people that filled London didn't worry Jack, he enjoyed being faceless, but the idea of small talk with an acquaintance filled him with terror.

He went to stand and leave when two men left the shop with records under their arms.

'Yes, it's an original pressing. You can tell because the last track isn't listed on the sleeve. Instead...' The man, dressed entirely in red corduroy, pulled the disc from the sleeve and pointed to something Jack couldn't see. 'You see, the last track name is etched into the vinyl itself. They recorded it after the sleeve had been printed.'

'Wow, I love it. May I?' The second man, dressed in blue suede, held out his hand.

The man in red winced. 'Maybe later. What did you get?'

'Japanese issue of *Rumours*. There was a problem with the translation and in Japan, the album is called *Scandal*.' The second man seemed very proud of this fact.

The man in red snorted. 'That album *is* a scandal. God awful, the only good thing about it is it helps me separate the morons from the Philistines.'

Jack tried not to look like he was listening and stared at the ground in front of them. At first, he thought it was a trick of the light or the uneven pavement. Jack leaned to the left to see if it changed with the angle. It didn't. Both men were floating, only half an inch or so off the ground but definitely floating. Muriel hadn't mentioned creatures that could float but this seemed magical. He crossed the street. 'Excuse me.'

Both men turned and horror dawned on their faces as they watched a man covered in mud walk towards them. The man in red put his hand out in front to stop Jack. 'Sorry, I don't have any change.'

Jack tried an awkward laugh to show he meant no harm, 'Oh no, I just wanted to ask if you're magical.'

'Honey, you've got no idea.'

'You see, I'm trying to find a friend of mine. Muriel? I don't know her last name but I thought you might know her. She works for The Laurels?'

The second man smirked at the mention of The Laurels.

'Please leave,' the man in red said, dragging his friend away by the arm.

Jack stepped in behind them. 'Please, it's important. You see I was rude to her when she was looking out for me. There was this wild animal, well, semi-domesticated really, but it all started in the men's loos at Charing Cross and then I was taken to a shed near Surrey.'

Both men stopped and turned as one. The man in red offered a patient smile. 'I don't know Muriel but a lot of the pond life hang around in The Squinting Lizzie pub off Marshall Street.'

'Marshall Street?'

'I won't say it again,' the man said, walking off.

'Down there and to the left,' the second man said. 'You'll walk past ten clothes shops before you get to it. Any of them will do,' he added with a finger pointed at Jack's suit.

Jack, still in his muddy suit, followed his phone down an alley off Marshall Street to a pub with a peeling paint job that left little to the imagination. The name was unreadable behind epochs of grime but on the sign, faded but just about discernible, was a woman walking with her arms in front of her. The Squinting Lizzie.

His mother was right, you can always judge a pub by its cover. Jack opened the door to the bar and found the air thick with atmosphere. Its inhabitants were standard for a Saturday afternoon: lost tourists, families who had tried to find "somewhere nice" and failed, and a few that didn't know it was Saturday afternoon but did know the pubs were open. The beanie-wearing population was well represented, *goblins,* Jack thought, *or bald people.* He headed for the bar. The room filled Jack with the faintest memory of having been in it before.

'What can I get you?' the woman behind the counter asked. Jack tried to get a look at her ears but her hair covered any bits that would give her away as an elf.

'Do you know Muriel?'

'I think we've got Old Rosie.'

'Sorry?'

'The cider? Old Rosie? We've got it.'

'No, she's a friend of mine, I think she comes in here a lot. Cheap suit. A bit mean and to the point.'

'This is London, you'll have to be more specific.'

'I know Muriel,' a voice said. It belonged to a small man in his seventies wearing a cassock. Holding a large pewter tankard of beer in one hand, he coughed into a hankie held in the other before continuing. 'She helped me out of a bind a few years ago when I accidentally swept away London Bridge.' The man headed further into the pub and gestured for Jack to follow.

'London Bridge is still there, it never wasn't there,' Jack said as delicately as he could.

The man gave Jack a knowing wink. 'Of course.' He coughed again.

'Are you ok?'

'Yes,' the old man said, putting his hankie away. 'It's the dry weather, sets me off. Just need a bit of rain. Drinking helps.'

The pub sprawled from one room to the next. The builders seemed to have taken the idea of buildings having floors as no more than a vague notion. Steps, slopes and staircases appeared at random. Stools and tables had been fitted in wherever possible. If someone could drink there, there was a seat, and it was filled. They walked further and further into the pub and the air became cool and refreshing away from the glare of the sun. They came to a windowless room which news of the smoking ban had failed to reach. Another bar did a roaring trade at the far end, drinkers sat in small groups around smaller tables.

First, but not second glances, were given to Jack and the old man as they weaved their way towards a corner table.

Muriel appeared through the smoke. She sat alone nursing a

pint. A pool of water from her still-wet clothes pooled beneath her on the floor. Her soaking wet coat sat next to her.

'There she is,' the old man said. 'And remember, it never wasn't there.' He winked again and was gone.

Jack approached with caution. 'I just met a friend of yours.'

She looked at him with just the right amount of indifference to let him know he had work to do.

'Some mad bloke who reckoned he destroyed London Bridge.'

'He did,' she said before taking a sip of her beer. 'But Father Thames is a nice man so I didn't mind sorting it out for him. I'm nice to nice people.'

Jack sorted and filed away all the questions he had about Father Thames for later and carried on with his apology. 'I'm sorry. It was just a bit of a shock, with the Mudlark. I'd never even been in a fight before I met you so to be attacked by a semi-domesticated pig was a bit much. I lashed out and I wanted to go home.'

'So why are you here?'

'Because I was wrong to go home,' Jack said. 'I was scared. I know you're only putting up with me while The Laurels sort everything out but I want to help. I want to try to stop whoever is up to no good with The Dragon.'

She downed her pint. 'Is that an apology?'

'It can be the start of one. Would a drink be another step closer?'

She shrugged. 'Worth a try.'

Jack ordered another apology pint for Muriel and a redemption gin and tonic for himself at the bar in the backroom of The Squinting Lizzie. The room seemed to act as an inner sanctum for elves and goblins and all kinds of London's magic folk. Hair was pushed behind pointed ears and goblins went hatless, including the barman. It had taken a conscious effort by Jack not to stare when ordering drinks. Great bulbous transparent ridges, like bleached tortoiseshell, ran backwards across his forehead. When his drinks were poured, Jack thanked the barman's eyebrows.

'So what's next?' Jack said, returning to the table.

Muriel took the pint. 'What do you mean?'

'With the search for The Dragon and whoever has found it.'

Muriel took a deep breath. 'No idea.'

'No?'

'I've racked my brain, called in every favour and no one has any idea what the hell I'm talking about.'

'How have you done that if you've just been sitting here?'

'My phone,' she said, with a look of concern on her face that Jack didn't know how phones work. 'I can go stop a planned robbery of a garden centre out in Chiswick if I want, or look into a large amount of bile that's gone missing from some lab in King's College but dragon? No one knows what I'm talking about. I've even asked Simon, haven't I Simon,' she called across to the barman.

'That's right,' Simon said. 'And the only old dragon I know is my missus.'

Muriel reeled at this comment. 'That wasn't necessary Simon, was it?'

'Sorry,' Simon said, climbing back into his box and finding a glass at the other end of the bar to polish.

The Muriel here seemed different, she was relaxed and sparred with the bar staff. She seemed to be at home.

'Good,' Muriel finished her pint. 'Another? I've forgiven you so I can get this one.'

Jack looked into her eyes. She wasn't drunk, she was annoyed about work and she was annoyed about work because she cared about her job. He wanted that, he wanted to care about things and maybe, if he hung around with Muriel for long enough he might. Wanting and caring and wanting to care felt alien to Jack and filled him with fear. Faced with fear, he fell back on an old dependable. 'How about some food instead?'

'Brilliant idea. I know a great little place,' Muriel said, picking up her sopping wet coat.

The barrel of discarded cooking oil sat uneasy under Jack but it was the cleanest surface he could find amongst the bins. Smells of ancient civilisations meeting the sensibilities of Middle England drifted from the kitchen window and into the alley.

'When you said you knew a good Indian restaurant; I didn't picture eating a stolen curry in an alley.'

'It's not stealing, I'm using my connections to get an advantage. No different to that old boys club you teach at,' Muriel said without looking up from her phone and an article about the long-term effects of swimming in the Thames. Her clothes had dried somewhat on the walk over but were still damp.

Jack was too hungry to argue but had seen from the parents at St George's that the real advantage wasn't in the connections the rich had, it was in the extra time. Being rich gave you time to think, time to play and just plain time. If you're unfulfilled in your job, you can pack it in and take some time while you live off your other half's wage. Always wanted to try your hand at being a yoga teacher? That's what savings are for. To the rich, you can always earn more money. Having time to be a mediocre playwright is the real advantage the rich get. Your aunt being a trustee at The Old Vic helps but most people don't have time to think about how to portray a bout of erectile dysfunction in a three-act structure. The rich do.

Nisha pushed open the kitchen door and flooded the alley with light and steam. She balanced two plates of curry and cutlery and joined Jack and Muriel. 'Dinner!'

Muriel stood with purpose and a smile. Jack hadn't known Muriel for long but this may have been the first genuine smile he had seen on her face, the type you don't even realise you're doing, a smile as reaction.

'Thanks love,' Muriel said, giving Nisha a peck on the cheek.

Nisha blushed and quickly shut the door to the kitchen behind her. Jack took a plate under quiet protest and ate under a quieter one.

'Why are you wet?' Nisha asked Muriel, squeezing next to her so they shared an upturned mop bucket.

Jack became fascinated with a pile of spent cigarettes littering the ground. He had been told, under no circumstances, to mention mythical monsters or magic or mudlarks or anything Muriel did. She worked for the investigative branch of the tax office, as did Jack, which sometimes involved long hours and the odd bruise when people didn't want to pay their fair share.

'I got caught in the rain.'

Jack watched Nisha's face for a response, she had been inside all day and this seemed to make just enough sense for her to accept. The brain is excellent at taking partial information and making it whole. So, like conspiracy theorists everywhere, Nisha filled in the blanks to make her world sensible again.

'How's work?' Muriel asked through a mouthful of Rogan Josh.

'Same as always, Chef's his usual charming self.' Nisha

pulled a spoon from her pocket and helped herself to food from Muriel's plate. 'Although we had this weird couple in last night. Related I think or maybe business partners or both, private dining room, the works.' She swallowed. 'Anyway, they were talking about the weirdest stuff, channelling power, experiments, all sorts.'

Muriel had the look of someone listening to a loved one talk about their day. Not knowing Nisha, Jack listened to every word. 'That's weird, did they say anything else?'

Nisha put her hand in front of her mouth and finished her food. 'It seemed to involve flesh.' She said the last word in mock horror. 'Finished?'

Jack handed over his plate and thanked Nisha who headed back inside. Muriel sat in a post-curry stupor and seemed oblivious to what Nisha had been saying. He threw a discarded lighter at Muriel who threw it back twice as hard.

'Weren't you listening?' Jack said.

Her back straightened. 'Of course I was. Chef's been an idiot and the customers are rude.'

'No.' Jack went and sat next to her on an empty beer keg. 'She said some customers were talking about channelling power using flesh, maybe it's dragon flesh?'

Muriel seemed unconvinced.

'If there are loose scales floating about, why not flesh? Maybe someone is cutting it up?'

Nisha stood in the doorway. 'I've got to get back. You guys need anything else?'

The kitchen was a galaxy but not the Newtonian kind of perfect order. It was the Hawkins kind that would kill you if you stepped in the wrong place. Gravity ebbed and flowed, cook-shaped planets collided and made comments about each other's mothers while clouds of aromas formed new unknown elements above them before breaking down never to be discovered.

Within this maelstrom, Jack had been given the task of astronomer; he was meant to tell Nisha when Chef was approaching while she tried to find the name of the diners from the other night on the reservation system. They stood in Chef's office and tried not to draw attention to themselves, mainly because a large sign saying the office was not to be entered had been nailed to the door. The office seemed to double as storage overfill and cases of bottled water, beer and wine were stacked high in the corner. Jack's astronomical task was proving difficult as everyone in the kitchen was roughly the same age, male, and wearing identical chef whites.

It's been theorised that the moons of Jupiter were once asteroids that had been caught in the planet's gravity and left the freewheeling life of outer space for the comfortable existence of suburban satellite. Jack took comfort in this idea, If directionless space rocks drifting through the void can find purpose and reinvent themselves then Jack could too. If Europa could settle into a routine; Jack could be a dragon hunter.

Jack's eyes were pulled by a force greater than Jupiter's gravity to a man walking directly towards him. The man was a Chef and not a cook. He stalked the kitchen with the power of an asteroid yet to figure out what it's all about. He stopped only long enough to dispense culinary justice to any underling foolish enough to get in his way. A pot of rice was thrown, proper knife technique was reinforced and souls were destroyed.

'He's coming,' Jack said, too fearful to take his eyes off the celestial body descending on them.

'Nearly there.' Nisha grabbed a pen without taking her eyes off the computer screen.

Chef looked into the office and saw Nisha and two strangers at his desk. His face shifted to one of extreme prejudice.

Jack knew he had to act so stepped behind the door. He peered through the gap and watched Chef stop and mime something unpleasant with a potato peeler at a commis chef before throwing the utensil at some shelves. The peeler landed next to the deep-fat fryer. The fryer bubbled like a cautionary tale waiting to happen.

Chef picked up speed. 'Guys we need to go. Now,' Jack said without coming out from behind the door. 'He just did something very unprofessional with a potato peeler and I don't want him doing it to me.'

'He threatens someone with the peeler every night,' Nisha said. 'He just needs a drink.'

Drink. Water. Jack began to search the cases of bottles.

'What are you doing?' Muriel asked.

'Planning to give an impromptu science lesson,' Jack said with a smile.

Muriel crossed her arms. 'That doesn't make sense.'

It would have killed in the staff room, the art teachers loved Jack. He found it, a case of bottled water hidden under five boxes of red wine. Ignoring this scathing commentary on the drinking habits of the British, Jack ripped open the plastic casing and eased out a bottle of water.

Nisha tore a corner off a menu and placed it in Muriel's palm. Muriel read the name and swore.

Chef darkened their door. He began a brisk and energetic line of enquiry about why exactly Nisha was in his office and who these strangers were.

Muriel's fist became a ball but Jack stepped forward just in time and explained they were from the Campaign For Real Bottled Water and Nisha here had been a great help in allowing them to carry out their surprise inspection to ensure the Chef's fine establishment wasn't filling up old bottles with tap water. Well done on staying so honest in these trying times. Anyway, must be off.

Chef, of course, didn't buy any of it.

'Put it where?' Jack said.

'I said shove it up your ar-'

Time for plan B. Jack pushed past the Chef and ran into the kitchen. He undid the cap on the bottle of water and threw it towards the deep-fat fryer. The bottle spun as it flew through the air. It landed dead centre in the fryer, nozzle down. *The art teachers would have loved that.*

Water made its funnest reaction.

Fire and hot oil burst from the fryer. Flames whipped across the room, eager to consume everything in their path.

Chef's scream was punctuated by the fire alarm belting a warning. Its metallic ring brought Chef back to the room. He turned to face Jack, pulling a pairing knife from his apron.

Jack grabbed Muriel and barged past Chef, shoulder first and towards the exit.

FIVE

Drinkers from nearby pubs and bars spilled out into the street and huddled together like sheep. There was screaming and quite a lot of dry heaving. Nisha spotted the back of Muriel's head bobbing through the crowds towards The Strand. Jack, who, if he worked for the tax office then Nisha did too, led the way.

Nisha had left Chef and the others to deal with the blaze, slipping out without anyone realising she was gone.

She followed Muriel and Jack as they weaved through the crowd. *Something was happening*. Muriel had never really talked about her work which Nisha didn't mind. In fact, it was one of the things she loved about Muriel. She was someone who cared about who someone was or wanted to be, not what they did all day. But tax officers don't set fire to kitchens or break into reservations systems to steal customer information; the pension's too good to risk.

Muriel and Jack worked their way along The Strand towards the river and the footbridges that connected the north and south banks of the city.

Nisha shook her head as she followed them. Muriel hated

the South Bank. She avoided it at all costs, whenever they needed to go anywhere near it she insisted they skirt it as much as possible even if it meant taking strange alleys or side streets. On their first date, Nisha had tried to take her to the bar in the National Theatre and ended up trying to navigate a dual carriageway on foot after Muriel refused to take the simple route along the river. If Muriel was heading into its belly on a Saturday night, something was definitely wrong.

Nisha climbed the steps onto the footbridge that linked the north and south banks of the river and spied Muriel ahead. She was walking strange. She wasn't limping or shuffling, it was her normal walk but it lacked the confidence it should have.

Despite being open to the sun the bridge was cool, thanks to a steady breeze running down the river. Cool but crowded. Since the heatwave began, young Londoners had taken to hanging out on the bridge to avoid the worst of the heat, even jumping into the Thames to whoops and cheers from their friends. Nisha pushed and squeezed her way along. *This was the real currency, not stocks and shares* Nisha thought as she jostled her way down the bodies, all pressed up against one another trying to catch a wisp of wind. The great driving force of innovation throughout history isn't trade or war, it's trying to impress your cousin and his mates.

A space emerged among the limbs and torsos, and Nisha dived through, catching up with Muriel at the top of the stairs leading down to the South Bank.

'Muriel!' Nisha called.

Muriel did a double take. 'What are you doing here? Go back to work.'

'You mean the work you just set on fire?' Nisha said. 'What's going on?'

'Nothing, just work, and anyway, *Jack* set it on fire.' Muriel fixed a smile that said she was skirting between the truth and a lie.

'Right,' Nisha said, loading the word like a gun. '*At the tax office*. Yeah?'

The bullet hit Muriel square in the chest but she didn't flinch. 'You know my job can be a bit weird. And boring. Not worth-.'

'Not worth bothering me with?' Nisha interrupted, her legs became rigid, rooting her to the spot. 'This is different,' she continued, ignoring the bodies barging into her, sweating strangers tutting under their breath. 'Something is happening and you're worried and I want to know what it is. What's going on?'

'She did help us with getting the name,' Jack said before immediately coming to his senses and taking a step back and out of the conversation.

'I *did* help with the name,' Nisha said with a nod to Jack.

For a moment, no one spoke, the sound of a red-hot London was the only noise.

'Fine.' Muriel threw her hands up in the air. 'I don't work for the tax office and I know you know that, and you know that I know, but if I had said I worked for an underground cabal that tries to stop evil you would have thought I was mad. But that's the truth, and, right now, the woman from your restaurant, Mimi, is planning to do something very bad with a dragon. Yes, a dragon. Now, go back to work so I can too.'

She was scared, Nisha thought. Muriel would never admit it, she probably didn't even know it herself, but she was scared and needed help. Dragon sounded big. Nisha wanted big. She felt like life owed her some big. 'You've kept the fact that dragons are real from me? This is like the time you got that fringe without warning me.'

Muriel pointed a finger at Nisha. 'I've apologised for that.'

'Well, I accept your apology for this too. What's the plan? I'm coming with you and it's not up for discussion.'

Muriel stared at Nisha before she sighed and continued down the stairs.

Nisha smiled, *The artist goes on an adventure.*

Streetlight snuck in through the gap above Muriel's bedroom curtains and covered everything with a gentle orange glow, making it feel like you could see the heat that filled the room. When Muriel first moved to London the eternal light had stopped her sleeping. She had thought about putting up blackout blinds but a landlord with an excuse to keep the security deposit was a foe too great even for her.

Growing up in the countryside, night was black, but here, with the endless lamp posts and car headlights, her nights had become the colour of fire. Now, the idea of true darkness unsettled her. There was always light in the city and that was good.

Nisha's snoring, however, is something she had never gotten used to. Sprawled on her back, mouth open, Nisha roared like a moped.

Lying in bed, Muriel thought about the conversation on the bridge and her decision to tell Nisha about The Dragon. She knew if she lied to Nisha's face it would be over. Nisha put up with a lot from Muriel and her silence about how she spent her days. Nisha would say nothing when Muriel turned up late or not at all, she would drop off leftover food from the restaurant after work so there was always something in the fridge when Muriel got home. She had even collected her from the hospital once without asking what she was doing on the roof of a pet shop on a Tuesday afternoon.

Standing on that bridge, Nisha had asked her for the truth and Muriel knew there was only one answer she could give. Nisha had, for better or worse, always been honest with Muriel. She ran a hand through her hair. *The fringe hadn't been that bad.*

As if reading Muriel's mind, Nisha let rip a louder-than-normal snort.

Admitting to herself she wasn't getting any sleep, Muriel slipped out of bed and into some jeans. She kissed Nisha on the forehead and smiled. If there was anyone who could sneak onto a dragon hunt, it was Nisha.

The street was just as hot as her flat but the space made it bearable. The trouble with calling it 'the greenhouse effect' was most people hadn't spent enough time in greenhouses. They're truly terrible places if you aren't a tomato plant.

Muriel walked and tried to think about what she needed to do tomorrow. When she worked alone it was simple: turn up, break stuff, leave. Now she had people to look after. The key would be control. If she could keep everything in her control it would be ok. Nothing unexpected or not according to the plan. She needed a plan.

Without thinking, she headed down a side street and regretted it immediately. Tomorrow must be bin day — she always forgot — and dozens of bins with house numbers painted on the side lined the road. *Two.* Each one filled with spoiled food heated by the endless sun for a week before being placed on the street for collection. It smelt like Satan's Rumtopf. *Eight.*

She picked up her pace and searched her pockets for something to cover her nose and block the smell. *Sixteen.* She found the torn menu from the curry house with 'Mimi Kensington-Jones' written on it, but nothing to cover her nose.

Mimi's was a name Muriel knew by reputation alone but that was about it. She was the top of the ladder, nothing happened in London that couldn't be linked back to her. *Twenty-two.* If you wanted to break the law in a serious way you checked with Mimi and gave her a cut. In some ways, Muriel's job had always been to stop Mimi. *Twenty-six.* If you ignored the fact that Mimi would soon have the power of The Dragon on her side, Muriel might now have a chance.

Twenty-eight's bin was missing. That wasn't good. She looked in twenty-eight's garden to see if they'd forgotten to put it out. They hadn't. She walked as quickly as she dared to the end of the street and listened. The dull thud of contracting plastic came from an alley between two houses.

It's too hot for this. She entered the alley and saw the mum-to-be. Although that wasn't right — it was no more a mum than a butterfly cocoon was.

A wheelie bin leant against the fence that ran down the alley. Its sides swelling and contracting.

'Come on, let's get you on the ground,' Muriel said to the bin. She grabbed the handle and lowered the bin onto its front, making sure to keep the lid shut. A low growl came from inside which Muriel took as a sign everything was on track.

She looked around for anything that might help and saw a half-drunk bottle of cider. Reaching for it, she unscrewed the lid and poured a few glugs over the bin to keep it cool.

'There's no rush, ok. Take your time,' she said, stroking the handles as it seemed to be the least intimate part of the bin and she wasn't sure what the correct etiquette was. This was

Muriel's first birth and it seemed simple enough. Some of the regulars at The Squinting Lizzie had told her what to do and the secret seemed to be staying calm.

'I envy you in lots of ways,' she said, pouring the rest of the cider over the bin. 'You're born fully formed and knowing what you're meant to do and how to behave, you don't need to figure any of this out. You just get to walk down the street like you own it and do whatever you like. You're free. The rest of us have no idea.'

The contractions picked up pace.

Muriel made soothing sounds to try and keep everything and everyone calm. She envied the creature in lots of other ways too. It wouldn't need to stop a gangster doing god knows what with a dragon. It wouldn't have to make sure everyone followed the rules. Muriel knew that people were going to break the law, she wasn't stupid, but they were still meant to follow the rules. The rules are more important than the law, that was her job — make sure people follow the rules. Mimi should know that the rules trump the law and she should know a dragon is definitely against the rules. A troll would be fine but not a dragon, it wasn't fair.

The Dragon had ruined everything. There was a system in place, it wasn't perfect but it worked. London ran like an ecosystem with everything in balance. Yes, there were winners and losers but it was balanced. Then The Dragon had to come and tip the scales.

The lid opened for a fraction of a second and spat a concoction of egg yolks and curdled milk onto the ground that pooled around Muriel's boots.

'Let it out, no one's judging you.' She patted the bin's back and moved her feet out of the puddle.

Then there was Jack and Nisha. She wasn't sure how she

ended up with so many people in tow. It had been a long couple of days. Less lonely than normal, she conceded. Less lonely, but more complicated. Getting everyone out alive, that was her job before anything else. Nothing Mimi had planned would be worse than life without Nisha. The Laurels might be able to help — call on another agent for support — but they've got fingers in so many pies. Muriel imagined The Laurels' faces if she turned up at the shed with a second civilian. They had found Muriel and given her a chance, stopped her from being just another thug and now she was repaying them by letting Nisha tag along on missions and jeopardising the city. *It was less lonely though.*

The bin started to shake, lifting itself off the ground and threatening to roll onto its side. Muriel pinned the bin as best she could while she straddled it. Her weight resting on the bin, she raised her hands and got ready to catch the lid. The guys at the pub had said the final moments were key. You had to keep the bin firmly on the ground otherwise it buckled too much and you got pigeons and no one wanted any more of them. The shaking changed and became rhythmic like a cat coughing up a fur ball. This was it. Muriel put all her weight on the bin and sat, hands poised.

The lid flew up and she caught it by the handles and with a grin. Empty wine bottles, spent toilet roll tubes and countless bags of browning salad leaves shot out of the bin spraying the alley with rubbish. Sat amongst the debris was a fox. It stood, fully grown and already a bit mangy, and stared at Muriel.

Muriel smiled at the newborn. 'Hello.'

The fox turned and trotted off down the alley and away from Muriel without a word.

'You're welcome!' she called after it. 'I stopped you from being a pigeon,' she added to no one in particular.

The fox stopped at the entrance to the alley. Lit by half a dozen lampposts, its fur glimmered. Life born from chaos and neglect, it was a true creature of the city.

It cocked a leg and peed against a fence. It *was* the city.

Muriel dismounted the bin and kicked the rubbish back inside. It would be nice to be thanked at least once.

As the King Charles Spaniel ages, its brain — too large for its skull — starts to seep out of its ears. It felt like Theo's brain was doing something similar after Big Seb challenged him to a game of Whippet Snippets at yesterday's lunch. Lunch gave way to dinner which gave way to waking up on the bathroom floor stinking of single malt whisky and claret. The walk to the lab hadn't helped and now, approaching it, the idea of spending all day in a metal box in this heat was becoming too much.

Pulling back the container door, Theo was hit with a haze of acidic air. Beakers were broken, shelves collapsed and every surface was covered in thick brown faecal matter. Theo stuck his finger in it and gave it a sniff. A welcome reprieve from the hangover. He gave it another sniff: bird, or something just like it. Theo had locked the door when he left last night, he was sure of it. Taking careful steps to try and avoid the worst of the guano he checked the vat of stomach enzymes. The meat was gone. *Science had happened.* He had made birds or at least bird crap. This was progress.

The smell grew thick and made the room stuffy. Theo stepped outside and back into the fresh air. He would need a new lab, or someone to clean this one at least, but he had good news for Mimi so it wasn't all bad.

With nothing to do at the lab until it was tidied, he headed somewhere safe, somewhere he could fix his head, he headed to the pub. Theo joined the main road and instinctively headed west towards the smart part of town. He had once dated a girl from Pimlico who claimed never to have turned right out of her front door. Right was South London so she only went left. The same sense of direction guided Theo to a pub near London Bridge, it was still South London but was called the Viscount of Lumley. Theo was pretty sure an aunt had married the Viscount of Lumley so it couldn't be that bad of a place.

He ordered the handover cure his father taught him the morning after his fourteenth birthday: four Irish coffees and a plate of chips. The final element was a quiet cry which he performed quickly and admirably in the disabled loo.

Starting on his final Irish coffee, colour and courage returned to Theo's world. He messaged a summary of what had happened to Mimi and asked for new lab equipment and more meat.

His phone buzzed before he had put it down. Mimi's reply consisted of just an address to an industrial estate in the Midlands. He would need another Irish coffee.

Dagenham, it turned out, was not in the Midlands but in East London. Other than the detour to Euston train station, Theo found the address without too much bother. A warehouse tucked away down a few side streets. A transit van had been parked at the entrance, its backdoors open and shielding its contents from prying eyes. The sounds of something very large, very heavy, and very cumbersome being moved came from inside the van. Theo poked his head around the open doors. 'Knock knock.'

He found three men, dressed like they used their hands for a living, squeezed into small spaces around a large cube. The cube sat on a wooden pallet with its true nature hidden by layers of plastic wrapping. 'I'm looking for Ms Kensington-Jones?'

The men continued to rock the cube in an attempt to edge it closer to a waiting dolly. 'You're on the wrong side of London for Kensington. You'll need to get the District Line,' said a man who was just a floating head, the rest of his body hidden by their cargo.

'I'd get the bus to Seven King's and pick up the Elizabeth Line to take you most of the way. Worth it for the air conditioning on a day like today,' a voice from further in the van said.

'He means the boss.' The third man was using his back to try and pivot the cube.

'Mimi's in the office,' the first man said and directed a nod into the warehouse.

The cube refused to budge. 'Don't suppose you can give us a hand?' The third man asked, in between deep breaths.

Theo surveyed the van and cube. 'No, I don't think so, but be careful. Looks heavy.' He left.

The warehouse was cool and loud. Both sensations were caused by a row of large fans in the middle of the floor kicking out cold air. Surrounding the fans were more mystery cubes, all wrapped in plastic and sat on identical pallets.

An office sat on a raised platform with stairs leading up from the warehouse floor.

From a large window, Mimi stood looking out over her fiefdom. She beckoned Theo up with a tilt of the head. *Poor thing,* Theo thought. The finest education in the world, an upbringing and ancestry to rival kings and queens and she's working in a warehouse in East London. Mimi was proud and would hate the idea of him judging her for her choices, he would keep a lid on it.

Theo climbed the stairs to the office and met two men carrying a rolled-up carpet. He stood to one side and wasn't thanked for his politeness.

Opening the door with gusto, Theo faked a smile to hide his pity. 'Mimi darling, how are you? Lovely carpet, are you redecorating?'

She moved away from the window and sat behind her desk. Theo went to sit opposite her. 'I didn't offer you a seat, and no. What have you done to the lab?'

'Science my dear, big breakthroughs often require breakages,' Theo said, still standing. 'Not ready to share the results yet but I will be soon.'

A crowbar and hammer lay across Mimi's desk, the bottom of the crowbar was smeared in an inch of blood. She picked up a cloth and started to clean it.

'I've successfully manifested real things I think,' Theo said, staring at the crowbar and feeling compelled to keep talking, 'only temporarily, I admit, but you'll agree it's a big step for so early on in the program.'

'I don't need real things. If I wanted real things I would take them. I want to change people's minds.'

'Yes, I guess so. If you could tell me a bit more about what you want to do—' An almighty crash from below shook the office. Theo leapt to the window to see one of the men from the van crushed under the mystery cube. Dead beyond doubt. The other two men looked on in shock from the back of the van.

Mimi marched to the office door still holding the crowbar. She flung the door open. 'Clean him up before anyone sees and if that happens again you'll be joining him, understand?' She pointed the crowbar at the two men. Cursing under her breath, she returned to her seat. 'Idiots. Do you know what the biggest killer of humanity has been for the last ten thousand years?'

Stupid Man, I told him to be careful. Theo pulled his eyes away from the scene below. 'War? No, disease.'

'No. They are both side effects of the real cause. Which is humanity itself. We are a silly chaotic little species. Messy, childish and easily distracted. Not to mention hateful.

'We have killed billions of kin through stupidity alone. Stupid wars and stupid ideas and then killing each other over our stupid ideas being better than theirs. When we are not killing each other over stupid ideas we are killing each other *with* stupid ideas. Do you know how long it took doctors to be convinced to wash their hands? Too long.

'And the *mess*, people living and dying everywhere and all the drama in between.' Mimi, satisfied the crowbar was clean, started scrolling through her phone. 'Just stay where you're meant to be and everything will be easier, but do people listen? That's what I will use the monster for, to tidy everything away. To change people, Theo, to make them better, calmer.' A fountain pen jumped from the desk to her hand without occupying the space in between.

She had filled Theo in on magic and spells, goblins and boogeymen when the two of them were down in the cave. She had willed various objects into her hand and offered to teach Theo. He had turned her down. If he wanted something he would go and pick it up, there was no need to spend time messing about learning spells. However, after last night's Whippet Snippets game, Theo saw the advantage of willing aspirin into your hand.

She handed Theo a postcard with a handwritten phone number.

'Phone them now, outside not here, and tell them what you need. It will be at the lab before you are.'

Theo did as he was instructed and spoke to a man about the equipment he would need before heading back to Bermondsey and the lab.

Theo returned to the lab and found a prole sitting on the ground outside surrounded by boxes of various sizes. The last thing he needed was an altercation. 'Sorry, can I help you?' he said, trying to add a cockney slant to his immaculate accent.

The man stood, not that it made much difference. Standing, he barely came to Theo's chest.

'I'm Reece, Mimi sent me. I've got the stuff you ordered. I was told to wait and help with the project.' He took off his straw hat revealing two large ridges running back along his head. They were tinged red in the sunlight and looked like mutated snail shells growing from his temples. *Goblin*.

Reece looked at him expectantly. Mimi hadn't been impressed with Theo's progress but surely she knew it wasn't going to be quick. 'No, thank you. I'm fine.' Theo turned his back on the little man and opened the lab. His great scientific breakthrough hadn't mellowed since he left this morning and a wave of rancid air hit his nostrils. 'But as you're here, why don't you see if you can do anything about the smell.'

Reece unpacked all the equipment and even wrote up Theo's notes onto clean paper and made extra copies for safe-keeping. Beakers had been washed and sorted by size, rope had been found to tie back the lab door to allow some much-needed fresh air inside, Theo was impressed, he had been working with the door shut as it didn't seem to have a latch. A mishmash of tables and worktops had been pushed to the edges and formed into a horseshoe. Reece had called it the "golden triangle". Apparently, kitchen designers use it so you're never more than a few steps from any one key area.

Theo placed another slab of meat on the scales. The display read two hundred grams, double last time, so hopefully the event should last twice as long. His current hypothesis was that the substance contained either bacteria or a virus that temporarily mutated DNA in random ways giving the host what could be called magic powers, but he decided were temporary evolutionary advantages or TEA, for short. He liked 'tea', it made the job seem benign in the same way Blitz Spirit glossed over the death and looting. He was just making tea.

'Reece?' Theo asked the room.

'Yes, boss,' the voice appeared to come from four cool-boxes stacked on a pair of legs trying to squeeze through the lab door.

Theo took the top two boxes and congratulated himself that he no longer had to repress a grimace at the sight of Reece's swollen goblin forehead. He had no issue with the idea of dragons or goblins existing in principle. Dragons were too big to understand — they were like the Mariana Trench or a billion years. Ridiculous if you thought about it too much so you didn't. Yes, dragons existed, he kept saying to himself without quite believing it, but goblins were far stranger. Reece was almost human which was harder to shut out. Theo's worldview started with humans being on the top, the apex predator and master of nature. Within humans he knew, some were better than others and rose to the top but the worst human was still better than the best animal. But now there were other creatures capable of all the things humans can do, what if the best human wasn't a human? At least Reece seemed content to lug boxes and fill out paperwork which didn't surprise Theo. A state education didn't prepare you for much, human or goblin. 'Once you've done whatever it is you're doing with these boxes can you set up another trial for me?'

'Yes, boss.'

The meat sat in a frying pan on a camping stove. They were close to cracking it, Theo could tell. They had nearly burnt through all the meat Mimi had sent over in one afternoon but it would be worth it, besides, he had seen a mountain of it down in the cave. They had shut the lab door in case they created something that needed containing. Reece had got lucky and figured out that heat was the extra element needed to activate the TEA. Being left in the hot shipping container overnight had caused the first batch of meat to warm up and trigger a flock of birds to fill the container, or at least fill it with a good source of fertiliser. The hard work would be figuring out how to make it last as long as possible and do the same thing every time and, more importantly, make it controllable and bend it to their will.

Theo stepped behind the protective screen and signalled Reece forward. Reece pulled on rubber gloves and checked his goggles. He picked up a box of matches and turned to Theo. Theo picked up a stopwatch and nodded. Striking a match, Reece made his way to the camping stove. The flame erupted. He turned the dial down as low as it would go and poured a beaker of bile into the pan. A strawberry smell filled the lab, not real strawberries, the fake kind they inject into strawberry-shaped sweets. The air turned thick and sickly.

Reece ran back behind the screen and Theo gave him a pat on the back. 'Good work.' The bile got to work and the meat hissed. Silence settled over the two men as they waited.

Reece went to say something but was interrupted by a butterfly landing on his nose. They stood stock still. This was new. Every time they ran the experiment they got a different result but this was the first time they had confirmation of a living creature being created. In the course of an afternoon, it had rained rose petals, the lab had turned to ice and sent them crashing to the floor, and in the last experiment Theo and Reece had grown horns and felt an overwhelming desire to play the panpipes; thankfully they didn't have any to hand. *But butter-flies.* If they could create real things, they could create imaginary things. If they could create imaginary things they were on the right track; then Mimi might be happy and Theo could set sail for the Mediterranean.

The butterfly's wings were a single shade of opaque blue trimmed in pitch black. Two more appeared on Theo's arm, bright green and yellow. A laugh escaped his throat which sent all three creatures up into the air where they bobbed and weaved. A poet would describe it as a waltz or ballet but really it was closer to the jerky movements and energy of an indie disco. If God existed, he loved a mosh pit.

Hundreds of butterflies filled the room and joined the dancing of the first few, they chased and hunted, fell in and out of love and formed fleeting vortices of colour. Calmness left the room. The butterflies ceased to be and Theo felt like he had permission to exist again.

'Right.' Theo clicked the stopwatch. 'That was seven seconds,' he said, something in his throat. He was grateful he had already cried today. 'Shall we go again?'

Six

Theo waited and watched Mimi run a finger along the edge of the worktop and inspect the green dust that had collected on her fingertip. She glanced around the shipping container and took in the spores that covered every surface of the lab in an inch-thick layer. Their most successful experiment yet had been creating a large amount of mould and getting it to hang around overnight. Theo and Reece had slept on the lab floor in case there were any other changes. When Theo woke, he had messaged Mimi and she had come straight over.

Mimi continued to stare at the mould.

'It's penicillin,' Theo offered. 'We haven't been able to predict what the tissue will do but we have discovered if you subject it to direct infrared waves it stabilises for much longer.'

Her eyes locked on him.

Theo smiled. It was all he could do until she finished thinking. His progress had been impressive and she probably wasn't expecting him to make so much headway so quickly after his rough start. His smile became fixed, unsure what to do next. He felt sorry for his cousin, she had ended up in a life of crime. In charge but being the best criminal is like being the best chef. At the end of the day, you still work in the service industry.

She prowled the lab surveying everything with a cold stare. 'There is only one use for this much penicillin and I hope you're not implying what I think you're implying?'

'Ha, yes I mean no. What's interesting is it's still here.'

Her hands lingered on a set of scalpels. 'I'm beginning to wonder why you're still here.'

Theo laughed. 'It's a big step, everything else has disappeared in less than a minute. This may not be the most impressive TEA but it is still here. I think the key is radiation.'

'What.' It wasn't a question; it was a demand.

'Radiation, if we irradiate the tissue it seems to allow the TEA to stick around for longer. It might not last forever, but it could extend it for hours, days even, and allow you to use the TEA for your plans, I think once you've changed someone's mind it won't change back. I know mine doesn't.'

Her fingers circled over the scalpels before selecting a blade with an edge that kicked out into a crescent moon. 'You want me to eat irradiated meat?'

'Yes.' Theo said, forgetting he wasn't speaking to someone as educated as himself. 'But all cooked food is irradiated, after a few different experiments I discovered that open flames work best.' This wasn't strictly true. He hadn't so much discovered fire worked best as dropped the last piece of meat into the open flame of the camping stove, panicked, and thrown the bile on top in an attempt to put out the flame. He said a short prayer to the universe and the universe answered in the only way it knew how — with a large amount of decaying matter.

Mimi dragged the blade of the scalpel across the stainless-steel worktop and it screeched an evil song. 'You mean you cooked it?'

'You could put it like that. But what it means is, I've found a way to extend the TEA. I just need to find a way to make the right TEA come out,' he said.

'Right,' Mimi said, the scalpel dancing between her fingers. 'You've bought yourself some time.'

By some unspoken command, a coltish elf in a hideous paisley suit walked through the lab door struggling with a cool box. Her tapered ears sat amongst an expensive pixie cut. Reece, who, up till now had been doing a sterling impression of a wall, cleared a space and took the box the rest of the way. Reece smiled at the elf who flashed him some eyebrows.

Mimi lifted the lid revealing chunks of a death-black living matter, it was soft and eased into every corner of the container. Theo bent low to inspect the new specimen and watched reflections of the strip lights above dance on its surface. A metallic smell reached his nostrils — it was tinged with another odour that he couldn't place at first. It was the scent of damp, mud, and dew. A memory of walking through a glade picking bluebells flashed through Theo's mind. A memory he didn't have.

'What am I looking at?' He asked.

Mimi leaned over his shoulder and looked in the box. Her features reflected off the specimen and became distorted and gross. 'Not sure, but it's from the creature and likely an organ, possibly liver.'

'Liver?'

'Well, a bit of liver. We found it where a liver should be but who can fathom what goes on inside a creature like that. That's just a sample but I can get you more if needed.'

'Do you know how it died?' Theo asked.

'Why?'

He repressed an eye roll at the stupidity of the question. 'Well, if it met a violent end then the liver should be healthy but if it just fell over for no reason then I might be looking at a diseased organ and will need to tread more carefully.'

Mimi nodded at The Elf In The Paisley Suit who replied with a curt nod of her own. 'My assistant here will look into it.'

The Paisley Elf tapped her watch.

Mimi checked her own. 'Yes, off you go, and don't be late. You know how Foresight gets.'

Theo picked up the dragon liver and held it up to his face for a closer look. Filtering things even a dragon couldn't consume. It could change everything. Theo began sketching the acceptance speech in his head. *Your Majesties, your Royal Highnesses, Esteemed Nobel Prize Laureates, I accept this prize...*

———

To the casual observer, Muriel was listening to a busker at the entrance to Brixton Tube Station. She stood a few feet in front of a woman who was giving a heartfelt rendition of Wonderwall and swayed gently to the music. This was, of course, an absolutely mad thing to be doing so everyone gave her a wide berth and squeezed down the furthest flight of stairs from Muriel instead of using the two available. Jack and Nisha stood off to one side and watched on in morbid fascination.

Last night, after the curry house, Jack and Muriel had caught Nisha up to speed on the last few days: being chased through Soho, Muriel's outrageous opinions about the work of JRR Tolkien, the search for The Dragon and more importantly, the search for whoever had found it and what they were going to do with it. Oh, and magic is real. Nisha had taken the news that her girlfriend of three years had been lying about the nature of reality well. If anything, she seemed relieved Muriel didn't actually work for the tax office. Nisha had filled them in on what she could remember of the dinner: Mimi had talked vaguely of a desire to bring order to the country, everything being too messy and needed sorting out, the country had once been firm and rigid, but it had grown weak and fat. Nisha said she had heard worse in the run-up to a general election and if it wasn't said alongside talk of organs and experiments she wouldn't have paid much attention.

Getting Mimi's name was a big step forward, they had The Who and just needed The Why and How now. What they really needed was The Where, but Jack was optimistic. This was why Muriel was dancing in the street. Hopefully.

'And the people she works for never leave their shed?' Nisha asked Jack.

'Yes.' Jack clicked his neck, if he had to spend another night on Muriel's sofa he would need to buy a pillow. She had insisted he stay over in case The Elf In The Paisley Suit, or the people she worked for, tracked down where he lived. Jack thought this was unlikely as she had very little to go on. He was just some guy who ordered some dumplings and didn't kick up a fuss when it had a bit of dragon in it.

'And they asked Muriel to keep you safe at the same time?'

'Yes. But I've decided I don't need protecting, I'm a dragon hunter.'

Nisha looked at the science teacher, covered in mud, and camping out on her girlfriend's sofa. 'Of course you are. And they are now talking to her through the music being produced by that busker?'

'I think so.' Muriel had explained it to both of them, but it didn't make much sense. Before mobile phones became commonplace, magic folk devised a way of communicating over vast distances in the city using song. She had explained it was like a network of two-way Indian smoke signals except it used overplayed pop songs so most people would try and block it out. The message would jump from busker to busker until it reached the intended recipient. Wonderwall had proven to be the most effective to the point that the technique had become known as "Wonderwalling". Hidden in the simple melody would be a message that anyone could hear if they wanted to, it was just most people tried not to hear the melody, let alone any messages hidden in it.

'And they don't use mobile phones?'

'Apparently not.'

Nisha growled a concern under her breath but said nothing to Jack.

The busker ended the song by holding the acoustic guitar above her head and letting the final notes fade out. Jack applauded out of awkwardness. The crowds started to avoid him too.

Muriel dropped a twenty pound note in the open guitar case and joined Jack and Nisha. If it was possible, she looked nervous.

'Well?' Jack asked.

'The Laurels are pleased with our progress but no luck with getting you off the hook I'm afraid,' Muriel said.

'Oh,' Jack said. Last night he had laid on the sofa in the dark and thought about the last few days. When he wasn't fearing for his life he was enjoying it. He couldn't remember the last time he felt like that, so had decided to become a full-time dragon hunter. When it was over, and if he was still alive, he would ask Muriel if he could tag along on more jobs. He couldn't make things move with his mind but he could run and that was a useful skill. 'That's ok. Where to next?'

Muriel looked him up and down. He had been wearing the same clothes since they met. A heat wave will push a polyester suit to its limit. Throw in the last few days and it was a wonder the suit hadn't turned back into a barrel of crude oil. Jack tried to pick the mudlark off his sleeve as best he could.

'The Laurels have arranged a meeting with The Seer. He's very important so you're buying some new clothes and meeting us at The Wolseley,' Muriel said.

Piccadilly was its usual busy self as Jack tried to tuck his new shirt into his new jeans on his way to meet Muriel and Nisha. The stiff material was uncompromising in that way only shirts straight from the packet can be. He spotted Muriel pacing in front of The Wolseley while Nisha stood to one side with the face of someone whose loved one was facing a self-induced apocalypse: utter bemusement.

'Are you sure it's necessary for me to wear a shirt and tie?' Jack asked.

'Yes,' Muriel said. 'Foresight is very particular about the company he keeps.' She adjusted his tie and murmured something about him needing a haircut.

He tucked his hair behind his ears as best he could. 'Better?'

'No, but it will have to do,' Muriel said.

Nisha stepped forward and broke Muriel from her fretting by putting an arm around her waist. 'What's so special about this guy anyway?'

Muriel turned as if Nisha had questioned gravity itself. 'He is The Seer.' The words left her mouth in a high gothic font and cast in iron. 'He can see into the future, guide, and answer your questions about what lies ahead and he's the only one left. There used to be hundreds of them in the city, but they died one way or another and no one came through with the talent to replace them.'

'A bit like politicians then?' Nisha asked.

'No, less of that. Getting to see him is a big deal as he's fussy about who he works for, and one false move and I could be banned for life. The Laurels are important enough to get us a meeting so we can't muck it up otherwise they could get blacklisted.'

They stepped into The Wolseley and entered a world of monochrome wealth. Everything in the restaurant was black and white or marble. Light reflected off every surface, designed to dazzle and confuse newcomers. The maître d' looked up from his pulpit. He had the tired expression of someone who saw it all. Everyday.

'Hello,' Muriel said. 'We're here to see Mr Foresight.'

The maître d's finger scanned the diary. An old-fashioned paper ledger to give the impression of old-world charm. The rich like nothing more than to pretend things like universal suffrage and the civil rights movement hadn't happened.

'Mr?' Jack asked.

'Yes, like I said, he's very formal and big on etiquette so make sure you call him Mr Foresight or The Seer.'

Nisha and Jack both knew now was not the time and nodded.

'Are you his eleven o'clock or his half past?' The maître d' asked.

'His eleven o'clock,' Muriel replied.

'Right this way please,' the maître d' said, leading them into the main dining room.

The diners were a mix of the rich and the almost rich. The rich filled the room with boisterous laughter. Jack knew the laugh. The laugh filled St George's at every PTA meeting, every sports day and graduation. A laugh of comfort and ease. It belonged to people born knowing who they were and their place in the world. Jack longed to be able to do the laugh. He wanted all the things that came with it: the confidence, the happiness, the direction. It all seemed so easy when you had the laugh. Now, as an apprentice dragon hunter he might finally be able to get the laugh and everything else that goes with it. He'll come back here with a friend at the weekend, sit at a table in the window and laugh between mouthfuls of scrambled egg.

Meanwhile, the almost-rich spoke in hushed tones scared they would be discovered and asked to leave.

Jack leant forward and spoke into Muriel's ear as they walked. 'I thought you said there was only one spell?'

'There is.'

'So how does he see into the future or that guitar thing work.'

'That's magic.'

'What's the difference?'

She thought for a moment. 'A spell is like a shadow puppet you make with your hand sitting around a campfire.'

'And magic?'

'Using magic, like Foresight, means picking logs out of the fire and juggling with them.'

Jack had always liked shadow puppets. 'And the guitar thing?'

'That's not really magic,' Muriel said, 'it just relies on people not wanting to listen to Wonderwall on the acoustic guitar again.'

A middle-aged man in a deep blue suit sat alone at a corner booth. His hand lingered on a champagne flute. An untouched plate of steak tartare sat in front of him. He saw them approached, removed the napkin from his lap and stood.

'Your party Mr Foresight,' the maître d' said, before making a swift exit.

Hands were shaken and cheeks kissed.

'It's nice to see you, Ms Sprout. What can I do for you?' he said.

'Thank you for seeing us at such short notice,' Muriel said, her hands fidgeting in her lap until Nisha held one tight. 'We need your help to find the whereabouts of Mimi Kensington-Jones.'

Mr Foresight took a sip of champagne while the waiter handed out drinks menus. 'Mimi is a very big fish, my darling. Why do you want to tangle with her?'

'Is she?' Nisha asked.

Mr Foresight touched his chest. 'Well, you are fresh to Oz aren't you, my dear? Mimi is one of the foremost employers of witches and wizards in London.'

'Employed to run protection rackets and steal things, she's basically a gangster.' Muriel said.

'There's nothing basic about it. She is a gangster and she's very good at it and you would be best to stay away. I'm not sure it would be wise for me to help you.'

Muriel rifled through her jacket pockets and placed a gold bar about the size of a matchbox on the table.

'I'm not sure what that has to do with anything,' Foresight said. He held the gold bar up to the light before sliding it into his breast pocket.

She continued searching and finally pulled out a package from her inside jacket pocket, about the size of a fist, it was wrapped in layers of newsprint, wet patches of red had started to seep through from whatever lay at the centre. She passed the parcel over and wiped her hands on her trousers. Mr Foresight gave it a sniff and seemed to approve. He placed the package next to him on the seat. 'I guess it's no business of mine what you do with any information I give you.' He pulled a deck of playing cards from his jacket pocket. He placed five cards face down on the table. The back of the cards were monogrammed with the letters B and F in crimson art deco letters. 'Are you ready to peer into the ether?'

Muriel nodded and gripped Nisha's hand.

One by one he turned the cards over. Jack of Clubs, Jack of Spades. He tilted his head and mumbled something under his breath. Two of Hearts, Ace of Diamonds and finally the Three of Hearts. The hearts and diamonds had faded to brown and the spades and clubs light grey.

He leant back. 'Interesting.'

'Do you know where she is?' Muriel asked.

'No, my dear, I never know where someone is, I only know where they will be. I predict the future, *not* the present.'

Muriel leant in expecting more. 'Yes? Where will she be?'

A marble started to roll in Jack's mind. It gained speed, took a sharp left and tapped a domino. The domino nudged another and started a cascade of hundreds of dominos falling in perfect formation across a table. The formation spread out to be ten-wide before returning to a single row. The final domino hit a bag of sugar balanced on the very edge of the table. The bag of sugar fell onto a waiting seesaw. The seesaw fulfilled its destiny and sent a dull copper disc into the air where it hung motionless for a brief moment.

Mr Foresight took another sip of champagne. 'Somewhere called Jones and Jones and she'll be there this afternoon at—.'

B and F. The penny dropped. 'Is your name Bruce Foresight?' Jack asked.

Nisha let out an involuntary cackle and the temperature dropped.

Mr Foresight (first name Bruce) made himself large. 'Three hundred years I have lived and worked in this city. Building a name and reputation as a seer of unparalleled brilliance, one who is not only accurate but discreet. I worked my way up from nothing only for some,' the word stuck in his throat, 'entertainer to come along and reduce my name to a joke.' Bruce swept the steak tartare onto the floor. Nisha climbed out of the booth and mumbled something about it being time to leave. Jack followed while Muriel froze along with the rest of the restaurant.

'Three hundred years!'

Jack covered his eyes as they adjusted to the sun. He twisted on the pavement looking for Nisha. She leaned against the Wolseley, biting her thumb to try and stop the laughter.

'Are you ok?'

She nodded, unable to articulate. Through the window, Muriel still seemed to be in shock and nodding along to every word of Bruce's ongoing rant. Jack turned to see a sweat-soaked doorman sensing a chance to use some of his power and move them on. Jack grabbed Nisha's arm and walked to the corner of the street and out of the jurisdiction of the doorman. He thought it best to wait for Muriel so he could apologise and try to keep his job as dragon hunter.

An infinite stream of people passed through Piccadilly; workers barging past tourists and the tourists getting annoyed at their travel companions for stopping to look at things. Everyone seemed to be flagging in the heat and wearing as little as their current roles in society would allow. He tried to imagine the business dress of the future once the heat became never-ending:

houndstooth ponchos replacing herringbone suit jackets, the Hawaiian replacing the Oxford, the Birkenstock the brogue.

It wouldn't last, though. If the heat continued, there would be no business dress; there would be no business. The city couldn't survive this; it was a fragile thing that relied on unspoken rules and kindness to work but the heat would evaporate all that. Heat changed people — it twisted them — just a bit, but enough so that when push came to shove, they would push and shove. If the heat didn't break soon, the city would.

Car horns blared and Jack turned to see The Elf In The Paisley Suit step into traffic and head directly for The Wolseley. Fear exploded in his chest. Maybe she hadn't seen him? Hope offered in an attempt to calm him.

The Paisley Elf, as if answering hope's question, locked eyes with Jack and gave the game away. He had been spotted. Jack pulled Nisha further down the street as fist-sized pieces of masonry disappeared from the wall behind them. The Elf in The Paisley Suit stood in traffic and aimed spell after spell at them.

Nisha sobered up quickly and caught on even quicker. Jack took the lead and they headed West towards Green Park Station. Jack shouted for tourists to move and they took the steps into the station two at a time. He approached the ticket barrier and got his debit card ready. He tapped and waited for Nisha. She fumbled with her card at the barrier.

'Hurry up,' Jack said, jumping on the spot.

She tried again, again the barrier taunted her. 'It's no good, I'm out of money.'

A small man in a TFL uniform started to walk towards them with a look that said he would unleash hell on anyone who so much as thought about jumping the barriers.

The Elf In The Paisley Suit fought her way down through the crowds and into the ticket hall followed by outraged yelling.

Jack took a run up and jumped back over the barrier. To his surprise, he made it and let out a victorious yelp. The TFL man, not used to seeing people pay and then jump back, stood helpless.

'Come on.' Nisha grabbed Jack's arm and they headed for another exit. They came up on the north side of Piccadilly and headed into the quagmire of Mayfair.

The Regency-lined streets of Mayfair gave Jack and Nisha little room to hide. The Paisley Elf's footsteps matched Jack's heart rate. Lumps of ironwork from balconies and cornices fell in their path, pulled down after their supporting counterparts had vanished into the hands of their pursuer. Nisha sped up avoiding the projectiles and headed straight across a main road that cut across their path. A lump of Portland stone, not having got the hang of its new career as an improvised weapon performed a strange piece of geometry, missed Jack's head and went for his ankle instead. He hit the ground hard but had time to be thankful it was one of the nicer streets in London. Jack had lost most of his lead on The Paisley Elf but Nisha waited at the lights for him. He carried on straight over the crossing and mumbled a thanks to the gods of traffic flow, reaching the other side just as the lights turned red.

Using the last of their strength to stay upright, Jack and Nisha emerged on a street lined with shops. Flagpoles jutted out into the road like a commercial honour guard. Jack wasn't sure where they were but he recognised the names on the flags from perfume ads so knew it was somewhere they couldn't afford.

'We can hide in there.' Jack headed for the least intimidating shop. Standing just inside the glass plate doors, stood the most stylish security guard Jack had ever seen. His haircut cost more than Jack's entire wardrobe. They went to enter and were met with a gentle shake of the head from the guard.

'No?' Jack asked.

The guard looked at Jack's shoes. Much like Jack, they were built for comfort over style, the shoes were moulded from a single piece of plastic and barely lasted more than a few months. They were the toothbrushes of footwear.

'No?' Jack asked again.

The guard nodded towards the window. Shoes, expensive shoes made from cows that had a better standard of living than most humans. Jack was not their target demographic and wouldn't be buying anything.

Nisha stepped up. 'We just want to have a look—'

The shop window exploded with a crack and showered the pavement with glass.

The Paisley Elf stood across the street, a fistful of glass in her hand and a smile on her face.

Jack and Nisha pushed past the guard and into the shop. The other staff offered no resistance as they looked on at the scene. When you're paid by the hour, standing around for ten minutes pays the same as getting into a fight with two crazy people off the street who really want to buy shoes.

While the front was velvet, perfume and smiles, the back of the shop was like any other, fluorescent lights flickering over damp corridors, passive-aggressive messages from management stuck to every surface and a staff room that smelt of instant noodles and reprieve. They found the stock room. It was a sartorial catacomb. Shoes on racks towered above them and were sorted five deep by gender, then size and finally style. Shoe horns and corrective insoles hung from pillars as grim reminders of what was to come. *Memento mori.* Jack dragged a rack of shelves across the door as a body thudded against it.

'We need a plan,' Jack said, trying not to sound panicked.

The Paisley Elf charged the door again.

'I know!' Nisha yelled, searching the stock room for an out.

They heard the muffled shouts of the security guard outside. Nisha swept boxes onto the floor and climbed onto the shelving.

The shouts had become screams. Then silence.

A panel on the door disappeared revealing The Elf In The Paisley Suit. She leaned through to aim. Stock rained down on them as slabs of shelving were sliced away.

Nisha scrambled further along the shelves for cover.

Jack ducked as dismembered shoes rained down on him. A mutilated stiletto bounced off his head and landed in front of him. Picking up the shoe he swung hard and drew blood on The Elf's hand. She cursed and withdrew out of sight.

'Jack!'

He scrambled onto the shelving towards Nisha, expecting the worst. Instead, she had uncovered an ancient door; lacking in health and safety notices it must have been forgotten about long ago.

Jack tried the handle but his sweat-drenched palms couldn't find purchase. The door burst from its hinges behind them.

'Nisha? Jack?' It was Muriel.

Jack let out a hysterical laugh at the realisation of rescue.

. . .

Jack stepped back onto the shop floor. The screams and panic of moments ago lingered in the air like dust. Outside, the security guard sat on the kerb, watched by a powerless crowd, he cradled the side of his blood-soaked head.

Nisha pushed past Jack and hugged Muriel. 'What happened?' she asked, her tone implying she was unsure if she wanted to know the answer.

'That trail,' Muriel said, nodding to a patch of blood in front of the stock room, 'was me scaring off an old friend of mine and Jack's. That trail I'm not sure, but I think it's his.' Muriel nodded at the guard.

'What's that?' Nisha had noticed a small chunk missing from Muriel's hand. It looked like someone had shaved a few millimetres from the side of her palm.

'Nothing, I got clipped that's all.'

Nisha grabbed Muriel's hand to get a closer look but she pulled away.

'I said it's nothing, it's not like it's my magic hand.'

Jack surveyed the damage, blood, broken glass, and mutilated hands. It was all real and he could do nothing but run. Surrounded by people with a power he didn't possess and his only options were to claw at locked doors or hide. *It wasn't much different to work after all.* He had survived, which seemed to be the most basic requirement of his new life. It was the same as his old, so maybe he could do this.

Sirens interrupted his thoughts. Muriel signalled for them to leave and they made for the street.

They headed east as fast as they could without drawing attention to themselves. Avoiding Oxford Street, they stuck to the strange roads to the north that were always quiet and barely met a soul until they burst onto Tottenham Court Road. Jack insisted on a rest and Muriel and Nisha didn't object.

Nisha tried to get Muriel to go to the hospital for her hand. More sirens interrupted the brewing argument and a coffee shop toilet was the compromise.

The main selling point of the coffee shop seemed to be pale wood veneer, lots of it, and the fact the sandwiches had been made that day. Yes, *that* day, never before have humans had such luxury. With Muriel's hand bandaged in napkins, they fought their way through the tail end of the lunch rush and found only a few sandwiches left. Nisha picked out a fancy ham baguette for Muriel while picking something veggie and filled with olive paste for herself.

Jack, who normally ate whatever was available in the school canteen froze at the choice before him.

'Jack, come on, it's just a sandwich,' Muriel said.

He had narrowed it down to four options when a man who looked the wrong side of hungry slid next to him, pocketed a sandwich and turned to leave.

Muriel's eyes tracked him to the exit. He reached the threshold and she went to intercept but Nisha grabbed her arm. 'He just stole a sandwich,' Muriel said, her voice filled with barely contained outrage.

'It doesn't matter,' Nisha said, directing Muriel into the queue.

'Yes it does, it's against the law.'

Jack panicked and picked tuna sweetcorn.

Nisha held Muriel's arm tight. 'It's just a sandwich.'

It wasn't though, was it? It was the halfway point, a

breathing space. As long as there had been humans, there had been lunch, and Jack had picked tuna sweetcorn.

'That doesn't matter, it's still against the law.'

They edged closer to the front of the queue.

'So is cutting off someone's hand in a train station toilet.'

Muriel burnt a hole in Jack with her eyes for a moment. 'That's different I was... He's just hungry.'

'Yeah, he's hungry,' Nisha said.

Jack looked back at the smoked salmon rolls and some form of beef with gherkins thing. This must be how Ingrid Bergman felt at the end of Casablanca. He had chosen Victor when he could've had Rick.

'No sorry, you don't steal. You go to a soup kitchen or something, there are people out there to help. He just has to ask.'

Jack and Nisha locked eyes for a moment as they approached the till. There were many types of intelligence and Muriel excelled in nearly all of them but surely she wasn't that stupid?

Nisha rubbed the small of Muriel's back and guided her towards the till. 'Let's forget it. We don't want a repeat of what happened in Majorca with the pedalo.'

This only seemed to add fuel to Muriel's fire. 'We had hired that thing for an hour. Time theft is still theft!'

They approached the cashier.

'Someone stole a sandwich.' Muriel dropped the words on the counter along with her lunch.

The cashier looked at the door and shrugged.

'Don't you care?'

. . .

What happened next was a blur. Jack remembered the sensation of wanting to collapse in on himself and a lot of indignant yelling. Someone had quoted Hobbes. Jack came to on a bench in Russell Park with his regretful sandwich halfway to his mouth.

'I think deep down the manager was happy to be reminded of the rules,' Muriel said to no one, 'and it got us a free lunch.'

'Yes,' Nisha said. 'A free lunch and a lifetime ban.'

Muriel threw the crusts of her sandwich to the pigeons and stood. 'A lifetime ban is rarely honoured, trust me. Anyway, we've got a gangster to find.'

SEVEN

Theo watched London drift past the taxi window and tried to block out whatever the driver was prattling on about. Theo didn't make it a habit of getting taxis nowadays due to the cost but he was meeting Mimi and needed to make a good impression. His parents had imparted the strange rules that govern the world to Theo through a mixture of yelling, ridicule and when it was really important sitting him down and talking calmly. Taxis were one of the calm chats, it was serious business. You had, in this order: Buses (not to be used under any circumstances), tubes (if you have to, only during the day but not to get to or from Kensington, walk from Victoria Station if you need to), and taxis (always the preference but black cabs only — no chauffeur driven nonsense. Only a non-U getting ideas above their station would go in for that).

A less calm conversation was over the choice of Theo's degree. For Theo's family, the idea of going to university was a new one. Within living memory, they had no use for knowledge or learning. Degrees were considered things that your accountant needed but not you. When you are at the top of the pile all you need is instincts for the best stocks to buy and tups to breed — a lucky streak at cards helped too. The fact that Theo had wanted to waste three years studying animals instead of doing useful things like earning money or shooting poachers had caused a row. His parents had humoured him until the crash happened and it became more important for Theo to earn than to learn.

He had done the rounds, calling up friends and distant family looking for opportunities and found nothing. His father had lost a lot of people a lot of money and old ties and blood are only in play when backed up with a healthy bank account. Working his way down the list, past school friends, godparents, and old flames, he got to the bottom and phoned his old science teacher at St George's. Theo had wanted Director of Something or maybe Head of This or That but was offered Biology Teacher instead. What he actually wanted was to live off dividends and interest on a boat somewhere but a golden opportunity to discover something new stood in front of him. New medicine, new inventions, he could spearhead a whole new branch of science. *Then* live off the dividends and interest on a boat somewhere.

The taxi pulled up outside a hotel off Oxford Street. 'But I was glad I got to the hospital in time, despite everything that happened between us I would have regretted not saying good-bye,' the taxi driver said, finishing his story.

'Ha! Brilliant,' Theo replied. He always found it best to laugh along or agree with taxi drivers. Theo walked up the steps into the hotel lobby. The hotel had been recently refurbished and smelt of fresh paint and dust. The receptionist directed him to the bar and he found Mimi sitting in a dark corner on a sofa. Two very obvious bodyguards leaned against the bar and gave Theo the once over as he approached.

Theo took a seat on the sofa opposite Mimi. Orders were taken promptly and they were left alone.

'Progress?' Mimi asked.

'With the liver?'

'What else?'

'Some,' Theo said. 'We're running the same experiments as before but not getting any new results.'

Mimi offered a sceptical murmur in response.

'But I'm confident we'll have some answers for you soon.'

The waiter returned with an espresso for Mimi and a glass of champagne for Theo.

Theo's grandfather had once shot a lion and rendered the fat to make soap so his platoon could wash away the North African desert. Theo had inherited one of the last bars and would wash with it when he needed to invoke the spirit of a man who shot lions. He had used it before this meeting and his nose caught a trace of the beast, tightening his muscles and filling his capillaries with ancestral vigour. 'But I had a question for you,' he said.

Mimi raised an eyebrow. 'This isn't a two-way relationship.'

'Well, that's part of my question. What if it was? I mean, you may not see it, but there is so much potential in the creature beyond changing minds. I wanted to ask: When you're done with the monster, can I have it? If there is any left.'

Mimi laughed. 'Did you just ask me for a dragon? Bold, I'll give you that.'

Theo nodded. 'We could do bold things with it. We could change everyone's lives, there's so much to explore in there, there could be medicine, new ways of understanding the world. We could get rich in the process.'

Mimi's coffee cup stopped on its way to her mouth. 'We?'

'Yes, we can work together.' Theo took a sip of champagne and crossed his legs, hoping to look confident and businesslike.

'And how would that work?' Mimi asked.

'Brains and capital. A tale as old as time.' The soap was doing the talking now.

Mimi downed her coffee. 'Yes, but what will you bring to the table?'

'Exactly,' Theo said.

Mimi stared at him. 'I'm already rich,' she said, with a slow blink and an intake of breath. 'You want more money. I want power. Will inventing a new aspirin give me power?'

'In the world of pharmaceutical companies yes, but you wouldn't need it. I'm talking billions here. You could just retire and never worry.'

'The thing about money Theo, and I mean real money, is it's a lot like love. When you don't have it you want it. When you see other people with it you're filled with envy and rage. But then you get it and you realise it's not this powerful thing with the ability to make or break you. It doesn't define you. What defines you is how much power you have. Money can give you power but it's finite, all the money in the world can't fix every problem or make things better. Power can, so you can keep your aspirin. I want power, not money. But I'll tell you what,' she stood before continuing, 'when I'm done with The Dragon, I promise you, money will be the least of your worries.'

Theo relaxed, he thought it would be a hard sell but Mimi seemed surprisingly open-minded about his idea. 'That's good to hear,' he said. 'I'll start drawing up some plans on possible avenues of research.'

She looked confused, no doubt unable to fathom what use a monster like that could have beyond her own simple ideas.

Education in this country was getting worse by the day. 'I'm standing because I want you to leave. Leave,' she said.

'Right yes, sorry.' Theo stood, downed the last of his champagne and left Mimi for the lobby. This was good, things were happening, he would still get his boat but first, he would change the world and get rich doing it. Then he'd be back on top where he belonged.

Theo stepped out of the hotel into the glorious heat. The city used to be so damp and dreary but now it glowed with possibility and sunshine. Maybe he wouldn't need to go to the South of France after all. It was all going to happen, the money, the respect, and he'd do it on his terms — with science and pushing the realms of knowledge, not by sitting on unearned wealth like his father or teaching useless children. Theo The Explorer — but the best kind of explorer, the kind that didn't need to leave London. But before all that, he would celebrate.

The building housing the Jones and Jones offices tried to give off the impression of unbridled power with its double-height windows and soulless lobby, but with every other building on the street going for the same look it ended up less Capitalist Powerhouse and more An Alright Place To Work.

'You sure this is the right office?' Jack asked.

Muriel scratched her eyebrow. 'No, Bruce was light on details after you two shat the bed.'

'So, we hide over the road in that coffee shop and wait for Mimi to turn up?' Jack said.

'Yeah,' Nisha added. 'And then follow her to The Dragon. Job done.'

Muriel shifted on the spot. 'No. We should go in and see

what we can find out. There could be useful information in there.'

Jack had never worked in an office, unless you count the job at the shoe shop while he was at university, but he knew places like this had security guards and swipe cards to keep people out. 'I'm not sure we can get in. What's wrong with just scoping the place out? You point her out to us and then we follow her when she leaves.'

Muriel took a deep breath but said nothing.

'What?' Nisha said.

'I don't know what she looks like,' Muriel said, suddenly finding a passing cloud fascinating.

'Isn't it your job to know all the fish in the city? Are you not Muriel The Vigilante? Muriel: Scourge Of The Underworld?' Nisha said.

Muriel offered a smile that came with thoughts of violence. 'I am. But London is big. There's lots of fish. I mean, I've heard of Mimi. Everyone has, I've just not seen her before.

'But Brucie Bonus back there,' Nisha pointed west towards The Wolseley, 'said she was the foremost gangster. Why don't you know what she looks like?'

Victory lit up Muriel's face. 'That doesn't matter because you've seen her, haven't you? You served her at the restaurant. What does she look like?'

'Well,' Nisha said, crossing her arms in defence. 'Tall, smelt good — rich. Wearing a red suit.'

'Great, so we'll stand by the entrance and sniff every tall woman that goes past.'

'Just the ones wearing red suits.'

'Why would she be wearing the same suit? It's been days.'

'Most people own a couple of suits at most. It's likely,' Nisha said.

'What if we say we have a meeting?' Jack offered as a way out for everyone. 'We could sneak in, hide... somewhere and see who turns up. Someone as important as Mimi is bound to cause a stir when she arrives.'

'And when they ask us who the meeting is with, and we don't know and even if we did know the name of anyone they would check and then what?' Nisha said.

Jack shrugged.

'I like it,' Muriel said, heading inside without waiting for a reply.

They followed without a word. Muriel hadn't said much on the walk over. She was meant to be a lone agent. The tip of the spear and she was having to drag the work experience kids around with her. The worst part was they were showing her up.

The lobby smelt good, not acceptable but virtuous, as if only beautiful things happen here. Everyone who works here is whole and jogs every morning. They buy fair trade coffee and if they can't get it, they go without. They phone their mum every Saturday and are always up to date on the news.

Muriel approached the gilded reception desk. 'Good morning, wow, what a lovely blouse,' she said with the cheeriness of a serial killer who just got away with another one.

The receptionist looked down, presumably to check if she was wearing a blouse and if it was lovely.

'Now,' Muriel said, not giving the receptionist a chance to speak, 'we've got a meeting at Jones and Jones and you're going to think we're the stupidest people ever, but my phone has died and we've forgotten who it's with.'

The receptionist's face straightened. 'Let me see if there's anything I can do.'

Muriel leant across the desk and caressed the lapel of the receptionist's blouse. 'Thank you. That blouse *is* marvellous, where did you get it?'

The receptionist laughed with a glint in her eye that said she didn't know why she was laughing. 'You know I'm not sure.'

Muriel threw her head back in mock despair. 'Fine, keep your secrets but we must be getting to our meeting. Can you let us through?'

'Right, yes, of course sorry, hang on.' A buzzer sounded and the gates opened. The security guard looked up from the football match playing on his phone and, due to the complete lack of sledgehammers or banners stating they were up to no good, looked down again. They walked through the barriers and headed for the lifts. Muriel stared straight ahead ignoring Nisha biting her tongue so hard you could practically smell blood.

The lifts were bright red, trimmed in gold and required a code to make them move. 'You charmed everything but the code off her,' Nisha said leaning against the back wall of the lift.

The security guard looked up from his phone again and seemed to be wondering why the lift doors were taking so long to close. Jack smiled at the guard. 'We need to do something before he figures us out,' he said through a fixed grin.

Muriel stood in front of the number pad and held out her hand.

'This isn't a film, that's not going to work,' Jack said.

The number pad and two sliced wires appeared in her palm. A welcoming ding filled the lift as the doors closed.

'That shouldn't work,' Jack said.

'Magic,' Muriel said with a wink. Sneaking into an office building had obviously put her in a good mood.

The lift set off at startling speed for the floor that housed Jones and Jones. 'So, what's the plan?' Muriel asked Jack.

'Me?'

'Yeah, this was your idea. You said we should say we have a meeting and sneak in, what's next?'

This was it. Jack's moment to prove to Muriel he could be useful and part of the gang. 'We,' he said, 'could hide in the toilets? No. We just walk about carrying stuff, people never question people carrying stuff at work, it's the very definition of work. People go: What's Jack up to? Oh, he's carrying stuff, he's *working*.'

Muriel took a moment to process this. 'You just want us to walk in circles around the office with reams of paper until Mimi turns up?'

'Well, you mutter too, no one ever bothers a mutterer at work.'

'You are good at muttering,' Nisha said to Muriel.

'The only reason I have to mutter so much—' The lift shunted to a stop. They stood still and tried to hear cables groaning and snapping.

'The lift has stopped,' Jack said.

Muriel breathed out through her nose and turned to Nisha. 'There should be an emergency call button somewhere.'

'And say what? Hello, we broke into your building and now we're stuck, can you let us out please?'

Muriel began scanning the lift for the button. 'They won't ask that. They'll just try and get us out. Where's the damn button?'

'It's there,' Jack said.

'Where?'

He pointed to the jumble of wires in Nisha's hand.

'That's a silly place to put it,' Muriel said. 'It should be somewhere else in case the number pad breaks.

Nisha nodded. 'Or someone rips it out of the wall.'

Muriel stood on her toes and tested the different ceiling panels.

'That's not a thing,' Jack said. 'Lifts don't really have panels that let you climb on top of them. Insurance companies would have a mare.'

With a clang, a panel popped out. Nisha gave Jack a sympathetic pat on the shoulder as they watched Muriel's legs disappear into the lift shaft. Her hand appeared. Nisha grabbed it and began to climb up.

Jack peered up into the gloom. 'Fine, but what's the plan once we're up there? There isn't going to be a ladder for us to climb up.'

Weak red lights lit the lift shaft. They had been placed every few feet but did little more than draw attention to the darkness. Vents and pipes ran up and down the shaft doing important but invisible jobs. Metal bars had been planted into the wall at regular intervals to allow people to climb up and down. 'It's not technically a ladder,' Jack said.

'Either way, start climbing,' Muriel said with a smile from ear to ear. If breaking into a building had put her in a good mood then the thought of climbing up a lift shaft had made her day.

'Does anyone feel that?' Nisha asked.

Muriel looked around. 'Feel what?'

'I don't know. Something just feels off.' Nisha shrugged. 'I'm sure it's nothing.'

Jack took the lead as they climbed up the technically-not-a-ladder. At each floor they tried to pry open the doors with no luck.

'I know what it is,' Nisha said somewhere between floors

seven and eight. She took their lack of interest as a sign to keep talking. 'The air conditioning is off but it's still cool.'

Muriel stopped climbing. 'What?'

'The air conditioning, these vents should be humming but someone's turned it off. Which is a bit weird as this whole building is basically a big glass tube on a hot day, we should be roasting.'

'Climb climb climb,' Muriel yelled. 'It's a pontificator!'

Nisha laughed. 'A what?'

'Is this like the mudlark?' Jack asked.

'Mudlark?' Nisha said.

Muriel pushed Jack up the ladder. She wasn't kidding. 'No, this is serious. They sneak into buildings, turn the air con off, and feed on the hot air that's produced in business meetings.' Panic laced her voice, her day ruined. 'They used to be rare, existing only at dinner parties, but with the invention of the meeting room their numbers exploded.'

A low drone spread over Jack as he climbed.

'But if it feeds on air why would it be after us?' Nisha called over the noise.

'They can never get enough; they want more and more. They enter people's minds and get them to produce more hot air, have you ever known someone who would just talk crap all day long for no reason? That's a pontificator possession,' Muriel said.

Nisha let out a gasp.

Jack turned, fearing the worst.

'What is it?' Muriel called out.

'Nothing, it's just lucky I got out of art school alive.'

A black square sat amongst the red light and offered an escape. A vent, small but big enough to climb through. The drone grew stronger. Jack's arms began to resist the ladder, muscles screamed and the strength drained from his hands. The tunnel grew near. The drone grew to be more than a noise. It became Jack's every thought and every memory. The drone existed at every point in time; it was at Jack's third birthday, it held his hand on his first day of school, and it was his first kiss. Every day of his life was filled with the drone. The drone was Jack and Jack was the drone.

With his last ounce of strength, Jack climbed into the tunnel. He crawled through the darkness and found another lift shaft and ladder. Deep below, a lift rose up towards them.

Nisha joined him, shaking and out of breath.

'Have you got the marketing reports?' Jack said when he meant to ask where Muriel was.

Nisha looked confused. 'Projections look good for the next quarter.'

'Let's take this offline,' Jack said. It was no good. He pointed to the rising lift.

Nisha nodded.

He put a finger in the air and pointed to himself, two fingers and pointed at Nisha then three fingers and shrugged.

Nisha pointed back down the tunnel and returned the shrug.

The lift rattled closer. He could jump and leave Muriel to fight the thing alone. He could run into the street while she wrestled in the darkness. He could return home and leave Muriel to all this. *But then what?*

A bang overpowered the drone. Something had landed in the tunnel behind them. It crawled towards them with the fire and fury of a beast unleashed. The lift drew close. Jack grabbed Nisha and pulled her onto the top of the lift. The thing leapt out of the darkness and landed next to them. Jack stood and stepped in front of Nisha, palm open. Bathed in red light, rage poured from the monster. *Don't move the can, it was always there.* Fire burned in its eyes and it was Muriel.

'Everyone ok?' she asked.

'Let's circle back on that,' Jack said, collapsing onto the floor.

She gave him a questioning look.

'Sorry yes, I'm fine. Is it gone?'

Muriel nodded. 'For now, I scared it off.' She helped Nisha to her feet and brushed her hair out of her face. 'You good?'

Nisha dusted herself down. 'Never better, but how?'

'You just have to be direct. Nothing stops a pontificator like purpose.' Muriel lifted the trapdoor leading into the lift and signalled for them to jump down.

'Mimi Kensington-Jones?' A smartly dressed woman asked as the lift doors opened.

'Yes, that's me,' Muriel said, stepping into the offices of Jones and Jones. This was not the plan. The plan was for Jack and Muriel to be lost on the wrong floor and distract anyone that needed distracting while Nisha snuck past and tried to find out what she could.

'Oh, you've got a little something.' The woman pointed to Muriel's cheek.

Jack stood to one side and tried to block the woman's view of Nisha sneaking past.

Muriel rubbed the lift grease off as best she could. 'Just been to a spa, Icelandic mud. Shall we?'

Nisha stood behind the woman and gave Jack a thumbs-up before disappearing down a corridor.

The smartly dressed woman was called Sarah, who, as they quickly learnt, thought it was so great to meet face to face at last and she was a junior executive and had been with the company for a few years and was super excited to be working on the project but don't worry some really talented people were taking the lead but she was super excited and it doesn't matter that you're a bit early as they are all set up and ready to go.

They walked down a corridor lined with offices and meeting rooms, floor-to-ceiling glass separating The Us from The Them. Sarah opened a glass door that led into a conference room with a view of the city looking west. The sky was hot and clear, the steel and glass of London seemed to wilt under its violence, it needed rain as much as the grass did.

A man and woman stood as they entered and fixed professional smiles. They introduced themselves with firm handshakes as Joe and Jo, both wore expensive suits tailored for their bodies.

Jack felt sorry for people in suits, not due to any counter-culture leanings but because people who worked in offices like this seemed very gullible. Someone had got hold of them at an impressionable age and convinced them that synergising marketing streams was what it was all about. When what the person had really done was convince them to make someone else a lot of money. Like the emperor in his new clothes teaching you how to play strip poker. Jack didn't know what it was all about but he knew it wasn't synergising marketing streams.

He pulled back a chair and it glided like it was on ice, the only noise was a slight whisper of money as the chair's chrome runner slid against the thick carpet. He glanced at the air conditioning vent. There was no sign of life.

'Your brief really got the team thinking. It was probably the most exciting thing that's come across our desk in quite some time,' Joe said. He sounded like an old-fashioned news presenter except for the occasional northern consonant. He would probably regale colleagues with tales of a simple childhood in a small mining town in Cumbria except if you probed a bit deeper, you discover both his parents were solicitors and he grew up with a holiday house in France.

'I would say the most exciting thing on anyone's desk since PR was invented. It's the type of project you dream about working on,' Jo added.

Joe nodded. 'Not a dictatorship, but—'

'A new way of organising ourselves. A benevolent voice taking the stress out of everyday living.' Jo added. 'You can't be stressed if you don't have a choice, can you?'

'Very Tao,' Joe said. 'I can see the poster now.' His thumbs and index fingers made two corners of the poster. 'Better living through consistency.'

Jack's body tensed an imperceptible amount.

Jo continued. 'When you told us your great idea and this new technology you had, we started by looking back at other great, er, shall we say, shifts in history and how we could bring about the next one.'

'The Black Death,' Joe added.

Jo nodded. 'Millions died but it brought about The Renaissance.'

'The French Revolution,' he continued.

'Liberty, Equality, Fraternity.'

Jack bobbed along to the verbal tennis.

'Yes, but we wanted something different for this project. Here at J and J we always push the envelope.'

Jack suppressed a grimace.

'We thought: there is so much bloodshed in history, what's a new way of doing this? How can we be better?'

Joe stood and pulled a rubber-band ball from his pocket and bounced it in a piece of well-rehearsed stagecraft. 'That's right. You can try and convince people of course but you'll never get everyone. There'll always be some stick-in-the-mud who wants to do it a different way or just likes a moan.'

'We bounced some things about. Brainstormed a bit and tried to think outside the box,' Jo, still seated, said.

'And I think we did. The key to bringing about a real paradigm-shifting change is to have vision and freedom. Vision you bring to the table, of course.'

Muriel nodded.

'But freedom is the hurdle you face, Mimi,' Jo leaned in, her face just the right amount of serious. God, they were good, Jack thought. 'Freedom to do the things that need doing and not being bogged down in all that red tape that is so often thrown at disruptors like yourself.'

'As well as freedom, the plan we've come up with allows for the removal of any opposition. I know people pause at the word monopoly, but every house owns a copy so it can't be all bad.'

Joe and Jo laughed.

'And with the removal of the moaners and the contrary, you'll have the vision and complete freedom to get this country where it needs to be.'

'And what a vision it is.' Joe moved to stand next to the TV.

'Now, the plan,' Jo said, joining her colleague, 'is, with the help of your device, to give the people the gift of a few bespoke memories — designed by Jones & Jones — that will help them see that real change is needed.'

An image of a sunrise flashed onto the TV.

'None of the events in themselves will be world-shattering. They'll seem isolated, one-offs, but they will slowly build.'

A policeman in riot gear raising a truncheon against a protestor in Trafalgar Square appeared on the TV.

'While your device changes the memories of the population my team will have doctored—'

'Enhanced,' Joe interrupted, winking.

Jo nodded. 'Sorry, yes. My team will have *enhanced* images and footage ready to plant into key archives such as BBC and Wikipedia.'

A miner, bleeding from his head, is being dragged away by a different policeman.

'Layers upon layers these events will build.'

Hostages — blindfolded and scared — are paraded in front of a camera.

'They'll linger in people's minds.'

Flames rising from a train station.

Empty supermarket shelves.

'The events have been planned to give the people a feeling of hopelessness, every week a new crisis.'

Bankers sipping champagne.

'Nothing changes for the better.'

Queues snaking into a food bank.

'With so many problems, where does one begin?'

A girl, four or five at most, attempts to cross The Channel in an inflatable boat.

'Soon people will question things. They'll become active in their own destiny.'

Rival gangs clash on a city street.

'Faced with these events they will call out for change. For someone with the power to do something. Anything.'

A politician throwing a punch in Parliament.

'This is where you come in. You emerge as a figure that can be trusted, you're thrust into the limelight against your will.'

A protest march with a white space where the leader should be.

'Campaigning for justice or some cause no one will remember or care about.'

The same white space on a late-night news show.

'But your following grows, you're down to earth and tell it like it is.'

The white space raises a pint of dark ale in a country pub.

'Soon you run for office with your own party.'

Megaphone in hand, the white space addresses a crowd of thousands in Hyde Park.

'You sweep the board.'

The King shakes hands with the cutout.

The screen goes black. The presentation finishes. Jack's eyes itch as he realises he hasn't blinked in minutes. His stomach twists and his bones feel hollow. Joe and Jo stand on either side of the TV, its final slide a back void. *They turn anger and sadness into money and sleep like babies every night.* Jack imagined the black void swallowing them, pulling in the whole office, tables, chairs, computers and all.

'The exact details on what happens next will be vague, of course,' Jo said. 'People will say how quick and welcome it was. They won't be able to explain why or how but no one will ask. They will only know things are better now.'

A moment passed.

'Any questions?'

Muriel sat with her mouth open.

'I don't think so. No,' Jack said. He pushed back his chair and stood.

'Fantastic,' Joe said. 'The next step will be—' The sound of the fire alarm burst into the room. *Nisha.*

'Oh dear,' Muriel said. 'It sounds like you're all going to die horrible deaths.'

'I'm sure it's just a test or a false alarm.' Jo opened the meeting room door and the noise doubled in volume. 'Sarah!' Jo was gone.

Workers started to file out past the meeting room towards the stairs.

'Perhaps we should go anyway,' Jack said. 'We've got a busy day ahead of us.'

Muriel pushed back her chair.

'I can assure you, there isn't a fire,' Joe said. 'If you're happy to wait outside for a bit we can get this all sorted.'

'You want me to stand *outside*? Like one of your *employees*?' Muriel said, enjoying herself a bit too much.

'That won't do at all. Let's go, I'll rearrange,' Jack said, making for the door. Through the glass, he saw Nisha looking the picture of innocence. She had procured a staff ID and some minor smoke damage. 'Mimi,' Jack said, turning to Muriel. 'Now.'

They left, catching up with Nisha on the stairs and catching her up on what they had heard once they were clear of the offices. They stood at a bus stop on The Strand and took turns in the shade offered by the doorway of a barbershop.

'Can The Dragon really allow her to do this?' Nisha asked.

Muriel ran her tongue along her teeth. 'It might. The Laurels said it allowed people to do great things they shouldn't have been able to do. If someone was able to channel all of it they might be able to pull this off.'

'What will she do once she's in power?' Jack asked, nudging Muriel out of the doorway. Jack's body had become acclimatised to the air conditioning offered by Jones and Jones and now sulked as it stood in the Dantean heat that hammered London.

Muriel rolled her eyes at Jack and moved into the sun. 'I don't think she'll be feeding the poor and hungry.'

'Did you find anything out?' Jack asked Nisha.

'I took a leaf out of Muriel's book and charmed my way into the finance office,' Nisha said with great satisfaction and a wink aimed at Muriel.

Muriel rolled her eyes again.

Jack tilted his head. 'Why?'

'Because, people who work in finance departments hate technology which means everything is still paper-based, including invoice details.'

'So?'

'So, if Mimi is using the services of Jones and Jones they would send her invoices.' Nisha pulled a copy of an invoice from her pocket. 'Which would have the client's address on it.'

'Well? What is it?' Muriel asked.

Nisha signalled to Jack it was her turn out of the sun. 'Addington Lane, number fifteen to be precise.'

'Wait, if it was that easy why did you start a fire?' Jack said, taking Muriel's place who had taken Nisha's.

Nisha shrugged. 'I needed to get a signal to you that I was ready to leave.'

Tapping on the window of the barbershop made them all jump. The barber made a gesture that informed them that the shade was for customers only. It was time to find Mimi.

EIGHT

Jack thought the houses on Addington Lane were called mews but wasn't sure. They were nice whatever they were called. Walking onto Addington Lane was like walking onto the set of a rom-com where the rich magazine editor falls for the humble lawyer and, after being distracted by a cad, wins back the lawyer with the help of a quirky yet loveable friend who seems to work in a pub but can somehow afford rent in Kensington.

'You're not listening to a word I'm saying, are you?' Muriel said. 'You've got no idea what I just said.'

'You asked what this kind of house is called,' Jack said with a straight face.

'What are these houses called?' Nisha asked.

'Mews, I think.'

Muriel ignored them both. 'What I actually said was, "I'm not sure how we're going to get past the builders."'

Mimi's house seemed to be a building site. Vans and skips lined the street with her front door as the epicentre. A steady stream of workmen filed out of the house and emptied wheelbarrows into the skips, others drank tea or got disapproving looks from locals. Some did all three at the same time.

Jack flapped his arms to try and generate a breeze. The air was thick and heavy with two hundred years of carbon. 'I don't care what we do as long as we get out of the sun soon.'

Nisha threw her phone in the air and it miraculously reappeared in her hand.

'Am I going to regret teaching you that?' Muriel said.

Nisha looked down at Muriel's mallard embroidered boots. 'What size shoe are you again?'

The only difference between a stupid idea and a genius one was if it worked. The Wright Brothers had a stupid idea until it wasn't, and this was up there. Nisha wore Muriel's boots, Jack's belt as well as her own, and some honeysuckle that had been growing up the side of a nearby house as a garland in her hair.

'This isn't going to work,' Muriel said.

'It will if you *believe* it will, do you believe?' Nisha's eyes widened.

Muriel tried to share a look with Jack but he was deep in character as Nisha's faithful but silent assistant. They walked past the tea drinkers and wheelbarrow handlers without comment. The door was within reach. Clear plastic sheeting lined the hallway into Mimi's house. They stepped over the threshold. The house was saturated with the smell of dust and sweat.

'Hard hat.'

Nisha turned and pulled a face she had seen on a thousand customers. The owner of the voice, a builder, took a step back.

'Hard hat,' he said again.

Nisha looked at Jack and Muriel as if to ask who this man was and why he felt he could speak in her presence.

'We're very busy,' Muriel said.

'You need to wear a hard hat.' He nodded to a notice. They did indeed need to wear hard hats. A crowd had gathered giving the gatekeeper confidence. His eyes narrowed 'And who are you?'

Nisha flinched as if shot. 'I'm the one who will be turning this building site into a work of art.' She took a moment to be absorbed by her own genius. 'I, am the interior designer and if our client.' Nisha's eyes darted upwards, 'Sandra, what's her name?'

Muriel missed the beat but recovered. She pretended to check her phone. 'Ms Kensington-Jones, Mimi Kensington-Jones.'

Two dots joined in Nisha's brain. 'Really, Kensington? And she lives in Kensington?' Nisha asked, forgetting where, and who, she was.

'Yes,' said Muriel, her eyes adding that this wasn't the time or place and maybe we should discuss the coincidence later.

Nisha saw their point. 'Right yes, Ms Kensington-Jones hears how you builders stopped us from making her dreams come true I will need a name?'

Suddenly the crowd had become a rabble, their society had broken down and one must be chosen for the volcano. No one left as the entertainment-to-danger ratio was still favourable.

'His name's Pablo,' a voice in the rabble called out.

'No it's not,' Probably Pablo said, his voice creeping up an octave. 'I'm just doing my job, it's health and safety. You've got to wear a hard hat.'

Nisha paced up and down in faux contemplation, 'I won't

give Mimi a name but as you have ruined my zen I will need the house to be silent while I work.'

Jack had seen the expression thousands of times on his students, the next few seconds were key. If one didn't buy it, none of them would. The entertainment-to-danger ratio had changed, the new calculation was: extended tea break to boss returning while on said tea break. Probably Pablo was the first to commit when he realised the merits of a group bollocking. He took off his compulsory hard hat. 'I could do with a cup of tea.'

The builders were a society again. A society of tea drinkers. A society of tea drinkers who would station a lookout on the corner to check for management returning.

Nisha slid off the honeysuckle garland and slumped on a paint can as the last builder left. 'I might need a minute.'

'No time.' Muriel put on a hard hat and headed into the front room.

Every room on the ground floor had been gutted and lay empty except for a film of white dust that followed all building work. Half the rooms upstairs were in the state of being ripped apart while others had been filled with supplies and materials for the work. And unless you could install yourself as dictator with paint brushes and bags of plaster it was a dead end. Every room had a trail of dust leading to the front door. The dust was joined by a trail of mud coming from the basement.

They settled into the soon-to-be kitchen that was acting as a makeshift war room for the builders. Blueprints lay on a trestle table, held in place with empty mugs and screwdrivers.

'Can you feel anything?' Nisha asked.

'It's a dragon, not a draught,' Muriel said.

Jack flicked through the blueprints.

Nisha began poking the newly plastered walls. 'Maybe there's a secret door or passage.'

Jack traced his index finger over the master plan and got his bearings. The whole house was being taken apart and rebuilt from the inside out.

'What are you talking about, you're looking at bare walls. You don't plaster then install a secret door that's double bubble for the plasterer,' Muriel said.

Under the master plan were more detailed drawings of each room. From what Jack could figure out everything was being replaced like for like: cabinets, doors, light fittings. An exercise in work for work's sake. *An excuse to make a lot of noise and mess.*

Nisha turned, her face lit up like a parent who had just seen their baby take its first steps. 'Double bubble? Since when do you say double bubble?'

Every room had a corresponding blueprint.

'I've always said double bubble,' Muriel said in a tone that insisted she had been able to walk for years.

He stuck his head under the table. *Nothing.*

'I have never heard you say double bubble. Farm girls from Kent don't say double bubble.'

He picked up the plans and left.

'We do, it's what we got if we helped Mum clear out the chickens at the weekend.'

'Basement,' he said.

They turned. 'What?'

The basement was locked but Muriel made short work of the door. It was another shell of a room. Plasterboards had been screwed in place without much care, scuff marks and mud covered every surface. The plastic sheeting to protect the floor continued down into the basement but had collected pools of muddy water giving the room a Cambrian odour. The only light came from a lamp set up in the corner, rendering their shadows large on the walls. A dozen flatbed trolleys, the type you get in DIY shops, were pushed against one wall. Their decks stained dark brown.

'They have plans for every room except the basement but they are clearly doing work down here,' Jack said. 'There was mud leading from the basement door to the front door. Someone has moved stuff in or out of this room.'

'Maybe the plans are somewhere else or it's just where they are storing those trolleys,' Muriel said, dipping a toe in a pool of water.

'I don't think so, the plans are numbered. One of ten, two of ten.'

Nisha carried on her systematic poking.

Muriel bent down and dipped her finger in the water and tasted it.

'What are you hoping to find out from that?' Jack asked.

She screwed up her face. 'Eggy.'

Jack looked up. 'Bad plumbing?'

They searched but couldn't see any signs of water damage on the ceiling.

A sheet of plasterboard slipped forward when it came under Nisha's scrutiny. Her arms lurched forward and she caught it but it was too awkward for one person to hold for long. She slowed its fall and placed it on the floor. The plasterboard had been hiding a tunnel that headed deep underground. Nisha turned, looking very pleased with herself.

Jack brought the lamp over and they peered. The tunnel

was manmade, its sides ragged and erratic from spades and pick-axes. Scaffold poles had been placed at intervals as supports, water seeped through the clay walls and collected on the ground.

Muriel stepped into the tunnel.

Jack sensed this was the end. If he took one more step there was no going back to his old life. The story that he was just tagging along until The Laurels could fix things for him would fall apart; even the story where he joined Muriel on a trial basis as an apprentice wouldn't hold water. This was him committing, he would be *involved*. Most of his life had been spent trying not to be involved and he had done pretty well out of it. The desire to press the big red button wasn't one he understood, *not anymore*. It's why he liked physics; it was all theoretical. A theoretical life for a theoretical man.

'Jack?' Muriel said, waiting for him.

'I want it on the record that I think this is a bad idea. Shouldn't we go back and report this to The Laurels?' he said, stepping into the tunnel.

'What, and say: The bad news is we annoyed Foresight to the point where he probably won't work with you again but the good news is we found a big hole?' Muriel gestured for the sheet of plasterboard.

Jack and Muriel held the board, enabling Nisha to squeeze through the gap. Muriel pulled out her phone and turned the torch on. 'Come on, it won't take them long to figure out where we went. We'll find The Dragon then report in with The Laurels.'

They descended into the darkness. The ground was compacted earth that made the sounds of their footsteps menacing and deep. Grooves have been worked into the ground where hundreds of wheels had made the trip before them. Hundreds of wheels or the same dozen hundreds of times. The torchlight did little to relieve the pressure of the blackness. The air became hot and thick the further they went. They stopped to catch their breath where slick London clay gave way to bedrock. Jack ran his hands along the walls of the tunnel, it had a honeycomb structure with sections taken out in neat circles. 'This can't be natural,' he said.

Muriel joined him with her hands on her hips, her breath short. 'You're right.' She held out a hand and a cylinder of rock appeared in her palm. 'Lorry drivers and miners.'

After an hour or so, the tunnel opened into a natural cavern. The light from their phones became unnecessary. Millions of specks of white light danced and weaved above them. The lights moved to an unknown rhythm but moved as one. The cavern was a forest, tall and dense. Beech trees reached up towards the light. Ferns, moss and bracken flowed like a great green river between the trees. Cool and fresh, the air smelt of the ocean, the countryside, and the mountains all at once.

An area had been cleared in front of the tunnel; life had been cut down to provide humans with a space to stand. More trolleys stood idle here too. From the clearing, a path twenty feet wide had been ripped through the forest. Trees felled and the ground upturned and compacted by boots passing back and forth. Drag marks from some kind of machinery or heavy equipment torn through the path disappearing into the darkness.

Nisha and Muriel both craned their necks upwards,

mesmerised by the lights. 'Did you know this was down here?' Jack asked Muriel.

She didn't reply, her eyes filled with white light. 'Muriel?' Jack said.

She returned to the world, embarrassed at being caught in awe. 'No. No, I didn't.'

They followed the path that had been hacked through the trees; Jack walking a few paces behind the other two. They saw no signs of life but heard them everywhere: birdsong, critters rustling and a thousand other forms of life all existing at once. Jack tramped and trundled along the path, his eyes fixed on the lights above. This was the closest thing he had had to a holiday in what seemed like years. Maybe it was. Since crashing and burning off his PhD, he had worked at a job he didn't like and wasn't suited to. When he wasn't working he was trying not to think about work. Every day took effort and force to get through. Every moment was considered and mulled over afterwards, which was no way to be. Living in the moment was for people who were already relaxed. But here, deep underground, watching the lights he could let the moments slip and glide over him. He purred.

'You ok?' Muriel asked without turning around. 'You just purred.'

'Did I? I was just watching the lights.'

'Is it me,' Nisha said. 'Or are we sloping upwards?'

They stopped and looked behind them. There was a slight slope to the path.

'So?' Muriel said.

'I don't know, but it might mean something,' Nisha said.

'Like what?'

The conversation continued. Jack half listened while he stared up and let the lights wash over him. Over the sound of

Muriel and Nisha debating the importance of the slope, Jack heard a rustle. The forest around them was full of sound and movement but this seemed different. It was a rustle with intent. He pulled out his phone, turned on the light and scanned the ferns and undergrowth. A thick layer of dew covered the plants, reflecting his torchlight back at him as a galaxy. There it was again. Rustling.

'Do you guys hear that?' Jack said to the other two. They ignored him.

He spun around but couldn't find the source.

Suddenly, a hound bounded out of the forest. Black as midnight and eyes filled with the hunt. It pounced and flew through the air. Jack didn't have time to yell before it was on him.

This is it.

It mauled and bit Jack's leg but was rather pleasant in an odd sort of way, like a massage from a colleague. The hound was, in fact, a very old and very toothless dog that had once been black as midnight but now speckled with grey and bald patches. Its eyes still longed for the kill. 'Guys,' Jack said. 'Guys. Guys!'

Nisha and Muriel turned to find a geriatric dog suckling on Jack's trouser leg. Muriel shook her head. 'Can't leave you alone for five minutes.'

'Can you help me?'

'How?' Muriel asked. 'If I pick it up it might crumble to dust.'

Nisha bent low to stroke the dog. 'Don't be mean.'

The dog, anticipating a flanking manoeuvre swooped on Nisha's outstretched hand and sucked. 'Well, aren't you lovely?' Nisha's pitch went up and her vocabulary went down. *God she's one of them,* thought Jack. *A dog person.*

'Where it's from?' Muriel asked, with a look that said she was reconsidering the most important relationship in her life.

'Over there,' Jack said and pointed into the bushes.

'I mean, how did it get down here.'

The dog continued to attack Nisha, it jumped onto her lap and pushed her to the ground.

'I doubt it came through the tunnel, there's no way it got through all those builders without a hard hat on. Maybe there is another way down or it might belong to Mimi's men? It could lead us to The Dragon?' Jack said.

The dog, thinking it had vanquished Nisha, began to pull on her sleeve, eager to take her somewhere to feast.

'I've got an idea,' Nisha said.

Nisha's second idea of the day consisted of Jack and Muriel picking her up by her arms and legs while the dog continued to think it was dragging Nisha back to its lair by her sleeve. The dog led them through the forest and up a steep hill. The hill became a sheer cliff in places and they were forced to weave and twist their way to the summit. The cliff gave way to become a wide plateau covered in more forest. The beech trees grew tall and straight here too but other trees were scattered amongst them: oaks, elms and dozens more. Natural paths seemed to wind and twist through the forest. Jack knew little about trees or forests but could sense this place was ancient.

'What should we name it?' Nisha asked about the dog.

'Nothing. It's not a pet.'

'I know. But if it was, what should we name it?'

'How about Gerry.' Jack said. 'Short for geriatric?'

Nisha shot him daggers. 'He's not a Gerry or geriatric.'

'Dusty?' Muriel suggested.

Up ahead, the flicker of faint orange light danced off the trees and a steady drumming overcame the sounds of the forest. Muriel dropped Nisha and crept forward through the ferns. She signalled for Jack and Nisha to stay back. Nisha stood, giving Gerry a fright as his dinner seemed to have come back from the dead. Slipping out of Jack's grasp when he tried to grab him, the dog headed towards the drumming. Muriel shot Jack a death stare due to his mistake. With nothing to lose, Jack and Nisha crept forward and joined Muriel to see what was making the music.

It was drums, well, drummers technically. A circle of them, twenty or so, dressed in faded tie dye and bell-bottom jeans. They sat on logs around a deep opening in the ground. The opening seemed to be the source of the light. Between the drummers and the hole, a middle-aged woman danced with more enthusiasm than skill. She possessed nothing but a poncho and the confidence to wear nothing but a poncho. Half hidden in the darkness, behind the group, sat a dilapidated Georgian townhouse.

Gerry reached the drummers and began to whine and signal for them to follow him.

'What do we do?' Nisha asked. 'They seem friendly, do we just stand up?'

'Friendly? They're hippies for god's sake, and besides, they might be working for Mimi,' Muriel said. 'Not to mention the random townhouse.'

'Hippies are friendly and don't work. That's their thing.'

'I don't like this. It's weird,' said Muriel.

'Right, but you lost the right to decide what was weird when you came to my work looking for a free curry and then set fire to the kitchen. I say we stand.' Nisha stood and waved. 'Hello.'

Muriel cursed under her breath before joining Nisha. Jack followed suit and offered a limp wave. *They were going to die.*

The drummers stood and stared. The woman in the poncho reacted first, she pushed past the drummers with her arms open. 'Welcome! Welcome strangers. It's been so long since we've had guests. Come.' She ran up to Jack and gave him a hug, her poncho and confidence rubbing against him. He mumbled a greeting or something, he couldn't remember.

'Yes,' Muriel said. 'Hello, it's nice to meet you. Who are you?'

The woman introduced herself as Dove and each of the drummers by name. Most Jack forgot straight away as they weren't real names, they were called things like Spring and Cloud and Midden — the type of names people give themselves in lieu of a personality. Dove insisted they sit by the hole and warm themselves. Jack had been enjoying the cool air for the first time in weeks but was too polite to say anything. The hole was closer now and Jack peered down. Heat and an orange light poured from the vent like a volcanic fissure. Jack caught Muriel's eye, she had spotted it as well. *Dragon.*

Nisha told Dove everything: The search for The Dragon, Mimi's plot to become a dictator, even about the tunnel. Muriel sat by the fire and stared into the middle distance, muttering to herself and trying to pretend that Nisha wasn't giving the whole game away. *Nisha was right, she was a good mutterer.* Jack attempted to curb Nisha's intelligence leak by asking Dove who the hell they were.

This was a mistake as the answer involved a poem. Dove, through the medium of bad prose and slightly better drumming, told the story of a West London commune in 1971. An abandoned Georgian townhouse turned into a happy place, free of prejudice, sexism and all the other isms that stop people from being whole. And by people, Dove meant university-educated white people who had decided to take a few years out from training to be dentists. The commune was popular and people came and went as they pleased. It was all so exciting. London was buzzing and alive with possibilities, again, if you were a university-educated white person. Carnaby Street swung, Big Ben tolled and Twiggy twigged.

Work began under the commune on what was to become the new Jubilee Tube Line. Due to an unknown structural fault with the house and some lacklustre Health and Safety regulations, the house, hippies and all, fell through a sinkhole and brought Dove and her people to this great and wondrous place.

'Sorry,' Muriel interrupted. 'You expect us to believe you fell a mile into this cavern and didn't die and the house just landed without a scratch?'

'The cavern provides, the cavern cares. The cavern is love,' Dove said. The drummers repeated this mantra.

Muriel pursed her lips. 'This has been lovely but I think we need to get going. Do you know if there is a dragon around here somewhere by any chance? Like in that hole.'

The group murmured at the word dragon. Dove calmed the group before speaking. 'You'll have to excuse everyone; we do not use that word anymore.'

'What? Dragon?' said Muriel.

Dove offered a thin smile. 'Yes, we prefer the word God.'

Jack's ears pricked up. *Oh no.*

'Right,' Muriel said. 'Why's that exactly?'

'Because he is the creator, the giver of all you see. When we first arrived there was only darkness. He gave us the light you see above you. We were cold so he directed us to this fire. It has burned for over a thousand years. All you see is him.'

'But it's only been about fifty. I think you've lost track of time a bit,' Muriel said.

'In the outside world perhaps but to us, it has been millennia in his presence. Here, we live forever.'

'Sure it didn't just feel like millennia? I've been to church and it does drag.'

Nisha patted Muriel on the arm and smiled at Dove. 'Can you tell us more about The Dra-God? What does he look like? If he had a house for example, where would it be?'

Dove turned to Nisha. 'He lives in every blade of grass, every plant and smile. But you must be tired and hungry. We should eat. Cloud, Midden,' she gestured for two drummers to step forward, a man and woman, 'bring our guests some food.' Cloud and Midden disappeared into the townhouse.

Carrying platters piled high with roasted vegetables and crisp ripe fruit, Cloud and Midden returned with enough food for everyone. The drumming and dancing started up again; small groups taking turns to entertain the others. Jack sat by the heat and ate. Dove talked of the cavern and how it provided for all of their needs, if they required anything they would find it amongst the trees and in the glades and pools of water. When they first arrived, they were cold but then the fire, she pointed to the hole again, warmed them. They were hungry and found fruit trees. They needed new life and the cavern provided new friends. A cheer went out from the drummers and they toasted the new arrivals.

Jack looked at the strange people who lived under London. They seemed friendly enough but their carefree attitude was unsettling. The townhouse was falling apart and ramshackle, but there isn't any rain underground so maybe it doesn't need to be watertight — just home. They seemed too young for people older than the Jubilee Line but then they didn't have jobs so maybe that made sense too.

Despite the humble ingredients the food calmed and satisfied Jack's stomach. Roast carrots and parsnips caramelised in some strange honey that tasted sweet and bitter at the same time, potatoes baked until their skins cracked and you could eat them like soft-boiled eggs, and Jack did. Peaches poached in lavender and chamomile. Beer, so heavily hopped the air seemed to grow thick and fuggy whenever you took a sip, flowed freely. The meal continued and the music slowed. The air grew warmer and warmer. Jack's eyes became heavy and slow; he stopped listening to the music.

Jack found himself a room. He hadn't checked into a hotel but had become a room. He was four walls, a ceiling and a floor. The room in question was a lab, his old lab, where he had worked on his PhD. The room was set aside for PhD students to run experiments and complain about their supervisors in private. He saw it from every angle at once, he looked inward as himself as a room and saw all. He saw under chairs and inside cupboards he saw the ceiling as the floor and the floor as the ceiling.

The door opened and Jack entered. A young Jack, Jack as a student. He was wearing his old football gear. *He used to play football; he was good. People wanted him on their team.* The walls sank and the ceiling groaned, they remembered what day this was. The day it happened.

Workbenches were set out in rows and every few feet a different experiment was set up. Being physics, most of these were boring and involved tumbles of wires and little plastic boxes that read the universe. But next to Jack's experiment was Sophie's. Jack liked Sophie. Everyone liked Sophie. When she smiled things were better. She was the star of the department and on track to change the world. Her experiment wasn't boring; it involved a glass flask filled with a green gas sitting above a Bunsen burner. Real old-school stuff that Jack didn't understand. Sophie had sat with him in the pub one night until closing trying to explain it to him, using shots of tequila as atoms. They sat side by side in a booth. Squeezing close and pretending the booth was smaller than it was, arms and knees touching. To this day, Jack would still unexpectedly get a whiff of her shampoo, like a molecule had clung to him for all these years.

Young Jack whistled to himself as he tinkered with his experiment. *I used to whistle.* The whole room screamed at him to leave but he didn't hear.

Sophie's experiment belched and young Jack looked over. He peered into the glass flask and the experiment belched again. The flask shook. The sound of fingernails on a blackboard emanated from deep within the glass. The shaking continued, the flask started to rock back and forth.

Young Jack stepped back. *Yes, leave! Run!* He scratched his chin and saw it. The thing that would change Jack's life. A pressure valve. He reached for the valve and decided to give it a gentle twist. There it was: the decision that changed everything. By the end of that day, he would no longer be a PhD student, he would no longer have a plan or bring himself to talk to Sophie again.

The day Jack turned the valve, he was meant to go to Sophie's birthday party. She said he was still welcome. He had stood outside her flat, listening to the music and laughter, and couldn't face it. He pictured the disappointment on her face, the anger in her eyes and words not said on her lips. He had fled, ending up at St George's. Where he stayed, becoming a gas, floating and inert.

Sophie's gas turned a dark green then black. It swelled on new currents. Young Jack stepped back. The glass cracked.

The lab was empty. The workbenches cleared and the air still. Dove entered with the other hippies. Together they began stripping the lab; they removed Jack's walls and ceiling. Piece by piece they took him apart. He became screws and nails, plaster and bricks, ceiling tiles and vents until they put him back together as Jack who sat by the campfire. Jack was alone until the hippies joined him. He asked why they had shown him that. He had shown himself, they had said. He asked where Muriel and Nisha were. Dove said they had seen what he had done. He was reckless and untrustworthy. They would go on without him. Dove smiled and said he was welcome to stay here until they returned. Jack would wait.

NINE

Days sent out tiny roots into the ground. The roots spread further and further into the mud where they found pockets of nutrients and water. Soon the roots had spread so far the Days became Weeks. The beginning of a stem burst through the soil, unfurled and reached for the sky turning Weeks into Years. Years flowered into Decades and Jack had grown old by the warmth deep underground. The threat of The Dragon and Mimi forgotten. He ate and slept and ate and slept. Sometimes he danced with the hippies but mainly he let the roots spread over his body, drawing life from him. He lived as a drummer and became one with the group. He wore tie-dye and bell-bottom jeans. He forgot his name, so Dove gave him a new one, she called him Lamb. She was young again, no more than eighteen, her face full of brightness and joy. All the drummers were young again, everyone but Jack who had grown old. His bones creaked and his muscles flagged. He could no longer dance so he sat by the fire and waited for death.

. . .

An aeon passed and death hadn't come. Jack stared up at a face. It wasn't Dove or anyone else from the group. The face was mean and serious but with kindness behind its eyes. An ancient memory resurfaced. *Muriel.* She spoke but each word took minutes to reach Jack. Slowed and drawn out, he didn't understand what she said. She tried again, but again Jack didn't understand. Her face was the same, she hadn't aged like Jack.

A second face joined Muriel. *Nisha.* Jack watched Muriel and Nisha. They seemed to be arguing but it was hard to tell as everything moved so slow. Muriel was holding a branch, the end ablaze. Nisha disappeared. Jack tried to lift his head but he was too weak and too old.

Nisha returned.

Lovely, caring Nisha. She kicked him squarely in the ribs and threw a pint of beer over him.

Time flowed in reverse. Centuries flooded back into Jack and filled him with energy and opportunity as Years became Weeks and Weeks became Days. Muriel grabbed the scruff of his neck. 'Get up, you idiot! We need to leave.'

Fire swept through the old Georgian Townhouse and lit up the windows like a ghoulish face. Drummers lay on the ground, limbs missing and perfectly still. The food from earlier lay scattered everywhere. *Food from earlier?* Jack touched his face, he looked at his hands. They were only decades old and not centuries. 'How long has it been?' He asked. 'Why did you leave me behind?'

Dove ran at Muriel brandishing a flint knife. Muriel swung her flaming branch and Dove rolled to the left. 'It's been twenty minutes! And no one left you!' Muriel threw the branch at Dove but missed. Her wrist flicked out and took the top of Dove's skull. Dove dropped to the floor. Dead. 'They put something in the food. A drug or something. Get up!' Muriel shouted, dropping the top of Dove's head.

Jack stood and ran with Muriel and Nisha into the forest. Under the canopy, the light from above grew dim and they ran in twilight. Once the chaos had calmed and they were sure they weren't being followed they slowed and walked in silence.

'That wasn't a drug,' Jack said at last. 'It was real, I was old. I lived a life amongst them.'

Nisha agreed with him, she had undergone a similar experience until Muriel woke her from her trance.

'Maybe,' Muriel said.

Jack shook his head. 'No, it was real. If there is only one spell then what the hell was that?'

Muriel didn't say anything at first. 'I'm not sure. The spell works by you thinking the object was always in your hand. They said the cavern provided anything they needed, maybe it's the same. They think of fire and they get fire, they need food they get food.'

If magic is just willing things to happen then it made sense Jack couldn't do it. He hadn't been raised to will things into happening, it was unnatural. Things happen to you, you don't make them happen. That's for other people. That's what that day in the lab had taught him.

'It could be the same with Foresight, he pictures you somewhere and that's where you are,' Nisha said.

'Yeah,' Jack said. 'Even what The Laurels said The Dragon did for the country. All the factories and stuff, The Dragon gave people what they needed, or at least what they wanted.'

'Maybe,' Muriel said. 'But then why did they need to do all that to be young again?'

'Remember what you told me?' Jack said. '"The actual answer is: it's magic." But how come they can do things you can't?'

This was met with silence. Teaching physics had taught Jack to spot different kinds of silence: There was "if we don't say anything we get to go for lunch" silence, every once in a while he got "I understand now and I am at peace" silence, and there was the silence he was in now which was: "This is all so stupid it either proves there isn't a higher power or if there is one they're as dumb as the rest of us" silence.

'Why didn't it effect you?' Nisha said to Muriel. 'The drug or spell or whatever?'

'I don't like parsnips.'

Talk soon turned to finding The Dragon. They agreed they were lost and any direction away from what remained of Dove's people was as good as the next.

Thick undergrowth made progress slow but by late afternoon they found the edge of the plateau. Standing on the edge, they watched the lights spread out for miles. They must have been at least three hundred meters up judging by how small the trees at the bottom, highlighted by the floating lights, were. The cavern must be as big as London. Jack tried to imagine the Thames snaking over their heads, he placed The Eye, The Shard and a thousand other landmarks. Millions of people walking above them, oblivious to the wonder under their feet. If there was a dragon here it could take years to find.

They headed down off the plateau. The going was steep and halfway down the slope, they spotted a great scar running through the forest: Mimi's path. Once they were on the cavern floor, Muriel walked ahead while Jack hung back with Nisha.

'I reckon The Dragon is in the plateau somewhere,' Jack

said. 'There's a cave system running through it and it's in there. It would explain the fire pit back at the drummers, The Dragon's down there being all fiery or whatever.'

'But The Dragon is dead, how can it be all fiery?'

'It's decomposing, that's how. Things give off heat when they rot and it was already pretty hot to begin with,' Jack said, in no way guessing.

'Look at you coming up with ideas and plans,' Nisha said.

'I know, I'm being involved.'

Nisha winked at him. 'It suits you.'

The path curved and disappeared behind an outcrop of rocks. Muriel had stopped and started to climb.

'What is it?' Nisha called.

Muriel told her to be quiet with a wave of her hand.

'Shh me,' Nisha said under her breath. Jack and Nisha caught up with Muriel and heard it. Laughter.

The outcrop was red sandstone and hard to climb. Jack made it to the top with great difficulty. Muriel and Nisha had beaten him and were lying low to stay out of sight. Jack followed suit and squeezed on the end. Below, the path finally ended at the entrance to a cave. *Dragon*. In the mouth of the cave, a fire had been lit, small and man-made. Three goblins sat around the flames; their ridges proudly displayed and catching the firelight.

One goblin, dressed in waders, fed the fire with twigs and fern leaves. The fire flashed blue whenever the fuel caught. A cube, taller than Jack, was off to one side. The light from the fire didn't reach far and Jack couldn't make out what the cube was made of.

'Do it again. Do it again,' one of the goblins started chanting.

The fire feeder joined in with the encouragement and the third goblin stood and embraced his inner showman. He ripped something from the cube, presented it to his audience before biting into it like a lion. It was meat. Silence and wonder fell over the goblins. Fish, barrel, parakeet, spatula, potato masher, the third goblin transformed into each for a moment before settling on a sofa. The other two leapt over the flames and sat on the new piece of furniture.

'I'm jealous,' one said.

'Why? You can command animals, that's superhero-type powers.'

'No, I can talk to animals, I still need to convince them to do stuff. And trust me, if you could hear what moths were saying you wouldn't want to owe one a favour.'

'Still—'

The sofa started to buckle and shake. The two goblins jumped up as the sofa disappeared and became their friend again.

A light appeared in the mouth of the cave behind the goblins, it grew from a pale yellow to incandescent orange until a fourth figure appeared holding the type of torch that could be handy in a bind. *No, your honour, I was going for an evening stroll and merely used whatever was at hand to defend myself. Premeditated? Not with my knees your honour, why do you ask?*

'Stop wasting the meat and give me a hand with the next shipment,' The torch-bearer said. 'The company's been doing double shifts to stay on track and you lot are out here pissing about.'

The goblins fell in line and headed into the cave.

A moment passed where the only movement was the crackle of the fire.

Muriel climbed down from the outcrop and signalled for Jack and Nisha to follow. They passed by the fire and Jack stopped in front of the cube of meat. He reached out. The meat was warm and gave off a sweet smell of spring pasture and fresh milk that overcame the wet smoke from the fire. Jack stood on an alpine glade, the sun warmed his face and birds sang.

'Jack, come on,' Muriel said. She was waiting further down the path with Nisha.

Jack turned back to the mass of tissue. It was too big. It had been butchered into a block bigger than a cow but lacked any features. No bones, no organs, nothing to tell you what it came from. It was pure muscle. 'This is dragon meat, isn't it? The Dragon's in that cave and they're stripping it for parts. It changes things and Mimi is going to eat it. She'll have the power to change everything for everyone.'

'Obviously,' Muriel said, beckoning him over. 'But let's not get caught. We need to find a way out and let the Laurels know, then come back or something.'

'We've come all this way, let's go in,' Jack said. 'See what else we can find out, go back with some evidence.'

'I don't think that's a good idea, we've got everything we need. The Laurels are better equipped to deal with this kind of thing. We're just meant to be finding out what's going on. That's my plan.'

Jack knew Muriel was right but there was a dragon in that cave and he wanted to see it. He had spent a decade doing nothing. He had floated since the day of Sophie's experiment but now he was a dragon hunter and dragon hunters are meant to find dragons. He wasn't a reckless student anymore. 'I won't be a sec.'

Jack didn't see, but he did hear Muriel's reaction.

Moss, lichen and all those other things that grow in nature that aren't quite plants or animals covered the cave mouth and surrounding cliff face. The cave was dark away from the floating lights outside and Jack turned on his phone torch. The walls of the caves were red, but a darker red than the sandstone outside, thick veins of white ran through them. *Marble?* The walls reflected the torchlight back at Jack as if wet. He reached out and ran a finger down the wall and felt moisture. A line where his finger had been appeared, only to be filled in a second later, replaced by more water.

'When is the boss getting us better equipment?' a voice called from further in the cave. Jack jumped at the sudden noise and dropped his phone.

'Yeah, if she wanted this done quick then we need more than the trolleys she's nicked.'

'Shut up and get back to work! She's planning another job out near Chiswick later this week. Then you'll have all the equipment you could need and no excuses.'

Jack bent to pick up his phone and when he stood the four goblins from before were watching him with the same curiosity that a librarian gives a misfiled book. *How did you get here, little one?* Much like librarians in certain parts of London, they carried bloodied saws, knives, and pickaxes.

They all moved as one.

Jack bolted out of the cave and jumped over the fire. He yelled a warning to Muriel and Nisha but it wasn't needed. They were on the move.

Jack ran, following Muriel. He jumped over fallen branches and sidestepped uneven ground. Jack dared a glance back and saw the torchlights of the goblins gaining. He bumped into Nisha. She had stopped dead, her eyes fixed on something ahead. Sitting amongst the ferns and trees was an elliptical wall of yellow. Cutting through the elliptical wall of yellow, was a slit as deep and unknowing as a singularity. It wasn't an eye, at least not as Jack knew them. It didn't give anything away or offer any insight. It merely existed to respond to light and movement. As if a mountain had been given sight. It arched above, disappearing into the darkness. Jack stepped closer and his vision filled with the dead iris. He was suddenly nine and standing under the dome of St Paul's Cathedral.

'This—' Jack said.

'Yes,' Muriel said, she had taken a few steps back to try and see it all.

'The cave is—'

'It. The old hippie was right. The Dragon is everywhere.'

The sound of footsteps woke Jack from his awe. Muriel and Nisha stood, still spellbound. 'Come on,' he said. He pulled on Nisha's arm and they clambered up to the socket, grabbing tree roots and ferns as handholds. Standing on The Dragon's eyelid, the iris became their world. A bright yellow sun in the dark. Voices joined the footsteps behind them. They crawled along the eyelid. The bright yellow sun had been replaced with the darkness of the singularity. They crawled into The Dragon's pupil.

The goblins stopped in front of the eye.

'Go back and get some meat, they could be waiting to ambush us,' The Torch-bearer said.

The Goblin formally known as Sofa nodded and ran back towards their camp.

The three of them crouched in the void. Jack put his hand on his chest to try to calm his heart.

'What are we going to do?' Jack asked as quietly as he could.

Muriel put a finger to her lips.

The Torch-bearer spun and stared straight into the dragon's

eye. Straight at Jack. A gasp escaped Jack's lips. The Torch-bearer stepped closer.

Deep in the darkest dark, a neuron fired.

The Torch-bearer stood, his eyes unmoving. He stepped over a fallen tree trunk and peered into the pupil. Jack began to crawl backwards when he felt Muriel's hand on his shoulder. Any movement could be a mistake.

After centuries of slumber, the next neurones were slow to react, but the message was gaining speed.

'What do we do now?' Jack said with a gesture.

'I don't know,' Muriel replied with a shrug.

Jack mimed a wand.

'It will give us away immediately,' she articulated with a shake of the head.

'What if we caused a distraction and slipped out?' Nisha suggested with a thumb over her shoulder.

'What kind of distraction?' Muriel shrugged.

The chain of neurons was at full speed now, lighting up long dormant passages.

Sofa Goblin returned and handed out fist-sized chunks of meat to eagerly waiting hands. Moth Whisper seemed ambivalent about the meat and slipped it into his pocket.

'Right,' Torch-bearer said, 'now that's sorted you can come out.'

Jack's heart sank.

'You're in the eye, I heard you.'

Nisha and Muriel gave Jack a look women had given him before, although not in situations quite like this.

The neurons delivered their message.

Muriel held up three fingers and then punched her palm.

'Seriously, you're outnumbered don't be stupid,' Torch-bearer said.

Jack swallowed hard and Nisha nodded.

Torch-bearer signalled for two of the goblins to start climbing.

Muriel counted down. The goblins climbed. The Dragon blinked.

TEN

Reece was lying on the floor of the lab trying to get the last of the penicillin out from under the cupboards with a brush while listening to Theo speak on the great advantages of a private education and how it was actually more unethical to deprive some people of those advantages in the name of fairness. The real issue he said, was how the ad men had got hold of the private schools and made them compete with one another which led to them building ridiculous new sports halls and theatres and hiring famous poets to teach English which inevitably led to fees going up. When he was a pupil at St George's School for Boys in the 1990s his father had been able to afford the fees from the interest accrued in a savings account alone. What was he talking about? Oh yes, just because some people can't afford private school why should that mean that those who can, can't? There was a silence. The first in ten minutes and Reece realised he was meant to fill it. 'You know, it would never occur to me to say any of that to another person,' he said after a moment of restraint.

Theo took off his lab coat and threw it on the worktop

nearest the door. 'This is what I mean, the country needs people who are educated in such a way that they will say whatever's on their mind to anyone.' Theo opened the door letting in a cloud of dust from the once-green courtyard. 'Right, I'm off, see you tomorrow. We did well today, I can almost smell that Nobel Prize.'

Reece surveyed the dust but decided it was a small price to pay for silence. He stood and hung Theo's coat on the hooks he had installed, straightening the arms and lapels to ensure they wouldn't crease. Theo may be an idiot but an idiot in a crease-free coat was the better of the two. Reece picked up the broom and made short work of the floor. Next, he heated up some water on the camping stove to wash up. While the water heated, he collected the beakers, pipettes, stirrers, flasks and test tubes they had been using. He loved them all. There was a logic to science that he enjoyed, you put things in an order to see what happens and then you put them in a different order to see if something else happens. If you were lucky something would change colour or catch fire. That's why he had volunteered for the assignment. Besides, he had learnt everything he could collecting dues for Mimi.

He poured the hot water into a bowl and began to wash up.

Reece snapped the padlock to the lab shut. A shadow passed over him.

'You took your time.'

Mimi's sidekick, The Elf In The Paisley Suit stepped out from the shadows. Parts of Reece tensed that he didn't know had muscles to tense.

'Don't look so worried. I come in peace.' She moved closer

and the scent of sandalwood soap threatened to overwhelm him.

Reece Walker was an anomaly in his family in that he was a boy. Every other member of his family was female, which isn't to say he didn't have a dad, he just didn't know him and there were no uncles or brothers or even male cousins. By sheer fluke, every baby born to a Walker had been female for the last two hundred years until Reece had come along. Every man who came into contact with the Walkers either died young or was quickly chucked once they were deemed useless. It wasn't that the Walker women picked useless men, it was that the women were so competent all men paled in comparison and weren't worth their time. This meant Reece was raised in a family where women undertook every role imaginable from breadwinner to carer to sage. Women, especially the one in front of him, were not to be trifled with or objectified. Having said all that, he couldn't help but admire how well her terrible suit fitted. 'I'm not worried,' he said. 'I'm about to go home but can I help you with something?'

'You're a natural employee, aren't you?'

'What does that mean?' He pocketed the key to the lab.

'It means you'll help even if you're not getting paid.'

'What's the alternative?'

'To be the boss.'

Reece shrugged, bosses get blamed and fired. 'I'm happy with a steady pay cheque.'

'Shame, you'd make a good boss.' She flicked her hair out of her eyes and Reece saw fresh bandages on her wrist poking out from under her jacket cuff. He knew what that meant. A close call. In the circles they ran in, slicing someone's hand was a standard tactic for taking them out of the game. No hand no spell no threat.

'I can't imagine you've come all this way to discuss my long-term career goals.' He started walking towards the main road and witnesses.

The Paisley Elf half-sprinted and half-skipped to keep a few steps ahead. 'I had a bit of free time and thought I'd see what's happening at my favourite test kitchen.'

Reece smiled. Maybe she liked the cut of his suit too, or at least his lab coat. 'I can fill you in over a drink if you like?'

Whenever it's warm the pub inverts. It peels back its doors and drinkers spill out onto the street leaving the inside dark and empty but also cool and quiet.

Reece stood at the bar and watched the news while the bartender made a jug of Pimms. Copernicus 6, a satellite funded by a host of nations with cutting-edge technology from many more, had reached Saturn and was set to send back high-resolution photos of its moon, Titan, in the next few days. Drinks ready, Reece returned to the table to find The Paisley Elf writing something on a piece of paper and whistling quietly to herself.

'What's that?'

She folded the paper and slid it into her jacket pocket. 'Nothing,' she said with a hint of embarrassment.

'Are you writing down the exact date, time and location your life changed forever?' Reece asked, filling two tumblers with Pimms.

'If you mean the day I gave up on men, then yes.' She nodded at the TV. 'What do you think they'll find on Titan?'

He turned to watch the screen for a moment. 'If we're lucky, some violent alien race hellbent on destroying us.'

'Lucky?'

'The way I see it,' Reece leaned in, 'the human race is social, kind and cooperative but also has a big "us and them" problem. We like to be included but love excluding others more. So, what we need is to move the "us and them" off planet and fight aliens. Then we'll stop fighting each other.'

'What about the aliens?'

'Well, it won't be pretty but it will end in a stalemate.'

'And we'll agree the only way forward is love and kindness?' she said.

'Exactly.'

'If you don't mind me asking you don't seem like the other blokes in Mimi's company?' She said, clinking Reece's glass.

It seemed more like a transit van held together with fear and duct tape than a company. 'I guess I'm not,' he said. 'But there aren't many opportunities for a goblin from Bexleyheath with two GCSEs.'

She nearly choked on her drink. 'You're from Bexley? So am I.'

'Shut up.'

'My dad runs the bowling alley,' she said.

'Your dad's Greg the manager? With the limp and the Christmas jumpers all year round?'

She laughed and nodded.

They looked at each other and realised they shared a history and a place. Thousands of tiny things in common that others won't understand. Ways of being and thinking that other people couldn't comprehend. Reece had spent so much time with Theo, using his words and ways of being to try and fit in and be understood, that he had forgotten his own. To sit with someone and share an unspoken language was freeing, if only for a bit.

'You know he threw me out once for vomiting in the hole where the balls pop up from,' Reece said.

'That was you? He still tells that story.'

'Really?' He said in disbelief.

'No.'

Reece knew when he was beaten and changed the subject. 'If you don't mind me asking he's not an elf and I thought you know...'

She shifted in her seat. 'He's my stepdad really, but he raised me. He met my mum in winter so didn't think it strange she always wore a hat on dates. Come spring, Mum's starting to show but he doesn't care. He takes the news that elves and whatnot exist quite well, at least that's what he says, Mum says he asked if she could predict the lottery numbers.'

Reece furrowed his brow. 'Why would she be able to—'

'No idea,' she said, shaking her head.

They sat in a comfortable moment of silence and listened to the drunken chatter outside the pub.

Reece downed his drink. 'You're more friendly than I thought you'd be.'

The barman and a local sent in for a round looked over from the bar, a mix of shock and awe on their faces.

She, however, seemed impressed. 'Wow, do you want a second date?'

'I didn't realise we were on our first one,' he said, pouring them both another drink.

'That's just the work me. If people think you're going to take their fingers you normally don't have to. It's why I wear this ridiculous suit, it's just war paint.'

'And have you?'

'Taken fingers? Yes,' she said flatly.

Reece realised this wasn't good date talk. This is the trouble with dating a colleague, you can't pretend you don't spend all day losing your soul. 'So, what is it?' He asked, trying to steer the conversation away from the violent.

'What's what?' She asked.

'The magic meat, is it a mutant mudlark or something?'

'No, but I don't want to talk about work.' She leant back in her chair. 'I'm a strict nine-to-five girl, when I'm at work I do what needs doing and when I'm not I—'

'Do whoever needs doing?'

She laughed much harder than the line was funny.

'What did you want to be when you were a kid?' He winced as he said it, a tired question to ask on a date.

She didn't seem to mind and smiled as if remembering an old joke. 'I wanted to be so famous I could turn down an OBE.'

'Turn one down?'

She nodded. 'I wanted to get accepted into all that — the establishment — and then turn around at the last minute and...' She made a gesture that was the greatest thing to come out of the Battle of Agincourt after Calais.

'That would be good, it's a shame you didn't get to.'

She straightened her tie. 'Well, I don't like to brag but I have killed someone with an OBE so in some respects I have one by proxy.'

'So why didn't you try and get into "all that"?'

'It's difficult when you're a girl from Bexley with three GCSEs.'

He whistled a high-pitched note. 'Is that why you work for Mimi? Are you trying to get accepted so you can turn your back on it?'

'What do you mean?' She picked up her drink and drew it close.

He crossed his legs, he had started down a road and wasn't

sure how to turn back. 'Maybe you hadn't noticed but she's posh. Not doctor posh. Really posh, pile in the country posh.'

Intentional or not, she held her drink up to her face and hid her reaction. 'I've never really considered it. Maybe. I'm good at it and I enjoy it.'

'So, you don't want to turn your back on it after a point and you know—' He repeated the gesture in the hope of breaking the tension.

The glass lingered. 'Do you judge me for what I do? We work for the same person.'

'Not at all,' he said, forcing a laugh. 'I was just following a thread, there's some overlap between the OBE dream and what you ended up doing or at least who you ended up working for. Two hundred years ago you probably would be eligible for an OBE doing what you're doing. Hell, fifty years ago.'

The glass fulfilled its destiny and was emptied. She placed it back on the table with a smile. 'That's a nice thought but what did you want to be when you were young?'

'Bin man.'

'Helping people again, you're no better than me.'

They walked to the second nearest tube station together and talked of siblings, times they called the teacher mum, and got into a competition over whose parents were crazier. She won. Reece shared every inane thought he had and she seemed interested. She disagreed with most of it but she seemed to want to hear it anyway.

'Are you off home?' Reece asked as they stood under the station awning. It was missing large sections of cladding exposing wires and rat nests. A busker, like buskers everywhere, played Wonderwall on the acoustic guitar. Someone had relieved themselves against the bin recently but to Reece, it felt like the scene in the movie where the hero leans in for the kiss. He just wasn't sure if she would.

'No, back to work, I've got a few things to do for the boss.'

Tyres shouted and people screeched. Reece turned to see a bus driver climb out of his booth and begin berating a woman on a mobility scooter who had decided traffic lights were a guide and not a rule. The woman gave as good as she got and they squared off in the centre of the crossroad, both drenched in sweat and glowing from anger and the sun.

'Blimey,' Reece said, shaking his head and turning back to The Elf. 'This heat.'

She was gone, off to do things to people's fingers.

Reece understood. The mundane world of crime and magic returned.

The darkness was a never-ending nightmare until it wasn't. The eyelid slid back and the goblins were gone. Not paid enough to fight a dragon. Jack stood frozen. Muriel tried to shout for them to run but her voice rattled with fear. Enough of her command got through and Jack slid down the moss and lichen and hit the ground harder than intended. Nisha picked him up and they ran further into the cavern. The forest grew deep and they ran silent and blind.

It blinked. They must have stood on a nerve in the eye. Do eyes have nerves? Jack wasn't sure but it was an isolated event he told himself. *It couldn't be alive.* He remembered reading how Marie Antoinette blinked after they cut her head off. It's like that. An ancient bit of electricity still rattling around a long-dead dragon. *It blinked.*

Later, Jack would describe the sensation of your stomach slamming into your heart as feeling a lot like your stomach slamming into your heart, but in the moment he sang a brief sharp note as he fell down a slope further into the cavern. He grasped at ferns but his weight pulled them clean out of the ground and they only slowed his descent for a split second before gravity caught up and he continued skidding down into the abyss. He rolled to a stop and coughed.

'Jack?' Nisha said from above.

'I'm ok. I think.' He pulled out his phone and switched on the torch. The lights from the cavern roof were weak and pale now. He must have fallen at least fifty feet into a crevasse. Life continued down here, trees and bright green moss covered every surface. The other side of the crevasse seemed steeper but both sides were impossible to climb.

'I'm in a hole.' He cringed as he said it.

'We know.' Muriel said after a pause.

'It's too steep to come get you, so keep going and hopefully, it will become climbable,' Nisha said.

The trail seemed passable. 'Good idea. I think it's still dead and we just stepped on a nerve.'

'Maybe,' Muriel said, her voice short and curt. 'We need to tell The Laurels, they'll know what to do.'

'Like Marie Antoinette,' he said.

There was whispering.

'Just get walking and we can talk about it later.' Nisha said.

Jack tripped and stumbled over the rocks and plant life. He remembered his geography teacher, Mr Jones, trying to sign him up for the Duke of Edinburgh Award. Jack smirked the way only teenagers can at the idea of walking in the countryside being a useful skill. *It blinked.* Jack was going to be a world-famous physicist and would never need to leave campus;

walking was for mortals. Besides, he thought Kristen in year thirteen with her eye makeup and Doc Martens would be more impressed if he didn't have any hobbies or interests. *It couldn't be alive.* He apologised to Mr Jones for not taking him up on his offer. He also apologised to Kristen for trying to impress her on the bus by listing all the elements of the periodic table by boiling point. *It blinked.*

A boulder wedged by stones and gravel blocked Jack's path, no doubt fallout from some ancient landslide. He gave it a push with the same certainty he kicked tyres on second-hand cars. If he could move some of the stones at the bottom the rest might fall. His eyes narrowed. He breathed in. *Don't move the can, it was always there.* He reached out. *Don't move the can. Move the atoms.* His face turned red. Nothing. He breathed out.

With the grace and strength of a much older man, he began to climb. Landing on his back but on the right side he thought Mr Jones would be proud, he wasn't sure what Kristen would think. Once upright he saw them. Nestled under a tree sat a clutch of eggs, as tall as a man, copper green and untouched in centuries. He stroked the shell and felt a rush of sulphur and heat. They must be his, hers, he corrected himself. The Laurels had said there was only one dragon but this proved otherwise, or at least there might be others. Jack swallowed hard. It was just an animal, not some mythic beast bent on destruction and rampage. It just wanted to protect its young.

His hands danced in indecision before touching the shell. A rush of heat passed down Jack's palm. The scent of freshly cut grass washed over him in waves like he was rolling down a hill on a summer's day. He moved his hand over the egg. A small crack appeared, spreading like fire across the shell. The cracks circumnavigated the shell and collapsed inwards turning to dust. Its occupant long dead.

'Jack?' Muriel called from the darkness.

'It was a mum,' Jack said, he turned and saw their silhouettes against the lights, they weren't as high as before.

'What was?'

'The Dragon, there are eggs down here. I'm coming up.'

Jack wiped the dust on his trousers and said a silent apology to the remains. He grabbed plant life by the handful and climbed up the slope, following their torches to the top.

'What about eggs?' Muriel asked.

'I found a clutch of eggs down there, long dead but maybe that's what she was doing. She was protecting her young.'

'From who?' Muriel asked.

'Us maybe, we built a city on her nest, you remember what The Laurels said, she turns up and attacks cities. Well maybe she wasn't attacking cities, maybe we built cities on her nests. It's like the videos on the internet of bears going through bins in suburban America, the bears didn't come to town, the town came to the bears.'

Nisha nodded in agreement. 'Have you seen the one where the bear falls asleep in the hot tub?'

Muriel scratched her eyebrow. 'I think that's unlikely, it's a dragon. It attacks things. That's what The Laurels said and they know more about this stuff than we do.'

'But they can't know everything,' Jack said. 'They weren't there.'

Muriel signalled for them to start walking. 'You might be right, but we need to get out of here first, then we can talk about it. Mimi's men are still down here and they might be searching for us, besides we've got bigger problems now you woke The Dragon by making us climb into its eye.'

Jack laughed. 'You don't really think it's alive, do you? We just stood on a nerve or something. We just need to stop Mimi from going all Oliver Cromwell on us.'

Nisha stepped in behind and stayed silent.

'Mimi is nothing compared to The Dragon coming back and it has come back. It blinked, Jack,' Muriel said.

'You don't really believe that, do you?'

Muriel stopped and brandished a finger at Jack. 'You're right, I don't know for sure if it's alive but I do know it blinked and dead things don't blink and don't mention Marie Bloody Antoinette — if I'm wrong I'm wrong. If I'm right it will destroy the city and kill everyone in it. Remember what The Laurels said: it will return and keep attacking us. It's a dragon, that's what they do.'

Nisha stood between them. 'Maybe we—' Muriel stormed off before Nisha could finish.

They walked as fast as the forest allowed: geology, trees and the fact they had no idea where they were going slowed them down. The forest here grew thicker and wilder than up on the plateau. Except, it wasn't a plateau, it was The Dragon. Jack had stood inside a dragon, he had touched it with his finger. Great cubes of meat chiselled out of its mass. Jack poked a spot between his ribs, is this where he had stood? He pictured Lilliputians boring a tiny hole in his skin and slicing sugar-cube-sized blocks of muscle out of his torso.

Their journey continued in silence for an hour, Muriel tried to power through the forest as best she could but every time she met an obstacle she swore and led them down a different path chosen at random. She didn't acknowledge Jack or Nisha or their suggestions and the tension fused with the cool air making Jack want to shiver and sweat simultaneously.

'Wait,' Nisha said.

Muriel did not wait.

'What is it?' Jack asked.

'Do you hear that?'

Jack listened, there was a noise like a thousand tiny roars. 'What is that?'

'It's running water,' Nisha said.

Muriel stopped ten feet in front. 'So?'

'In case you've forgotten we're underground.'

Muriel wiped her brow. 'How could I forget? That's why I want to leave and that's why we need to keep walking.'

'That means it doesn't rain here,' Nisha said with threadbare patience. 'So, if there's water it might have come from above and above is where we want to be.'

'Nisha's right, we should try and find it and follow it.' Jack said.

'I'm not sure that's a good plan.' Muriel walked back to where they stood. 'We should just keep walking. In case you've forgotten there's a dragon over there about to wake up. I've got a plan and we should try and stick to it this time.'

'And what? Hope there's a second two-mile long tunnel under London? We should follow the water,' Nisha said.

Jack nodded.

Muriel ran her tongue along her teeth and gestured for Nisha to lead the way.

They listened for the water as best they could, it was faint and with every rustle of leaves or heavy footstep, they lost it.

They spread out, keeping each other in earshot. 'You know how those hippies thought The Dragon was God,' Nisha said.

'Yes,' Jack said while losing a fight with a fern that blocked his path.

'Do you think it might be God?'

'Sorry?'

'It can make things appear if you think about them hard

enough. That's prayer. It's really big and unknowable. That's
God-like. And it punishes people. That's God again.'

'Who did it punish?'

'Everyone in 1666.'

That was true. Jack pulled the fern out of the ground with
extreme vengeance. 'I'm not sure that's enough to make it God,
at most you could argue it's Father Christmas, he's all those
things. Gift giving, big and hands out punishments — in the
form of coal.'

'Is Father Christmas God?'

'Despite the deafening amount of stupidity. I've found the
water and it's running,'

Jack felt bad for the fern and placed it on the ground with
care. 'Muriel?'

'Who else? The tooth fairy?'

'Maybe, it's a big cave,' Nisha said.

Jack hadn't been to many babbling brooks in his life but
this was the nicest because it might rescue him from a lifetime
underground and endless metaphysical debates about the gift-
giving properties of various mythical creatures. The water
moved at pace, skimming over pebbles and rocks and weaving in
and out of trees. It also stank to high heaven.

'What is that?' Nisha asked, giving the air a sniff.

Muriel bent low and watched the water. 'If I had to guess,
crap.'

Jack took in a big noseful and agreed with Muriel. The
smell was compelling, it was the morning after a misjudged
kebab, it was every sick day and the human race at its most
basic. It was crap.

'But that's good,' Muriel said. 'London's full of crap. If we
follow it we might get out of here.'

Muriel led the way at speed and they marched against the

current and retraced the stream's path. Slowly, the ground became steep and they were walking uphill again. Muriel became silent but kept the pace quick. At times, Jack had to jog to catch up. It had been four hundred years, Jack thought. The Dragon was dead and Muriel was wrong. *It blinked.*

The stream ducked and weaved for miles without a care in the world. Not wanting to risk losing the source, they followed its whims.

Miles passed and they were level with the floating lights that illuminated the cavern. Jack would stretch out to grab one but it would be gone, as if never there. Like fog, the lights were always just out of reach. The higher they got, the less life they found. Trees stopped and bushes became sparse until just grass and mud covered the ground. The view, however, grew far and wide, you could see the whole cavern lit up by white light, the forest stretched below, rising up and over The Dragon. What came first: The Dragon or the forest? The other side of the cavern was much steeper as if The Dragon had skidded to a halt and swept the rock aside.

Once they passed the floating lights it became pitch black and torches were needed again. The plant life stopped and London Clay returned.

The source of the water was a spring near the very roof of the cavern, just a trickle of water seeping out of the ground. They clawed and pulled at the mud and, after some work, revealed an old brick sewer tunnel. It had burst its banks and water ran down into the cavern. Muriel clawed at the bricks and threw them back down the slope. Jack made himself useful and moved the bricks Muriel had missed. After some effort, they were able to make a hole big enough to climb through. The idea of climbing into a sewer tunnel seemed to lift everyone's spirits.

Jack ripped the sleeves off his jacket and gave one each to Muriel and Nisha to act as placebo masks. He tied the remains of his jacket around his mouth and they entered the tunnel.

Memory is just imagining things backwards. Jack would have liked the tunnel to have been an unimaginable horror because then he wouldn't remember it later. Instead, it was all so clear. The fecal water, the air you could cut with a knife. The potential for such an embarrassing death, to slip and drown in someone else's crap.

They walked for miles and Jack made a mental list of what they would need to do when they got to the surface: Check in with The Laurels, change and burn their clothes, eat. He would invite Muriel and Nisha to his for food. Apologise for the Foresight incident. If Mimi was planning to use dragon meat to change reality, then they would need to figure out how. Jack was new to the world of vigilantism and wondered if they would need to kill Mimi or just stop her. He was ready to be a suffragette if needed.

And then it happened. Modern infrastructure. A ladder, a manhole cover. The surface. Jack climbed the ladder first and tried to push the cover off but it wouldn't budge. *Don't move the can, it was always there.* Nothing. 'I can't move it,' he called down.

Muriel tutted and held out her palm.

Two holes appeared in the disc of metal and the evening sun shone down. Jack put his hands through and pushed the cover up and to one side.

They had come out on a quiet side street overlooking the river, somewhere in Wapping judging by the size of The Shard.

It had only been a few hours since Jack had last seen the city but it had changed beyond recognition. The glass and steel monuments to modern life had been replaced with precarious follies sticking like knives out the back of the creature that made them possible.

The air was so fresh it hurt. Jack took lungfuls anyway.

Muriel's head emerged from the sewer with a great intake of breath. She crawled onto the road and lay on her back. Nisha wasn't far behind and rested her head on Muriel's stomach.

Muriel pushed Nisha off and stood. 'Everyone ok?'

Jack murmured a positive.

She seemed pleased with the answer and gestured for Jack to stand. He did. She faced him and placed her hands on his shoulders. She spun him around so he faced west and pushed him.

He stumbled before turning.

'Go home,' she said.

'Sorry?'

'I had a plan and a goal. Find out what's happening and get out. At no point did it involve being seen by Mimi's men or poking about inside a dragon.'

'I was just—'

'Waking up a dragon? I know,' she said. 'I've got to clean that up as well now.'

Maybe he was still that same reckless student as before. 'What about The Laurels? They said—'

'I'll tell them you died.' She crossed her arms. 'I'll say you got hit by one of those tour buses that serve afternoon tea. Death by Wowcher.'

'Muriel,' Nisha said, trying to keep the peace.

Muriel turned to Nisha. 'And you're going home as well.

Go make art or whatever. This is my job, not yours. There's no room for amateurs.'

Nisha got to her feet and stood next to Jack, drawing a battle line. '"Or whatever?" No, we're staying. Aren't we Jack? We're a team.'

'I do have this work meeting I was meant to go to,' Jack said. 'I've got a promotion and...'

Nisha turned to face Jack, they each became a battle line of one. 'Jack, don't go to work, the world is ending,' she said.

Jack looked at Muriel and knew there would be no discussion, no compromise. Her eyes were as deep and unknowable as The Dragon's. She was right, maybe this wasn't the life for him. All he had done was make things worse — like Sophie's experiment — he had run away from a mudlark and ruined the meeting with Foresight. He wasn't anybody, just a science teacher. He would go home. Rest. Work. He would go to meetings, drink coffee and nod along. In a few years, he could be the real Head of Physics. Under a dictator though, a small voice added. Jack stood and got his bearings, he headed west.

Nisha called after him, asking him to stay and to fight. This wasn't his fight, it never was.

ELEVEN

Jack stared out of his kitchen window at the square of turf that served as a communal garden to his block of flats. To call it a lawn would be a mistake. It was to a lawn what a drunken argument was to opera.

The garden was never used, even on nice days as it was overlooked on all sides and the residents' association were sticklers for The Rules. You needed to own a flat to join and as most people rented, including Jack, it was really a junta of two. Mr Fitzwallace in 6A, who, if the rumours were to be believed, didn't win any of the medals permanently pinned to his chest, and Mrs Pickers in 5C, whose outdated views on mixed fruit jam had got her thrown out of the local WI. Between them, they ruled the block with an iron fist. Jack would spend his holidays lying in bed and when he heard the buzz and crackle of walkie-talkies he knew Fitzwallace and Pickers were on the prowl for wrongdoers. This was his life now. A lifeless view, a steady job and knowing that things could only get worse.

A soft but determined scratching noise woke Jack from his stupor. He walked to his bedroom to find a black cat perched on the window sill. It meowed at the sight of Jack. Jack opened the window just enough to let the cat in. 'Hello,' Jack said. The cat would visit every few days and sit at Jack's window until Jack relented and let him in. This arrangement had been decided on by the cat without any consultation from Jack who wasn't sure who to complain to about such matters. The residents' association had more important things to attend to.

The cat was nameless as Jack didn't feel like he had a right to choose one for it; if the cat had an owner then it already had a name and if it was a stray then it had chosen a life beyond petty bourgeois conventions like names. Jack hoped it was the second, someone should be living life the way they wanted. Far from the turf.

Jack followed the cat to the kitchen where it jumped onto the counter and waited by the sink.

'Hang on,' Jack said. 'How have you been?'

The cat licked itself.

'As long as you're keeping busy.' Jack opened the cupboard under the sink and fished out the bag of dry cat food he kept for the visits. Every time he felt compelled to give the bag a sniff and every time he was rewarded with the same smell of dried offal and abattoir sweepings.

He tipped some food into a cereal bowl and slid it across the counter. Stroking the cat while it ate, Jack wondered if he should tell it about the last few days. He hadn't told anyone about what he had seen and experienced, about the life he could have led. Muriel had only banished him that afternoon but he hadn't seen or spoken to anyone, nor would he until his work meeting tomorrow. He thought about telling someone. He wanted to shout about everything he had learnt, peel the lid back on the world and bring it all into the sun. To most people, Jack was a stranger and most people were strange to Jack.

The cat, its meal finished, jumped down onto the floor and walked back to the window knowing that Jack would follow. The cat left without saying goodbye.

Jack's phone buzzed. An email saying his knitted duck tea cosy had been dispatched. There was nothing left to do but wait for work.

The bus jolted to a stop as two mopeds, headlights blaring, attempted to overtake a car and swerved towards the bus on the wrong side of the road. The roads of South London weren't designed for buses, two-car families, and children with access to combustion engines. The Elf In The Paisley Suit grabbed the handrail to balance herself without taking her eyes off her phone. The government website said she would need to make achievements in public life or help Britain to get offered an OBE. Her achievements were awesome but mainly criminal and she couldn't think of anything worse than helping Britain, at least the version of Britain that the website imagined. She closed the browser and reread the text from Mimi, it contained an address and a terrible pun about cracking heads and omelettes. Text messages like this made her think they needed a reading comprehension test for new company members. You can say what you like about the criminal class but they can read context clues like no one else. If they compared the reading comprehension scores of prisoners to the general public she'd bet the prisoners would score higher, being a criminal means living *and* reading between the lines.

The bus pulled into her stop. She stood and checked her suit in the window before thanking the driver with a wave of the hand and stepping off the bus. The Elf's job used to be simple: Kill this person, scare that guy, but ever since Mimi's grand idea to be ruler of the universe she kept being sent to *question* people before killing them. It wasn't what she signed up for and was frankly, boring. She didn't care how The Dragon died and this seemed like a waste of time.

She arrived at the beaten-down house and checked she had the right address. The house of the oldest living Londoner loomed large in her mind and she expected it to be all pillars and servants quarters, not in need of repointing with the recycling out front. She approached the front door and, with a flick of the wrist, the lock was in her hand and the door fell open. The sounds of London at night filtered into her ears but the house was silent.

At this point, some of her colleagues would run up the stairs, grab the old girl and get her to tell them everything she knows about The Dragon. The Elf preferred to take things slow. Make some noise, get them worried and creeping down the stairs in their dressing gown. Perhaps it was the romantic in her.

Light from the lamp post outside the kitchen window lit up the room giving her just enough light to make a cup of tea. She searched the worktop for a kettle but found only discarded mixing bowls and half-eaten cake. *Who doesn't have a kettle?* She opened the fridge and settled for a beer. She fished in her pocket for the bottle opener she kept on her keyring. The beer was good and tasted like rosemary. Making herself comfortable at the kitchen table; she knocked some books onto the floor. The thud spread through the house.

A open notebook sat on the table. Turning the book over,

there was a strip of masking tape with 'baking soda/powder' written on it stuck to the spine. Each page was filled with hand-written recipes, written and rewritten with changes. Scones, rock cake, soda bread, the recipes took a step back in time with each page. An urge came over her and she gave the book a sniff, *home*. She took another swig of beer and listened for movement upstairs. Suze must be a heavy sleeper. Bottle in hand, she started going through the piles of cookbooks that covered the room. Flans, sponges, cupcakes, loaves, gateaux and blood pancakes, there were books on every kind of cake that she had heard of and more that she hadn't. She flicked through a pamphlet on the Chickpea War of 1862 — between Italy and France over who invented the chickpea flour pancake. She moved onto a book bound in leather with pages as thick as card. The book seemed heavier than the others. She stroked its cover to check it was ok for her to pick it up. It didn't object so she opened it at a random page.

Thick black lines ran over the page like tears in space weaving and dancing to form drawings of the most wonderful cakes she had ever seen. The artist had used such joyful colours that she knew how the cake tasted without needing to read the ingredients. She listened to the house again but heard nothing. Taking trophies from crime scenes was for amateurs but surely one page wouldn't hurt? She took a breath and ripped the page from the book in a quick clean movement.

'You really shouldn't tear books, my dear.'

The Elf In The Paisley Suit jumped back and fell onto the slate floor, sending her beer flying in the process. 'Sorry,' The Elf said and began to mop the beer with her sleeve. The books had made her forget where she was and who she was, she couldn't remember the last time she had been distracted. To be completely lost in something other than yourself, to not be aware of everything and to watch time pass over you like sunlight seen from the bottom of a river.

'I know you weren't raised to use your sleeve,' the voice said. It entered the room and belonged to Suze. She looked about thirty but The Elf knew she was much older. Suze wore an apron over a plain white nightie that went from chin to toe and left everything to the imagination. She handed The Elf a roll of paper towels and helped herself to a beer. 'If this is the calibre of assassin nowadays no wonder the country's going to pot.'

'Sorry.' The Elf repeated, unsure if she was apologising for the spill or not killing her quickly enough. 'I just got engrossed in your books and how did you know I was sent here to kill you?'

Suze searched in a drawer for a bottle opener before taking a seat on a pile of Nigellas. 'People break into houses for three reasons.' The bottle hissed. 'And judging by your farcical clothes you're not short of a few quid so it's not number one, I've met Saint Nick and you're not him so that leaves the third option. What book caught your attention?'

The Paisley Elf gestured to the book between them before she gave the floor one last wipe.

The book appeared in Suze's palm and she inspected it. '*Malleus Pistorum*, the hammer of bakers,' she said with a hint of drama in her voice. 'When the Duke of Aquitaine died of gout his wife wrote this as an attack on bakers everywhere. She blamed them for his early demise. She filled it with the most wicked examples of cake she could find to prove they were in league with the devil and trying to bring down the Right and the Good and return the Dark Lord to his rightful place as ruler of the world. Nonsense of course, but it proved very popular and was an early prototype of what you would call a cookbook.'

'And that's a copy?' The Elf asked, perching herself on a pile of books.

'No,' Suze said, inspecting the torn edge in the book. A siren passed, filling the room with its call. 'So, why are you here to kill me?'

'I meant to ask you some questions first,' the Elf said as if this made it acceptable.

'Do you want to make it?' Suze said, putting the book down.

'Make what?'

'The cake.'

The Elf licked her lips.

'Put the oven on high and grab those two bowls,' Suze said.

The Elf greased a baking tin while Suze gathered the ingredients. The recipe didn't call for anything fancy, just eggs, flour, butter and sugar. The secret Suze said, was love, not picturing those you love eating it or pouring your love into it but to love doing it. If you love baking, if you find joy in it then it will be good. The same is true with most things Suze found. If you love life it will be a good life. The Elf folded flour into the eggs and turned Suze's baking philosophy over in her mind. It was rubbish. She loved what she did and was under no illusion it was a good life. A joyful life and a good life weren't the same thing at all. It was the kind of rubbish people spouted to explain their crap lot in life or by those so well off they don't realise what everyone else was putting up with. Power and money were what made a good life and if that meant the odd violent act then it seemed a small price to pay.

The cake was ready for the oven. Suze opened the door

while The Elf slid the cake tin onto the middle shelf. The blast of heat from the oven caused her eyes to water.

'You haven't asked me yet,' Suze said.

'Asked you what?'

'Whatever it was you were sent here to find out. Take that and pour when I say pour.' Suze handed her a box of icing sugar before tipping a whole bottle of rose water into a small bowl.

Hadn't she? 'I'm meant to ask you about The Dragon, you were there weren't you?'

'Pour and yes and stop,' Suze said, mixing the sugar into the rose water with a wooden spoon.

'How did it die?'

'Pour and like everything else scared and alone and stop.'

The Elf watched in horror at the amount of sugar going into the bowl. 'I know *that*, but was it killed or did it just fall over?'

'Pour. Yes, really, more, and let me think.' Suze tried some of the icing but seemed unsure. 'Try that. There was cannon fire from the Tower and some idiots were taking potshots at it so it's possible someone got lucky.'

The rose water smacked the Elf across the face but once she recovered from the shock it was surprisingly good. 'It's lovely. So you don't think it looked ill?'

'I can no more tell if it was ill than I can tell what the ocean wants for dinner, and I think we can take a break. Beer?'

'Yes please.' The Elf took another finger full of icing while Suze sorted the drinks.

'A popular topic at the moment,' Suze said from the fridge.

The Elf swallowed. 'What is?'

'The Dragon, you're the second person to ask me about it in as many days.'

The Elf froze. 'Really?' She just needed to nudge her into saying more, too much and she'd shut down.

'Yes, a friend of mine and some odd fellow came by. He had the deranged look of a teacher or dog sitter about him. Do you know what I mean?'

'I do know what you mean. Who's your friend?' *A teacher,* she knew a teacher, a very odd teacher.

'Just a friend,' Suze said with a knowing smile. She handed The Elf a beer. 'But that's enough talk of that. Did you know that James Watt invented the steam engine while attempting to find a way to keep his oven humid enough?' Suze filled the next forty minutes with tales from the history of cake and how it was really the history of humanity. Since we first crawled out of the ocean everything humans have done has been an attempt to get sugar and fat or impress someone with the amount of sugar and fat you have. Cake, was the how and why of civilization.

The first signs of day appeared in the night sky when the cake was finally ready to eat. Suze had insisted they wait for it to completely cool before icing. The Elf had seen many tactics employed to delay death but this was the only one she had pretended to fall for.

A slice of the perfect cake was placed in front of The Elf. It had been decorated with dried fruit and a sugar syrup that she wasn't allowed to help with after a close call with a gas ring and a tea towel.

Suze joined her at the table. 'How is it?'

The Paisley Elf took a bite and adjusted her yellow swim cap. She made sure her paisley swimsuit wasn't riding up before taking her spot next to her twelve teammates at the edge of the mixing bowl. The opening notes of 'Dance of the Sugar Plum

Fairy' sang from somewhere. One by one, her teammates, all bright white chicken eggs, dived into the bowl with a gentle splash sending flour skyward. She bent her knees and joined them in the plain white, taking in a mouthful of flour as she broke the surface. Flying through the flour like it was water, she emerged in perfect time with her teammates to form a circle. Legs akimbo, the circle rotated a half turn. On an unspoken order, six of her teammates headed inwards and formed a second smaller circle. They shot their mouthfuls of flour high into the air and completed another half-turn. The Elf sunk under the surface and made her way through the flour until she reached the bottom of the bowl. She counted out four beats then pushed hard against the bottom of the ceramic bowl and flew upwards through the flour ready to become the glorious centre of a perfect creation when the lift doors opened.

'You're late.' Mimi stood in the lobby of Jones and Jones wiping blood from her hands with someone's shirt. The Elf very much doubted the shirt owner had been in a position to object.

'The baker wasn't very talkative,' The Elf said after taking a second to get her bearings.

Mimi grunted and directed The Elf down the corridor. 'You know Foresight won't meet with me after you missed your appointment the other day,' she said.

Bodies, broken glass and signs of struggle litter the corridor. The Elf tried to retrace her steps here. She had eaten the cake. And then? Nothing. No cake should make you lose time, no matter how good it is. 'As I said before, I bumped into the ones that stole the scale.'

'That's right, and you let them get away again.'

That will take a while to be forgotten. They stepped over a broken glass door into a meeting room that overlooked London. Dawn broke on the top of St Paul's. Two city types sat upright at a table. Their bodies missing all the important bits. Mimi took a seat and signalled for the Elf to do the same opposite her.

'Our two partners here had a lapse in security and leaked my entire plan like second-rate Bond villains. Everyone I hire is useless. Did you know Light Barry went mad? His crew too.'

'Light Barry?' The Elf asked.

'Miserable man, carries a torch everywhere? Anyway, him and his crew decide they've had enough of work and go walking off into the cavern, meaning that a shipment is missed. They come back after a few hours raving about the monster blinking. Madness.'

Two of Mimi's men dragged a body past the meeting room. 'Carry them, don't drag! You're getting glass everywhere!' Mimi shouted through the door. She rolled her eyes and returned her attention to The Elf.

The Elf took in the scene, no one had made it out alive. 'So you did the whole office?'

Mimi shrugged. 'What did the baker say?'

The Elf licked her lips at the thought of the icing. What other treasures were in the book?

'Well?'

The Elf shook her head and tried to forget the scent of rose water. 'Nothing about how it died but she said a teacher came round a few days ago asking questions about The Dragon.'

Mimi raised an eyebrow. 'A teacher?'

The Elf nodded knowingly.

Mimi considered this. 'How many teachers do you think there are in London?'

'A few thousand, maybe a handful know about magic, and

in theory, just the one knows about The Dragon,' The Elf said. 'Besides, I can't imagine many make it a habit to go around to Suze's place and ask about dragons.'

'Yes, perhaps it was a former teacher?'

'That was my thinking too,' the Elf said. 'One that got a job with better hours.'

Mimi seemed to file this away somewhere. 'I got a message from The Laurels earlier.'

The Elf laughed. 'The Laurels? Are they still a thing?'

'Yes, it took me a moment to place them, they said a teacher got caught up in one of their schemes the night you let the scale get away.'

You let the scale get away. 'Oh?'

'Yes, they want us to let him go back into the world. He's an innocent apparently, wrong time wrong place situation.'

A goblin and an elf joined them in the meeting room and stood by the door, attempting to subtly block The Elf's exit. They gave off the impression of being dumb but strong and she doubted she could take both of them and Mimi in a straight fight. She didn't recognise them and she had never heard of Light Barry or his crew. This was becoming more and more common since Mimi's operation had expanded to accommodate her plans, lots of new recruits with no history, no brains and loyal only to Mimi and her pay cheques. *Except Reece.* Mimi would have no use for the smart ones soon. Once she was everyone's glorious leader she wouldn't need anyone who could think. The Elf swung round in the chair and tried to make eye contact with the two newcomers but they stared straight ahead. 'Did you agree?' She said returning her attention to Mimi.

'They think I did. I gave my assurances that he'll be safe.'

'God, they think there are still rules.'

Mimi leaned back in her chair. 'What are the odds it's not Theo?'

Not zero, The Elf thought. The Napkin Guy was out there somewhere and he had bills to pay so why not a teacher? But she was on her second strike with Mimi, after losing the scale and missing the appointment with Foresight. The piece of theatre with the two at the door seemed to be for her benefit. She would let Mimi's mind run to wherever it wanted. 'Slim I would say.'

'I'm glad we agree,' Mimi said. 'But if it isn't Theo, what's The Laurel's angle? Why risk exposing Theo to keep a second teacher safe?'

'Honour?'

Mimi laughed. Her laugh had grated on The Elf since they first met, it was the laugh of someone who didn't know what a gas bill was.

'It's not conclusive but too strange to be nothing. I want you to join me tomorrow when I go and ask Theo and his side-kick some questions.'

'Reece? He's okay, he's been with us for ages.'

Mimi stood and went to the window. 'Fine, if you vouch for him, he can stay.' She looked out over the city. 'In a few hours this place will be crawling with people, they will come and work their sad little jobs and go back to their sad little flats. They will achieve nothing other than making the world that little bit more cramped and noisy. There's too many of them, there's no space anymore. No space to breathe or live. No space to think. It all needs to change.'

Despite it being close to midnight Nisha still checked the coast was clear before climbing over the railings and dropping down amongst the communal bins. Jumping the fence here saved five minutes on her journey and she desperately wanted to get home.

The bins were used by residents on this bit of the estate and her mum would often comment on how unkempt they were compared to the ones at their end. *What must people think?* Her mum would say.

Her feet felt heavy from the day and she realised she was still wedged into Muriel's duck boots. God, she hated the ducks. The idea of having to return them and face Muriel seemed impossible right now. Sleep would help. Everything is easier after sleep. Tomorrow she would think about all the things she had said to Muriel and what she needed to apologise for. There would be a lot. They had fought after Jack had left. This fight was different, not final but ending.

She left the bins behind and carried on towards home. She walked amongst the squat blocks of flats built quickly and with love after the war. Most people had placed blankets and sheets of cardboard in their windows to block out the sun.

Everything seemed small now, not because she had grown in the last few days but because she had seen it.

The Dragon.

She had wanted big and it was big. It was far bigger than anything humans had ever done and may ever do. Everything paled in comparison to The Dragon. Everything Nisha had ever done or could ever do. What was the point if nature could just take it all away in a blink of an eye?

Blinking slowly, she tried to imagine what The Dragon saw when they had hid in its eye. Three itchy specks of dust. If it could even see them, perhaps they were just a sensation. Nisha had always wanted to be a sensation.

This should have been her chance to prove herself. Her whole life, she knew she wasn't doing her best, she was capable of more and better. It's why she got up every morning, to see if this was the day she did more and did it better.

People got more than one shot at greatness of course, but Nisha was pretty sure you only got one chance to stop a gangster from using a dragon to change reality and she wasn't up to it. She had been sent home.

Nisha stopped dead. She thought she had done all the ones on the estate but the sign sat there, taunting her under a lamppost: NO PARKING. Forgetting everything, her steps became confident and she drew her marker pen from her pocket when she was in arm's reach. Four quick clean strokes and her work was done: NO KING!

She exhaled, for a fleeting moment she existed purely as a body that created things and forgot the world existed.

A loud crack surrounded her followed by a flash of blue light. She turned expecting a police car. A second green crack followed and Nisha saw a trail of sparks from a firework fall over the park at the centre of the estate. This scene must have played out on the patch of grass between Heron and Thornhill House countless times. For a moment, she thought she saw her younger self amongst the crowd of teenagers watching natural selection at work as the stupidest ones ran forward to light the rockets. She looked up at the walkways surrounding the park and half expected to see herself at sixty looking down. *The Artist looks at her younger self and worries.*

A scream leapt out of the crowd as a rocket flew too low and wedged itself in the branches of a plane tree. The wisest members of the crowd scattered immediately knowing that even if the sparks didn't spread, word would, and they needed to be home before it reached their matriarchs. An older boy started to throw stones, attempting to knock the firework free. Others caught on and joined in. Nisha tried to remember the last time it rained.

The rocket exploded in the tree. Leaves ignited and soon the whole tree was ablaze and as angry as God. The tree creaked. A person capable of greatness would save the idiot children from their folly. Nisha looked down at Muriel's boots, then up at the ghost of her future self. She was already worried so where was the harm?

In hindsight, trying to convince twenty surly teenagers to do something before a burning tree fell on them was always going to be a fool's errand. Nisha should have known better. Now, it was morning and she sat on a hospital bed staring at the bandages wrapped around her right forearm. She stared at the bandages with a mix of awe and annoyance. Awe because it could have been so much worse. Annoyance because they itched like hell.

Everything Muriel had said yesterday replayed in Nisha's brain in full technicolour. Muriel was right and this proved it. People who get to do things are from interesting places and grow up with parents with interesting jobs, not Streatham and dinner lady. The last few days had been luck, luck or Muriel propping her up. Alone, she was useless. She would go back to the restaurant.

A doctor entered Nisha's cubicle by saying knock knock. They didn't knock, they just said it which was somehow worse than just barging in. 'Hello Nisha, I'm Doctor Steenson. I'm just here to sign off your discharge papers and whatnot.'

'Hi,' Nisha said but he wasn't listening. He was knee-deep in the paperwork.

'It says here,' he said eventually, 'that you were playing with fireworks? A bit old for that aren't you?'

'Well no. The kids were playing with fireworks and—'

'And you thought you'd join in? Ridiculous at your age. You're lucky you didn't die.'

Nisha glanced at her phone next to her on the bed. It was already half-nine. She had been here all night and hadn't showered or slept. If she left right now and the buses were on her side she would only be twenty minutes late for work. She took a deep breath. 'You're right doctor, I am a fool and won't do it again.'

The doctor held her in his gaze, he had clearly been expecting a fight and seemed disappointed.

'So, can I go?'

The doctor flicked through the paperwork but couldn't find anything else to bring up. 'I guess so.'

Nisha jumped off the bed and marched out of the cubicle. Halfway down the corridor, she realised she had forgotten to ask something. She ran back to find the doctor about to leave. 'Hi again,' she said, 'What do I do about the itching?'

'Scratch it?' he said with a shrug.

The buses were not on Nisha's side and she arrived forty minutes late, drenched in sweat after having to run the whole way from the hospital in heat pushing forty. She ducked through the kitchen door and found it all as she had left it — minus the fire. It had been three days and it was like she had never left. *Maybe she never would.*

One of the commis chefs gave her a nod as he walked past. Then a strange look when he got close enough to smell her.

She went to freshen up and change into a spare uniform she kept for just such occasions. No one had noticed she was late and Chef was nowhere to be seen, she may have gotten away with it. In her locker, she found the pile of order slips with her ideas written on the back. Flicking through them, they were all so small and pointless. Maybe making art was small and pointless, at least the art Nisha made. She wasn't very good at it but she was good at finding dragons and getting in and out of scrapes. She was good with Muriel. She had enjoyed spending her days with her, those days made sense in a way that the days spent apart didn't. Hunting dragons was just a nice bonus.

Stepping out of the bathroom she came face to face with The Manager, Chef's number two and kind in all the ways Chef was mean.

'You've been in the cellar setting traps.' And he was gone.

'What?' Nisha said. But he didn't reply. Nisha turned and found her vision filled with Chef's spice-encrusted jacket.

'Where have you been?'

'In the cellar setting traps,' she said without missing a beat.

Chef sucked on his teeth and walked off.

Nisha slipped back into the routine of the restaurant with ease. Most people hadn't realised she hadn't been turning up for work. Waiting staff aren't just invisible to customers, it's their colleagues too. The restaurant wouldn't open for a few hours but Nisha kept busy. She polished cutlery, she listened to Chef talk about the specials, she cleaned the beer lines in the cellar. She volunteered for this, normally she hated the task but today the idea of sitting alone in the dark for half an hour appealed.

Staring at the damp walls of the cellar, Nisha tried to picture what Muriel was up to. She was probably already back in the cavern with a flaming sword smiting her enemies as she had been doing everyday for years without telling anyone. Meanwhile, Nisha made art and waited tables. There would be a point when she just waited tables and didn't make art anymore. That day wasn't today but it was near, she could feel it. She was close to letting her dreams be dreams and settling for the small. *The artist isn't anymore.*

Then what would Muriel see in her? Warrior queen and waitress. They were an odd pairing before and now Nisha had even less going for her. The day Nisha had approached Muriel it had almost been a dare with herself — go on, I dare you, go chat to that real person, that grown-up standing at the bar that could have anyone they wanted, go see if they'll acknowledge your existence. Muriel had acknowledged Nisha's existence and they became part of each others; but every day Nisha woke up with a little voice that said: *she'll figure you out today. Today, she realises you aren't special and realises you're just you.* Maybe it had already happened. Maybe that was why she never told Nisha about her job. Muriel had sent her away, banished her for being a hindrance, banished for being Nisha.

Having cleaned the lines and polished off a few bottles of beer, she returned to the surface feeling a lot less about everything.

The damage done to the kitchen by Jack's fire had reduced the usable space by a quarter. Add a few decorators trying to cover the worst of the smoke damage and the whole kitchen moved to an angry beat. Somebody was shouting her name.

Chef dropped a bucket of garlic cloves in her arms and told her to peel.

'Yes chef,' she said with resignation.

'What did you say?'

Nisha's eyes darted around the room for clues on what she may have done wrong. 'I said "Yes chef",' she said when no clues were forthcoming.

'Good,' he said. 'You don't normally say it like that. It's better, keep it up.'

'Yes chef.'

He turned to leave before stopping. He sniffed. 'Do you smell beer?'

'No chef.'

Chef eyed her with suspicion before leaving.

Alone, Nisha peeled garlic. This wasn't so bad. It was mindless, which was underrated as a task. Mindless jobs let you be mindless and she needed to not exist for a bit.

Garlic peeled, Nisha put the cloves back in the bucket by the handful. The clock said ten past twelve, the restaurant opened ten minutes ago and she was meant to be out front.

She ran to the walk-in with the bucket of garlic under her arm. Ducking and diving under hot pans and hotter temperaments she rounded in on the walk-in fridge and didn't spot the paint roller on the floor.

The next thing she knew, she was on her back and it was raining garlic cloves.

The kitchen stopped and stared.

'I'm ok,' she said from the floor. *I think.*

The kitchen returned to work.

She stood to find Chef, potato peeler in hand, doing his

best to occupy the same space as her. He backed her against the walk-in door. The blade of the potato peeler rested on her cheek. 'There is an often quoted piece of advice that keen home chefs give each other,' Chef said. 'You know the type: they buy Japanese knives and French Pans. One minute they are into falafel and the next it's kimchi. They tell each other "Don't buy a kitchen gadget that only does one thing". They smirk and roll their eyes at lemon zesters, garlic crushers and the like.' The peeler inched up her cheek. 'But you know what? They're right. You shouldn't buy a gadget that only does one thing. And now I know you're really confused as I'm holding a potato peeler as I tell you all this. A gadget that only does one thing. But you know what Nisha? This gadget has a second use and unless you get your head in the game I will show you its second use. Understand?'

Nisha stared at the pointed tip designed for digging out potato eyes and thought of her own. She went to nod when The Manager appeared next to them. 'Nisha, we have a customer. I need you out front.'

TWELVE

Muriel had relaxed since returning to the surface. With Nisha and Jack safely far away, she had the freedom to act as needed. Yes, The Dragon was waking up. Yes, it was going to destroy everything and everyone that Muriel held dear. It was also huge and needed time to get all its limbs and organs sorted before anything happened. This meant Muriel had time. Time to feel no regrets and to consult a friend about everything that had happened. Time to come up with a solution. If she was wrong and The Dragon was about to burst through the city at any moment then it was already too late and there was nothing she could do about it. Relax or die, an easy choice if you think about it.

She checked her phone again as she waited in the beer garden of an ancient pub on the edge of London. There was no word from Nisha which was fine, good in fact, it meant Nisha had listened and gone back to work.

It would have been a nice beer garden except the tall trees designed to block out modern life seemed to be struggling in the heat, their leaves limp and already turning brown. Lower branches had snapped and lay dead on the ground, the tree shedding the old to save its young.

'In Herefordshire, Hartford and Hampshire, hurricanes hardly ever happen,' said a voice behind her.

'The rain in Spain falls mainly on the plain,' she said without turning.

Reece, in a large straw hat, sat down with two pints of beer. 'Afternoon, how's tricks?'

'"How's tricks?" You've been undercover for too long.'

He slid a pint across to Muriel to join her half-empty glass. 'I know, I worry I'm forgetting where my persona of dim but lovable lackey ends and I begin.'

'So is the hat part of the dim persona you're putting on?'

Reece touched the brim of the hat. 'But how are tricks?'

Muriel sighed. 'Saving the world single-handedly as normal. You?'

'Same. Never knew it would involve moving so many boxes about or babysitting rich idiots though.'

The next words stuck in her throat. 'Can I run something past you?'

'Muriel asking for advice, this must be serious.'

'It is,' she said. 'What if I told you something big was happening that could only be fixed by killing an innocent creature?'

'How big and how innocent?'

Muriel took a mouthful of beer before saying the word. 'Dragon.'

Reece's face dropped, he pulled back his shoulders, his eyes became cold and serious. 'Please tell me you haven't made me come all the way out to the countryside in this heat for a bad joke.'

'We're in Zone Six,' Muriel said. 'But I am serious.'

'Really?'

'Really.'

'Piss off,' he said.

A young boy at the next table giggled. His mum gave Reece and Muriel a disapproving look. Muriel met her gaze. 'It's a pub, not a playground.' Although to be fair some idiot had decided to put a climbing frame in a beer garden.

Reece smiled an apology before turning back. 'Have you told The Laurels?'

Muriel mirrored his stance. She wouldn't go into 1666 and all that. 'They know bits. I wanted to say it out loud to someone else first to make sure I could. I think this is bigger than me.'

The young boy had found two girls to play with on the climbing frame and they settled on a game of monsters.

Reece gulped down half his pint. 'It is to be fair. I mean how do you even begin to kill a dragon? You're going to need a team.'

The children crept around the back of the slide, each taking turns to giggle and be shushed by the other two.

'Maybe.'

The older girl led the charge up the steps and onto the climbing frame.

'I'm also not sure killing it is right,' Muriel said.

They fought valiantly and made their way to the monkey bars.

'What else is there?'

The children weren't strong enough and one by one the girls fell. The boy stood alone with the monster.

'I don't know, but we found a clutch of eggs which makes it different somehow.'

The boy fell to his knees. The girls, forgetting they were dead, cheered him on.

Reece's eyes narrowed. 'You once told me you took a man's kneecap off and threw it at him.'

Muriel smiled. That had been a good day. 'But he was asking for it. This is just...' she struggled to find the words '... just sitting there.'

'I see what you mean,' Reece said with a nod.

They sat in silence while they searched for an answer. Muriel hadn't taken anything as formal as an oath to protect the city and its inhabitants but she liked to think she had rules she worked to. Was killing one creature to keep everyone happy and free the right thing to do? She had no issue fighting and occasionally killing criminals. That made things better and they deserved it. The Dragon didn't deserve it. Then there was the city itself, she knew the city was more than buildings but if The Dragon escaped, destroyed London and then they rebuilt it, would it really be London? She liked London. She liked how stupidly it was laid out and how the roads didn't work but the tube did, she liked how friendly everyone was providing you didn't try and make small talk. She liked being in a crowd, it was the closest thing to infinity she was likely to experience.

'I think you should take it to The Shed and talk to The Laurels,' Reece said. 'The only way to get anything done is to work together and trust those above. It's what makes us different from them.'

She stared at the trees surrounding the beer garden. 'If in doubt pass it up and follow the rules.' She downed the last of her beer. 'How's tricks with you anyway? What have The Laurels got you doing?'

The little boy jumped back onto his feet and with one final blow vanquished the monster. The children cheered and danced in a circle, the townspeople were safe. The boy stood at the top of the slide and yelled a newly learned swear word.

Muriel locked eyes with Reece. They turned as one to face the mother. It was time to leave.

Muriel decided she should walk off the pub and set off along a river path that would take her to The Laurels and their shed.

The sun reached its zenith and offered no quarter. Every inch of cement, tarmac and metal absorbed its fury ready to kick it out into the afternoon and beyond. The sun would rise early again tomorrow and begin the whole violent cycle over and over.

When she was young she had gone on holiday to California: two weeks of endless sun. She had found it so boring, she missed weather and the change that comes with it. Everyone in California seemed happy with the heat but here it turned people sour, they shrivelled and dried out in the heat like raisins. Other countries made grapes, the British made raisins. Maybe that's why Mimi's plan could work, the country was already halfway there. Muriel inspected her hands, she wasn't a raisin yet but her hands were starting to pucker, growing hard and uncompromising. She needed to be more grape. Nisha was a grape. Muriel stopped and checked her phone. No word. Good. Fine.

The path bent away from the river and took a detour inland to allow a row of houses to have riverside gardens. The houses seemed odd and out of place on the river. They were modest, with no more than a few bedrooms, built out of ubiquitous red brick in a time when having a garden that ran to the Thames was possible for the some and not just the reserve of the few.

Climbing over the wooden fence that ran between the path

and the garden were thick vines. Their tendrils licked and whipped the air searching for a handhold. They had finally reached the summit only to find a dank alleyway as their reward. Leaves like spades caught the sun's rays and on the end of each vine were grapes. Luscious green but tiny compared to a supermarket bunch, they seemed to glow with their own internal light.

Muriel cradled the grapes in her hand and wanted to roll her eyes at the universe for its lack of tact. She checked she was alone before picking the biggest off the vine. Her teeth pierced the soft skin filling her mouth with sour tart juice. She swallowed but the taste lingered, as did the skin, too thin for her teeth to chew but too thick to swallow. She spat out the skin along with a hard pip. It was still better than a raisin.

<hr>

The fridges of alcohol were being emptied as fast as staff in the supermarket could restock them. Burger buns, burgers and little squares of plastic cheese were in a similar state. It hadn't rained in two months or dropped below twenty-four, but the thirst for barbecues hadn't been sated. A cage of beer emerged from the stockroom and shoppers looked on like true believers beholding a sign from their creator. Cans and bottles rattled like psalms and a quiet reverence fell over the crowd. The crowd became a queue, ready to receive their ambrosia — which was also on the cage.

A man, a boy really, opened the cage while a manager tried to keep the shoppers at bay until the beer reached the fridges. They both sweated despite the air conditioning.

Reece hung near the back.

'Can everyone stand back while we put the stock out? You

can't take it from the cage,' the manager said, taking a stab at authority.

'Why not?' someone called out.

'We need to put it in the fridge so it's cold.'

'We're just going to take them straight out again, they won't have a chance to get cold.'

Reece checked his watch and did some quick maths. Theo said he was lighting the barbecue when he texted Reece to pick up supplies on his way to work, he didn't have long. When Reece asked for the morning off to meet a friend Theo had winked and nudged for so long he blasted through ironic to annoying to concerning. Theo had been in a perpetual good mood since he had met with Mimi the day before. He hadn't said what had been discussed but it had caused him to become driven and focused, willing to try anything that might bring success. Reece had only suggested the barbecue as a joke but Theo had latched on to it and now Reece had been sent to buy burger buns. The whims of management.

'It's for insurance reasons,' the manager said, trying a different tactic. 'Customers aren't allowed to take things from the cages, only shelves.'

'Just give us the beer,' someone shouted.

The manager straightened his back and stuck out a finger. 'Right, if you lot don't calm down I'll take all the beer back to the stock room.'

Their creator had turned on them and the shoppers repaid them in kind. The crowd lurched towards the cage. The manager had a look that said he knew what percentage of the profit went to the Cayman Islands, he stepped back and let the beer-thirsty crowd descend. Hands pushed and clawed at bottles and cans. Those at the back pushed forward and the cage rolled backwards, collided with the fridges and tipped over, sending beer and glass skidding across the shop floor.

Three men jumped onto the cage and grabbed cases of beer and headed for the exit. A wall of bodies had formed around the scene and the last man attempted to push through. He was pushed back and fists were thrown.

Two cans of IPA rolled and stopped in front of Reece. He picked them up and placed them in the basket before anyone realised. The scuffle over beer threatened to turn into a full-scale looting. Customers fought each other for prized items, or in fact, anything they could grab. London was Reece's home and always would be, however in the last few weeks it had begun to change, becoming the place people from other places said it was.

Reece looked at the chaos in front of him and the beer sitting quietly unharassed and thought it was worth the risk. He sneaked forward and placed a four-pack of Belgium beer in his basket. Theo was in a good mood and he would need more than a six beers. Reece spied a few more cans in, what was until a few moments ago, someone's trolley but was now acting as a battering ram. Walking at pace and with confidence towards the trolley, he moved the cans from the cart to his hand and then to his basket in one quick movement. Others would do magic and slice the beers into their possession, but Reece had to use wit and guile in lieu of magic. The slow path was only slow if you were too scared to take the odd shortcut.

Knowing he had pushed his luck, Reece headed to the veg aisle where the riot hadn't reached — *it would though* — and picked up a couple of heads of lettuce. Burger buns were next on the list, he skirted past an affray over the last unclaimed French stick and took two packets in case he lost one on the way to the checkout.

Reece crossed the road by Bermondsey Station and watched people bask in the sun. They had been calling it a heat wave but it wasn't moving. What do you call a wave that doesn't move? An ocean perhaps or a stagnant pond depending on the size. The country sat under a stagnant pond of heat and no one seemed to care.

Reece bent down and opened the fridge in the lab. The blast of cold air washed over him like an ocean wave. The fridge was filled with a hodgepodge of science experiments and the edible, today they would combine the two. He placed half the beers on a shelf and picked up the ketchup before returning to the smell of cooking liver outside.

The sky was flawless. Reece couldn't remember the last time he saw a cloud. He welcomed the heat at first but soon the clear blue skies had become as soul-destroying as endless overcast days where the grey concrete blends into the murky sky. Reece had never left the city but knew somewhere out there someone was trying to grow food and wasn't getting any rain.

'Reece! Grab yourself a beer. That's an order,' Theo said. He stood by the barbecue, giving a slab of dragon's liver the occasional poke with a spatula.

Reece knew he wasn't The Laurels' best agent, he wasn't the fastest or strongest, he definitely wasn't the most intelligent but, earlier that day, standing in the blazing sun and explaining to Theo what a spatula was, he knew he must be the most patient.

He put the ketchup with the rest of the shopping on the table — the lettuce had already lost the fight with the heat and collapsed in a heap — and opened a can of beer.

'Glorious, isn't it?' Theo said. 'If this is what the scaremongers have been warning us about, I say bring it on.' Theo flipped the liver with the spatula in one quick jerky movement. The edges of the organ had become black and brittle. Taste wasn't important here. 'Bit crispy but I think it will work.'

Reece hoped so. He had heard rumours about what Mimi did with a crowbar to those who failed her and would prefer not to find out if they were true. It wasn't just the violence that Mimi could dole out that kept everyone in line, it was her connections. Mimi's roots went deeper than the oldest English oaks. She was related to everyone worth knowing and if she wasn't, she knew someone who was. The criminal underworld worked just like the one above but, down here at least, Reece could do something about it. Might ruled the underworld but that didn't mean other means of getting things done didn't work. When everyone is keeping one eye on the door being kicked in they don't notice someone slipping in through the window.

Reece took a sip of beer and drank in the view. The shipping container lay on a piece of scrubland near the river. Anyone else would have sold it to be turned into flats but Mimi knew the benefit of having a scrap of land conveniently located and deserted at night. It was surrounded by garages and the back of an old factory but if you stood at just the right point you could see the Walkie Talkie.

'On days like this, you can really forget your worries,' Theo said, downing half his beer. 'This is what it's all about. It takes me back to my uni days sitting in pubs, on my parent's boat, not studying.' He laughed at his own joke. 'You've got to stop every now and again and enjoy it.'

The liver was flipped again and was now equally charred on both sides. Using the spatula like a monkey uses a stick, Theo pushed the liver onto Reece's waiting plate.

They made their way to a trestle table Reece had found

around the back of the shipping container. Mismatched cutlery, paper plates and an array of condiments sat on top of a gingham tablecloth Reece had brought from home. There's no reason science experiments can't have a sense of occasion.

They cut the liver in half, covered it in ketchup and sandwiched it between their burger buns. Reece said a brief prayer to Charles Darwin and took a bite. It was mild and if it wasn't for the ketchup it would be almost tasteless. Reece was hoping for fireworks, new beginnings and first kisses. Instead, it was as disappointing as New Year's Eve.

Gulls circled overhead, drawn to the promise of food, however bad. Theo finished another beer. 'Have I ever told you about my parent's boat?' He didn't wait for a reply. 'It's a Mälar. Only a hundred and twenty were ever built. All wood, no engine, real classic design. The only thing they were able to keep after the big crash. The summer before university, I sailed it to the Med and spent my time going up and down the Côte d'Azur.' He opened a beer. 'It was a summer of equilibrium, right between childhood and adulthood you know? Anything is possible and everything seems balanced.' Theo nodded at his own perceived profound statement.

Reece took a bite of his burger and the birds closed in for the kill.

'At the time I was jealous of a friend who took their family's yacht to the Caribbean. I sulked the whole way to Portugal but slowly the sun and unending blue cheered me up.' Theo opened another beer for Reece. 'I grew up a lot that summer and realised that anyone, no matter their background, can enjoy themselves. God, I wish I had that boat right now.'

And I would sink it. Reece went to say something, stopped himself, and channelled his thoughts into another bite of liver.

A gull crashed onto the table attempting to mug them of

their sandwiches. The cutlery scattered across the floor with a clang. Reece fell backwards over his chair and landed with a thud, his sandwich gone. He dragged himself up and took a moment to realise the rocking wasn't his head. The courtyard had been replaced with antique planks and the shipping container with an actual ship. The barbecue and trestle table sat on the deck of a yacht as if it were the most normal thing in the world.

Boundless blue stretched in every direction; the horizon unbroken by land.

Theo stood, seeming to take it all in. 'This is my boat.' He ran into the cabin. 'This is my boat!' His voice carried far over the water.

Liver had become smeared across Reece's palm. Specks of blue glistered in the sun, half hidden in the liver. Engaging fully with the scientific method Reece gave his hand a sniff. He was in a desert for a moment, hot sand between his toes.

'This is my boat,' Theo said from the doorway, his eyes bright with excitement.

A hypothesis bobbed to the surface of Reece's mind. This was quickly capsized by a prediction and soon found a conclusion circling it in the water. A conclusion that wanted to drag them to the bottom of the ocean.

Reece pushed past Theo into the cabin and down into the bowels of the ship. The rooms were laid out like a maze, nothing was labelled or marked, if you needed to ask you didn't belong. He slammed open door after door finding only cabins and a galley filled with cases of wine and not a lot else. He stood in the doorway of the master bedroom and looked into the hallway. A faded Persian rug ran the length of the corridor. That's where he'd put it. He ran to the edge of the rug and threw it back exposing a trap door. A heavy iron ring with a padlock through it sat at one end. Reece twisted and pulled at the padlock but it wouldn't budge. Galley. He ran back to the galley and grabbed a fire extinguisher.

'It's really my boat!'

Using two hands Reece slammed the extinguisher into the lock with a dull thud.

'Reece, get up here and help me with the sails, I can teach you a useful skill.'

He hit the padlock again.

'Reece?'

The third strike sent the padlock skidding down the hallway. The heavy trapdoor took two hands to pry open.

Water roared in the darkness of the hull. Reece filled his lungs and jumped. The few inches of seawater did nothing to break his fall and pain shot through his ankle when he hit the floor. Cursing at his miscalculation, he limped to the light switch. The hull had been filled with various emergency supplies: flair guns, out-of-date rations and more wine. The sound of water filling the boat continued further into the hold.

The whole boat creaked a warning.

Reece threw boxes to the ground to reveal a hole in the hull. He was just in time to watch it implode inwards in a torrent of water. Just before the water hit, Reece observed how the hole, inexplicably, was the shape of a liver sandwich with a bite out of it.

Theo stood on the deck admiring the main sail, he tugged on ropes and smelt the varnished wood. The trestle table and chairs had listed to the back of the deck.

He had nearly finished his sandwich.

Limping across the deck, pain shot through Reece's leg. He watched as Theo raised the last bite of his sandwich to his mouth. Reece jumped.

THIRTEEN

Muriel stood outside The Laurels' shed waiting for them to open the door and tongued the grape skin stuck between her teeth. The skin lodged firm between two molars and she was finding it tricky to get her tongue into the right position to wiggle it free. This was good, it meant she could focus her attention on the grape instead of what happened after Jack had left and what she had said to Nisha — how the words had tumbled out of Muriel in the wrong order and made her seem mean and controlling instead of calm and caring. Nisha *should* go back to the restaurant and make her brilliant art, not because she thought Nisha wasn't capable of doing whatever needed doing next, but because Muriel was scared she, Muriel, wasn't capable of it and Nisha would end up dead in a ditch somewhere. There weren't any ditches in London but the point stood.

If only Jack had followed her plan. She would talk to The Laurels and it would all be like before. Nisha safe at the restaurant, Jack far, far away and Muriel on her own doing things her way. She'd fill The Laurels in, they would come up with a solution, she'd get it done, then home in time to apologise to Nisha and make it up to her. There was a lot to make up, they had both said things but Muriel had said more. She needed to make sure she didn't lose Nisha. These last few days had been magical, truly. Muriel knew a thing or two about magic and didn't use that word lightly. It had also been terrifying and frustrating but mostly magical.

'Muriel my love, how are you? Come in come in,' Nigel said, opening the shed door.

They went through the social dance of teas and biscuits, pink wafers this time. *Someone's in a good mood.*

'So, how's it going? Did you find out who's searching for The Dragon?' Denise asked, sipping her tea.

'Yes, but we've got a bit of a Pandora's box situation.'

'The Greek restaurant on the corner? Not my thing really,' Nigel said.

Muriel pressed her tongue against the grape skin and tried to push it up and out from between her teeth. It didn't budge. 'No, I mean things might be about to get big, nasty and irreversible.' She explained what she had found out, about the size of The Dragon, and most importantly how it had blinked. She lied and said Jack had decided to stay with family in the countryside until he was given the all clear it was safe. She filled them in on Mimi's plan to use The Dragon which they seemed less concerned about. At some point during her retelling of the last few days, Denise had gripped Nigel's hand and squeezed the colour from both their knuckles. Muriel finished her story and they sat in silence.

'This is it, love,' Denise said to Nigel.

'Let's not get too excited.'

'This is what?' Muriel asked. She had been expecting panic or at least mild surprise.

Nigel took the lead. 'Do you garden Muriel?'

'My parents grow apples if that counts.'

He nodded as if they spoke in code. 'A country is like a garden or a farm. It needs to be tended, cared for, loved. Recently we've noticed that we're missing a gardener, there is no one to focus the garden or give it some direction. There are all kinds of weeds coming up, you can't see where the path ends and the beds begin. Ants and other pests are crawling over everything. When a garden gets chaotic like that there's no choice but to strip it back to the earth, to its core. With The Dragon back and seeping magic again, we can start over. Do you understand?'

This wasn't Muriel's understanding of how it works at all. Her mum loved ants, she said they did good things to the soil. Weeds were all kinds of useful. 'I think I do.'

Nigel looked to Denise for permission before peeling back the Keep Calm and Carry On poster that had been stuck to the shed wall for as long as Muriel had worked for The Laurels. Behind the poster hung a rough oval mirror, hammered into shape and polished to a shine, reflecting a crude version of the shed back into the room.

'What is that?' Muriel asked.

'Don't you recognise it?' Denise said. 'It's the dragon scale you brought us the other day.'

'We just put it to use,' Nigel added. The Laurels stood and signalled for Muriel to do the same. 'With what you told us we can start to get the garden in order again. Return it to its proper state. Are you ready?'

Curiosity forced a reluctant nod from Muriel.

Denise instructed her to stand in front of the mirror. 'Don't worry, it will just take you home.'

The reflection was dull at first. She stepped closer and it all became startlingly clear. At first, Muriel stared at herself and thought it was someone else looking back. The reflection looked like Muriel but was younger. Her hair was tame and she was wearing a blouse.

Suddenly, Muriel stood in a living room wearing a polka dot blouse and an A-line skirt. The room was just like her gran's living room except it didn't smell of cigarettes and anti-depressants. Legions of strange porcelain creatures stared at her across various shades of brown furniture. She felt like she was sinking and she was. A giant sheepskin rug covered a brown carpet.

A service hatch in the wall opened with a bang and made Muriel jump. Denise peered through the opening. Gone were her faded pink cardigan and grass-stained shorts, instead, she wore a gingham dress and apron like a housewife in a gravy advert.

'Where am I?' Muriel asked.

'Home, love,' Denise said.

'What does that mean?'

'This is what we're talking about, people have forgotten what it's meant to be like. Come with me.' Denise led her to the front door and out into the street. The street matched the living room, rows of neat houses with freshly cut lawns and trees in blossom. Boys in shorts played in the road with a football, also brown, while girls sat to one side and had tea parties with porcelain dolls. None of them brown.

'This is how we're meant to be, how things were when The Dragon seeped magic into the ground. This is what we'll return to now it's back.'

Muriel took in the clingfilm world in front of her and saw no weeds or pests. She knew they must grow here but they had been pulled and burnt on the pyre of conformity. Maybe some sheltered under rose bushes or cracks in the pavement, weak and stilted but it was no life for anything. 'Where's Nigel?'

'At the farm, shall we drive?'

They headed north through town. Denise drove up Charing Cross Road. Its once grim Georgian fronts gleamed until they looked like facades. The gaggles of tourists and workers had been replaced with the cast of Dad's Army, cheeky chimney sweeps and shoeshine boys. Miles of Union Flag bunting hung from every conceivable surface. It was as if God had joined the National Trust. Making their way to the countryside, they saw milkmen in bright white coats dropping their wares off to housewives in hair curlers with rosy cheeked tikes underfoot. Coppers chasing lovable crooks who gave up at the end of the street. Muriel actually heard one say, "It's a fair cop." Teenagers still stood on street corners but now Lindy Hopped and helped old ladies cross the street. The voice of Vera Lynn filled Muriel's brain. Her music and this strange world were the same. If you took a microscope and examined a handful of dirt its atoms would read: *We'll meet again, Don't know where, Don't know when.* If you travelled to the stars in a spaceship the words: *But I know we'll meet again, some sunny day* would be etched across the Cosmos.

At first, Muriel thought it was a trick of the light as the sun dipped in the sky but objects were becoming flatter. Trees were no longer made up of thousands of individual leaves instead becoming smudges of green, the road became a single shade of grey and the sky lost its brilliance. By the time they pulled up to a thatched farmhouse, the world had become two-dimensional and dull. Nigel greeted them in jodhpurs and a red hunting jacket. The sound of Vera Lynn — real this time — mixed with their footsteps on gravel.

'Hello my loves,' Nigel said. 'So Muriel, what did you think of it?'

She took in the house and turned to the surrounding countryside but said nothing.

Denise cracked first. 'Shall we show her?'

She followed them to a barn at the back of the house where Vera grew louder. Muriel had grown up on a farm but this wasn't home. It lacked the smells and movement of farms, it lacked the noise. The countryside wasn't quiet, it was loud with machinery, work and death. She had lost count of the number of disillusioned faces she had seen on the lanes at home. They had come expecting silence and beauty and had found only engine grease and mud. This was their farm. A farm for people who knew little of how life was made or what it was made from.

The barn was cool but the air was stuffy with dust, at least they had got that right. On a table sat an old radio. Made of wood, it had a built-in speaker shaped like a tiny cathedral window.

We'll meet again
Don't know where
Don't know when

Nigel and Denise took up places next to the radio. 'So this is it.'

'A radio?' Muriel went to put her hand in her pockets only to realise she didn't have any.

'It's a bit more than that.'

'What is it?'

'Well, it is a radio,' Nigel said, 'but it won't run out of battery or play anything other than our girl Vera.'

Muriel toyed with the grape skin, she managed to rotate it a few degrees which gave her an extra couple of millimetres to work with. 'What does this have to do with The Dragon? And how did you make all this so quickly?'

'Another agent has been doing some work in parallel to you. He made copies of some research notes he had access to and got them out to us.' Denise said. 'It was just enough to go on but until you came back and said The Dragon was alive we didn't want to get our hopes up.'

'It's how we're going to fix the country, along with this.' Nigel pulled a syringe as big as Muriel's forearm from under the table and placed it next to the radio.

'It's simple,' Denise said. 'You take both of these down into the cavern and inject The Dragon with this.'

'And what is that?' Muriel asked.

Nigel stroked the syringe. 'Tranquilliser, the good stuff too. It should keep it asleep for another hundred years at least.'

'Right...'

'And then you set this up near its head,' Denise said. 'Then this wonderful music will seep into its dreams and the creature will dream beautiful dreams about rose bushes and clean-shaven men in suits and these images will seep out and up and into the world and turn it into this.' She gestured at the landscape beyond the barn doors. 'A place where people will know how things are going to work day after day and it will be safe to leave your house.'

The grape skin was loose, Muriel teased it out and swallowed the last of the grape. She now gave The Laurels her full attention. 'It's already safe to leave the house and you want me to make The Dragon dream about tailoring?'

Nigel and Denise both nodded. 'That's the short

version yes, but the only hurdle is the tranquilliser. You'll need to inject it into the beast's heart.'

'Sorry?'

'But that won't be a problem for you,' Nigel said. 'You're surprisingly capable.'

'I've always said you were,' Denise added. 'For a girl.'

'Why do we need the radio? Why can't we just put it back to sleep?'

They didn't seem to understand the question. 'So we can fix everything.'

'But I don't think it needs fixing. It's fine the way it is.'

Nigel chuckled. 'Surely you don't really think that? We need to go back to how things were.'

There was a dragon under the city about to wake up and The Laurels were playing around with radios and trying to undo the world. 'But this is bloody stupid. I mean it's just terrible, no one wants to live like this and no one ever did. This isn't turning the clock back, it's bulldozing everything that came before it and replacing it with a model village. People can't live in model villages. They need new ideas and new solutions, not a childish version of history that ignores the complicated bits.' A bright white chicken strolled towards them, its feet a single shade of yellow and its wattle cherry red. It turned to face them, becoming a single black line for a moment before heading out of the barn. 'They need a third dimension for God's sake.' She turned to leave.

The Laurels watched her walk away in stunned silence before she returned with her index finger leading the charge. 'You know what this is, don't you? It's Thatcher's wet dream.'

'Steady on love,' Nigel said, taking a step back.

'I'm taking this and doing it my way.' She snatched the syringe from the table. Nigel's hand leapt out to stop her and she sliced it at the wrist and slapped him across the face with his own hand. He collapsed on the floor.

'Muriel!' Denise said in horror.

'Piss off.' Muriel stormed out and headed back down the track away from the farm.

Walking away from the barn Muriel could see details that she'd missed on the drive to the farm. Everything was the same. Every tree a carbon copy of the one before, every blade of grass identical. No flowers grew on the side of the road. She was walking through The Laurels' dream world and it was as interesting as a golf course. She wondered how she missed it. Were they always weird fascists or had it happened slowly? Did they buy a vintage tea towel one day and before they knew it they wanted to escape reality with its shades of grey and terrible leaders to a world of retro necrosis? She understood, of course, things weren't better in the past. You just knew how they were going to end. It was like reading the last page of a book first to find out what happens to The Elf in The Paisley Suit.

She came across a village of cobbled streets and flat caps. Smoke drifted from chimneys and the air smelt of freshly baked bread. It was sickening. Against her better judgment, Muriel headed for the pub.

The pub was called The George and it was made of, in both senses, smoke and mirrors. Ornate mirrors covered every wall and tried to reflect what little light from outside made it through the thick clouds of cigarette smoke emanating from every patron. Eyes followed her every step on her way to the bar. The landlord, wearing a shirt and tie and polishing a glass, smiled as he approached. 'What can I get you, young lady?'

Muriel had a hunch that The Laurels' world wouldn't have lager in it so she ordered a pint of bitter.

'Might be a bit strong for you darling, how about a nice glass of sherry?'

She slapped her hand on the bar. 'Why not, and how about a pint for everyone else on me.'

They were five rounds into the newly introduced game of Whippet Snippets when they forgot Muriel wasn't a man and allowed her to order a pint of beer. She drank half in a single bound to much applause and collapsed onto a barstool. She watched the game unfold next to a man she had learnt was called Fred. 'The thing about people from other places,' Fred said, 'is they're not as logical as us. It's in our nature to look at things and make them better, to improve them. Other people can't do that. That's why we have to go in and sort them out. My grandfather told me when he first went there they didn't even have proper measurements.'

Fred was exactly what she was after. 'Tell me Fred, how much of my pint have I drunk?'

'Half?'

'And what's that in ounces, I always forget?' she said spinning on the stool.

Fred's eyes inspected the ceiling as he tried to remember.

'It's ten ounces,' someone called across the bar.

Muriel clicked her fingers. 'That's right, so that's sixty drams, isn't it?'

Fred knew this one. 'No, it's eighty.'

'So there's a hundred and sixty drams in a pint which is the same as twenty ounces.'

'And eight pints in a gallon,' Fred said. 'I think.'

'And what's bigger than a gallon?'

'Two gallons?' he replied after a pause.

The pub thought about this. They didn't know if it was meant as a joke but erupted into laughter anyway. A hairline crack appeared in the ceiling.

The barman rang the bell for closing time. It flashed between being a bell and being a pigeon with every ring. No one except Muriel seemed to notice. 'That's it, you've drunk us dry, we're out of beer. You don't have to go home but you can't stay here!'

The crowd booed and hissed.

Muriel squeezed through the throngs of people to find Fred. 'Fred, is there another pub in the village?'

'Of course, The Dragon's about half a mile down the road. How'd you not know that?' People started to push past them towards the exit.

'You know what us women are like Fred, if it wasn't for my girlfriend I'd forget to put clothes on, can you imagine?'

'Girlfriend?' Fred's face grew serious and the crowd froze. They lurched forward like a car starting in gear before coming back to life a second later.

Fred's face returned to its happy drunken self. He yelled for what seemed to be most of the village to head to The Dragon.

Muriel picked up the cauliflower, twine and shotgun shells used to play Whippet Snippets and stepped in with the crowd. She found herself next to the vicar. He had taken enthusiastically to Whippet Snippets and his face had the sheen of someone who had decided to pile all his worries and regrets onto tomorrow morning. 'Mary my dear,' he said through a burp. 'Where are we doing?'

'The Dragon, vicar.' She took his arm to steady him while he figured out the cobblestones.

'Wonderful,' he said. 'I do like dragons.'

The bright yellow eye deep under London loomed large in Muriel's mind and she wondered where her body was. Was it here with her or still standing in the shed looking in the mirror at someone's ideal version of herself? If she stayed here would The Dragon and Mimi's plans pass her by? She had pissed off The Laurels but they hadn't come after her so maybe they wouldn't mind her staying. They had a whole network of agents they could use. She could stay and drink sherry and knit or do whatever it is women were meant to do in the imagination of scared people. Alone though, she thought. A dangerous world with Nisha was better than this.

'Shall we stop at the pub first?' the vicar asked.

'Vicar?'

'Before we see the dragon shall we stop in at the pub?'

'It couldn't hurt,' Muriel said, directing the vicar down the path of least resistance and towards the entrance to a pub.

'So, tell me Vicar, who's the landlord here?'

He let out another wet burp and apologised. 'Noah Murphy, moved here from Little Wheezing a few years ago with his wife. I think her name is Mary too.'

Little Wheezing with its thatched roofs and cobblestones, every village in the new world will be the same as the last. If she asked The Laurels they would say they didn't go in for all that equality stuff and people needed to work hard to earn their keep but everyone here was taken care of. They were equal in their poverty but equal nonetheless. Three types of people wanted everyone to live in small cottages and be close to nature: Anarchists, fascists and people who had never lived in small cottages close to nature. Everyone else saw the appeal of bin men and indoor plumping.

A faint pink light replaced the mortar between the cobblestones as the last of the villagers passed down the road on their way to the pub. One by one the cobblestones fell into a pink void that sat under the village.

The Dragon pub was identical to The George right down to the nicotine-flavoured wallpaper and the landlord polishing a glass. The village poured in through the doors and the landlord's eyes grew wide with fear until he did a quick calculation and welcomed the influx of drinkers and their money. Muriel handed the cauliflower to the team setting up Whippet Snippets and they balanced it on the leg of an upturned barstool. She dropped the vicar on a bench by the door where he broke into a rendition of Danny Boy. The villagers gathered around the stool waiting for the game to begin when The Laurels burst in sending the shotgun shells scattering across the floor. The villagers straightened up and stood in silence. The Laurels had made themselves lord of the manor and why not? If you're going to live in a fantasy world why be the stable boy? Nigel cradled his handless arm in a swaddle of vintage tea towels. 'Get her!'

The crowd turned to Muriel. Then back to The Laurels. Fred stepped forward, cap in hand. 'What? Muriel?'

'Yes! She's trying to stop us,' Denise said.

Fred scrunched his hat tight. 'Stop you doing what, if you don't mind me asking?'

The Laurels stumbled, unsure how to explain their plan to change what was real to people who weren't real.

'Well?' Muriel asked with a smile.

'She's not from here, she's an intruder,' Nigel tried.

The villagers laughed. 'What do you mean "not here"?' Fred said. 'Everyone's from here. Or Little Wheezing.'

Muriel took a sip of beer and watched the faces in the pub. One by one the idea of "not here" seemed to dawn on the villagers. They talked in groups, some with raised voices while others whispered. Suddenly, The Laurel's world was as messy as the one they wanted to leave behind. They had created cookie-cutter people but like real people and real cookies, they had spilt over the edges and congealed into a mess at the first opportunity.

'Fine,' Denise said. 'I'll do it.' Her hand flicked out to slice at Muriel when a pink hue flooded the room through the windows.

The pub rocked, Muriel tried to keep her pint level but took a flying bar stool to the shin and fell hard onto the floor.

The pint survived.

Muriel stood and fought against the tide of villagers heading to the middle of the pub to see out of the window. The village, the countryside, the world had vanished. It had all been replaced with a rose-tinted void. The pub hung suspended over nothing. Roof tiles whipped off one by one as lampposts, cows and trees flew past and around them.

She turned to find everyone, including The Laurels, looking to her for guidance. 'Vicar, can I borrow your bel-?'

The vicar started undoing the buckle before she could finish the word 'belt'. Some of the female villagers watched through slanted fingers.

Muriel took hold of the belt at the buckle and threw the other end out of the window. The belt whipped and snaked through the air. It pulled on her arm and she let go. It flew up and joined the rest of the world, disappearing into the pink haze. They were falling or being pulled down towards something. The objects flying past had taken on a more urban feel. Trees and cows had been replaced with cars, lampposts and other bits of street furniture. They had entered through the mirror in the living room. It might be the way out. It might be the epicentre of a world collapsing back in on itself.

The roof began peeling away, flooding the pub with more pink light. She didn't have long and it was the best she had.

'What do we do?' Nigel screamed.

'Wait here!' Muriel climbed onto the window ledge and took a deep breath.

Muriel stood alone in The Laurels' shed. She had a vague notion of falling but no memory of how she got from the pub to here, *no difference there then*. She still had the syringe, which was good. She still had the ridiculous dress, which she could fix.

Taking a breath, she knew she needed a plan and not to panic. There was still time to save the city. The Laurels' network was cell-based and only they knew all the people who worked for them. She knew Reece because she had caught him climbing the allotment fence after forgetting his key a few years ago. She went to call Reece but didn't have her phone. It was in one of her jeans pockets and they had disappeared or been turned into a skirt.

Muriel would have to break protocol and contact the other agents somehow, but given the circumstances they'd understand. Searching the shed for anything that might give her clues to their identities, she turned over tools, checked packets of seeds for coded messages, and poked the walls for secret panels. It was just a shed. Out of ideas, she sat in a lawn chair and saw it. Sticking out behind an old paint can was a leather-bound ledger.

The ledger was filled with the inner workings of The Laurels' operation. Money in money out. Payments, wages and expenses. Muriel felt guilty and excited looking behind the curtain. A record of The Laurels' grand network laid out in black and white.

She scanned the names and saw the end of her world. Pages and pages of entries going back years but only two names. Muriel and Reece. So this was it? The Laurels' whole operation consisted of just two mad gardeners and a couple of naive idiots. No secret army of do-gooders keeping evil from the door. No grand plan to keep bad people in check. *There were no rules.* Just her and Reece and there was a reason Reece was given the job of moving boxes. Her whole identity was this job and it was gone. She had never been a weapon of justice, she was just another violent thug who did the bidding of a loon. Muriel was no one now, existing only in time and space without purpose. This job had cost her everything. She had tried to protect Nisha from it, to keep her in her life but squirrelled away. Worlds had collided and now it was over. Muriel had put work first and ended up with nothing.

Muriel gripped the page with both hands until it threatened to tear. She had sided with The Laurels because they seemed powerful and good. Instead, they were mad. Mimi had power and was likely mad. Muriel thought of herself as powerful so maybe she was too. After the last few days, it made sense; with what was to come, she saw the appeal.

The Dragon would escape and destroy the city or Mimi would succeed and a shadow would fall over the country. Either way, millions would die, they always do when someone wants absolute power. Madness could be an escape. Muriel pictured herself walking alone through a ruined London.

Muriel had escaped to London alone, she worked alone and lived alone. And then for a brief moment: Nisha. Nisha so full of — not life, Muriel was full of life — but bravery. Nisha was unexpectedly brave, fearless in fact. She made art and showed it to people, she stole paperwork and tricked builders. Nisha was Muriel's reason to be brave, and to see the centre of her world going toe to toe with gangsters and monsters was unnerving. Muriel had flinched and panicked, pushing Nisha away when she should have pulled her close and now Nisha was beyond her reach. Maybe forever.

Without a reason to be brave, Mimi and The Dragon seemed insurmountable. Muriel could just stay in the shed. Four flimsy walls and a magic mirror for company. The allotment was probably far enough from town to avoid being wrenched apart by The Dragon. Mimi was unlikely to be interested in allotments if it went the other way.

Muriel imagined Mimi in wellies arguing with the committee about some strange allotment bylaw she had infringed upon. Her carrots planted too close together or paths mulched with the wrong kind of wood chips. A giggle escaped. *The madness had already set in.*

The shed would be Muriel's home, not London. She scrunched the piece of paper, leaned back in her chair and put her feet on an upturned bucket. Hidden behind a bag of compost was a half-smoked packet of cigarettes and a lighter shaped like a lipstick. *Denise, you dark horse.* It had been a few years since Muriel had quit but it was the end of the world so why not? The cigarettes glowed bright before settling on a calming ember. It had been so long since she had sat with no idea what to do next. It was nice.

. . .

Halfway through her third cigarette, she lounged in the silence and her madness, and had a thought. A sane thought which was very annoying. It reminded her that although she was safe and a bit mad in a shed, Nisha wasn't. She was still in the city. The restaurant was right in the middle of town. If The Dragon woke, Nisha would be gone.

A life without Nisha would be torture but a world without Nisha wasn't worth living in. And Muriel wanted to live, to live in the same world as Nisha and to know she was there, somewhere.

Madness would have to wait. Stubbing out the cigarette and her feelings with it, she stood and took a breath of clean air. All her thoughts plunged through her lungs, through her feet and out into the ground. She waited for a moment, half expecting the ground to cough them back up.

The Dragon scale-cum-mirror-cum-magic portal looked at her from the wall, it had lost some of its sheen. She gave it a flick. Nothing. She put down the syringe and picked up the mirror and a spade. She put the spade and mirror down, picked up an olive-green gardening jacket that hung on the door and slipped it on over the dress. Properly dressed, she went outside with the mirror and spade.

It was still blistering hot outside and not good weather to be digging a hole. The rock-hard ground put up a fight but she won in the end. She placed the mirror face down in the hole. Muriel didn't really consider herself a witch, witches weren't real, magic was, but witches were made up. If someone asked her to explain that line of logic she couldn't but she knew it was correct. Looking down at the mirror, however, she felt the need to witch it up a bit, just to be sure. She slipped off her shoes and climbed the apple tree that took up most of The Laurels' allotment plot. Dead mistletoe clung to the upper branches. She placed a bunch on top of the mirror with care.

Not knowing any wards or hexes she hummed the National Anthem — reasoning it was the only song she knew about bargaining with an eldritch power — as she filled in the hole. To seal the deal, she placed a bird bath on top. It was done.

She returned to the shed and picked up the syringe, wrapping it in an old cloth and placing it in her jacket pocket. There was nothing else to do except everything. No plan or rules now, just impending madness and a life without Nisha.

FOURTEEN

Jack stepped out of his flat to go to work and his whole body flinched at the heat. A thin layer of sweat covered every inch of his skin before he closed the door behind him. For the last few summers he had taken to packing a spare T-shirt as well as deodorant and sunscreen whenever he left the house; each year it felt like he started the ritual earlier than the year before and ended it later. He had become a hat man, or at least he would be if there were any good summer hats for men. With straw hats you had two options: pair it with a button-down shirt which would add forty years and give you automatic membership to the RHS or embrace the look and match it with a linen shirt-chino combo. This was known as "The Full Del-monte". You had the cowboy hat which the less said about the better, and finally old dependable, the baseball cap. Jack had gone for the baseball cap. If he could design a nice summer hat for men he would be set for life; with summer going the way it was it was only a matter of time before they became a necessity. The air was different too, it was thick and made the world bend and blur.

As Acting Head of Physics, Jack was now expected to go to meetings during the school holidays. His usual half term of lesson plans, marking, and binge drinking in front of TV until he woke up in the middle of the night surrounded by course-work from a not-entirely unpleasant dream about a rough but kind-hearted police detective with a Scottish brogue, was over, but at least it got him out of the house.

Jack always found people who filled every waking moment with work or hobbies off-putting. It was as if they were running from something. Too lazy to run from anything Jack would rather let whatever it was catch him and do whatever it was it was going to do. *Just like Detective Campbell did.* After the last few days, he wasn't sure what would happen next with Mimi and The Dragon but he did know he was powerless to stop it. So he wouldn't try.

He walked to the bus stop, catching sight of things at the edge of his vision, a glimmer or flash of what was to come. Banners reminding people of their love for their glorious leader, armed thugs masquerading as the law on street corners and the great yellow eye blinking over the city. The only way to stop it was with distraction; he would throw himself into this new job and become one of those off-putting people who never stopped to look around.

Meeting Room C was on the first floor of St George's and was like every Meeting Room C everywhere. Grim white walls were lit by fluorescent bulbs tinged with sadness; dreams didn't die in Meeting Room C but they took a beating. Blue tack peppered the wall from countless, forgotten presentations and genera-tions of cobwebs sat unmoving in front of an air vent.

Jack took a seat in the meeting room only to be moved by

the Head of History. It turns out there was a rigid yet unspoken seating plan in play for the meeting. The Deputy Headteacher, who chaired, sat at the top of the table flanked by Maths and English. The sciences followed with Jack squeezed between Chemistry and Biology. History and Geography were next, followed by the Arts and finally, PE who stood by the door. Mrs Turner from the office, perched in the corner and tried to balance a notepad on her knee to take the minutes. 'Would you like my seat so you can use the table for your notes?' Jack asked Mrs Turner.

She looked like Jack had slapped her across the face. 'I don't think that would be appropriate, would it?'

That told you, History said with an eyebrow.

The Deputy Head coughed gently to get the room's attention. 'If Jack has finished with the jokes we can begin. I sent you all the agenda this morning and I trust you have all printed a copy.' On cue, they all produced a sheet of paper with a list of items to be discussed. Mild panic set in. Jack hadn't checked his emails before setting off. Anything important would be mentioned at the meeting, wouldn't it? Emails aren't for important things, meetings are. He budged his chair up next to Chemistry in the hope of seeing what was in store. Chemistry, having a long history of being overshadowed by Physics, slid the agenda out of Jack's eye-line. There was no point trying Biology, it was the redheaded stepchild of the world of science and resented the other two for all the attention they got.

'As you all know,' The Deputy Head said, 'each year we give two full scholarships to some local children to keep the pitchforks from the gates, so to speak. This year, the board of governors has decided to double the number of scholarships.'

This was met with murmurs of agreement.

'However, the amount given to each student will be halved.'

'But where will the rest come from?' Jack asked, trying out his new work persona.

'The parents will need to pay for it. Over the last few years the families have been, shall we say, not really understanding of how we do things. Not really St George's material and the hope is this new policy will keep the school's reputation intact.'

The work persona took on a life of its own. 'But the local families can't afford half the fees? It's not that kind of area.' The school was once surrounded by miles of countryside, cut off from the outside world to protect the boys from the world but also the world from the boys. Despite the best efforts of those with vested interests, the city had come to St George's and now the school was butted up against by houses of the wrong sort on one side and a dog food factory on the other. Legend has it that a planning officer was researching his family tree and discovered he was a direct descendant of Wat Tyler and, overcome with revolutionary fervour, he approved the construction of the factory and houses.

'It's sixteen thousand a year, which I'm not saying is nothing but any financially sensible family should be able to find it,' The Deputy Head said with growing impatience.

'That's over twelve hundred a month, how do we expect people to find that?'

'I don't know, grandparents? A few less takeaways?' This was meant with sycophantic laughter and nods from a few of the teachers. Jack had heard the laughter before. It was the laugh of someone who had never failed, the laugh of someone who mistook opportunity for talent, the laugh of someone who thinks advantage is work ethic. It was the type of laugh that couldn't be argued with or reasoned against. Not because it wasn't capable of logic or understanding but because it had no need for any of these things. It was the laugh of entrenched power. Jack's new work persona died, it slumped forward on the table leaving the old Jack alone. He would need to find a new way to distract himself from the future.

The next agenda point was changes to staff: Theo in biology had left and they would begin recruiting shortly. A great swell of relief filled the room. Theo had gone to school at St George's and had that unbridled confidence the school gives its pupils. The school worked on the assumption that pupils go off and do unbridled things in other places. TThey aren't meant to come back and challenge sixth formers to drinking contests or show new pupils the best places to sneak a cigarette.

The Deputy Head said he thought that Theo would be remembered for a long time and wished him well. They moved on to department updates.

Jack nodded along as he listened to his colleagues talk but thoughts of what would happen to Muriel when she went up against Mimi alone crept in.

Chemistry gave an update on the new beaker cleaning rota that was working much better than the last two attempts. Chemistry was also in the middle of a stock take and one of the labs would be out of bounds as it was being used as a holding area.

Muriel would die in the cavern under the city, forgotten. Mimi would rise and life would sink.

The room turned to Jack for an update on the Physics Department. He began to talk and stopped.

'Jack?' The Deputy Head asked.

Muriel was fighting alone in the dark while Jack sat in Meeting Room C and listened to department updates. He had to do something. His work persona was dead but maybe that was good, it meant Jack could do the right thing.

· · ·

Jack left the meeting room without giving an update and headed for the exit. This was Hero Jack who had would-be dictators to stop and a city to save. He took the stairs to the ground floor two at a time but could have floated if he wanted. He headed towards the outside world. Towards Muriel and Nisha and adventure. Towards purpose and certain death. Jack was going to live a hero's life. Adventure beckoned through a set of double doors. Sunlight burst through the glass panels, the outside world was drenched in possibility and hope.

Jack swaggered into the main reception. The main doors were locked at all times to stop the smaller children escaping and adults had to press a button at chest height to get out. Presumably, no one minded the larger children getting out. Jack got within reach of the button and gave it a kick. Hero Jack had style, he did things with flourishes. The receptionist shook her head at this blatant display of life and enthusiasm. She muttered something about these things having no place in a school.

The door crept open with the speed and urgency of a summer's day.

Jack looked through the glass pane on the door at the scorched grass and pristine blue sky beyond. Freedom, purpose. All his for the taking. He was going to grab life and beat it into submission. He was going to have faith in himself. Once this damn door opened. 'Can this thing go any faster?' he asked the receptionist.

'Be patient,' the receptionist said with a tone that rang with the inevitability of death.

He took a step forward to try and squeeze between the four-inch gap, then thought better of it and stopped.

'It won't be long.'

He gave it a nudge. The door stopped. Mocking him with its stillness. He locked eyes with the receptionist.

'I told you,' she said.

She did tell him. Jack tapped the button in the hope it would get the door moving. It didn't. This was ok, just a normal everyday thing. Even heroes must struggle to open doors sometimes. He bet Muriel forgot to put the bins out on bin day all the time.

'It just needs to reset, it will take a minute,' the receptionist said. 'Don't look at me like that, I didn't kick it.'

He didn't have time for this, he had to find Muriel and stop Mimi.

Spinning on his heels, he headed for his classroom. It was on the ground floor and you could squeeze through the windows if you were brave and didn't mind bending the wooden frame a bit. Jack had learnt this after a particularly fraught parents' evening when Lord Windermere hadn't taken too kindly at the suggestion his son would do rather well at university and could make a real go at having a job and contributing to society.

The lights were off in the corridor with only weak sunlight reflecting off the polished parquet floor. A low drone danced at the end of Jack's hearing. He had walked down the corridor countless times and never heard it before. A figment of his imagination, he pushed it aside.

The classroom door was locked. The drone was back, louder and heavier. Jack rubbed his eyes and pinched the bridge of his nose but the drone continued. He shook it off and stumbled into his pockets looking for his office keys.

'Hello Jack.'

Jack turned with a start. A man stood in the dark corridor but glowed like he was in full sun. He shone from within. Dressed in a sharp green suit, the man dripped power and purpose. He walked towards Jack. His features and mannerisms became more familiar the closer he got. He looked like Jack, he *was* Jack, but an older, wiser Jack. A successful Jack.

'Who are you?' Jack asked. The man was only a few feet away, he stood with perfect posture and was completely at ease.

'That is a complicated issue, one we will need a bit of time to really unpack. How's your week looking? I can do Thursday or if you're happy to walk and talk we can touch base now?'

Pontificator. Jack didn't have time to figure out why the creature looked like him but it felt mean that it did. Jack had a purpose now, that should have scared it off. He put the keys back in his pocket and made himself tall. *Leave now, I am a man with purpose and direction. I am no longer susceptible to your power. Begone! I have a city to save!* Is what Jack tried to say. Instead, he said: 'Now would be a great time to touch base.'

'Fantastic,' the pontificator said. It directed Jack down the corridor towards the newly built sports hall. 'I've been wanting to reach out for a few days now since we met at Jones and Jones. In my line of work, I see a lot of directionless people, you could say they're my bread and butter.' The creature let out a full-chested laugh that was so joyous Jack couldn't help but join in.

It felt good to laugh.

'Now, imagine my surprise when I'm sulking around my lift shaft and you wander in with your defenceless mind — open and so inviting. The young PhD student who spent his afternoons teaching simple physics to simpler children. So noble. Afternoons came and went and the young PhD student is now no longer young or a PhD student. Drifting along doing nothing, absorbing nothing.'

Their walk had taken them out of the science block and out onto the playground. The sun was evil today. It cooked.

'Anyway, I've never seen anyone like you before, so much potential for nothingness. With a bit of training, you could be one of the best. I said to myself, and I don't say this kind of thing lightly, with a bit of help you could lobby parliament on behalf of the gambling industry, or be head of recruitment at a horse charity.'

'Help?' Jack said.

'Yes, that friend of yours most likely told you horror stories about how I feed off people. And I do, I'm not going to lie. But it's two-way. I take a bit from you but I give something back. Do you want a nicer flat? Maybe one up high with a view? I can do that for you Jacky boy. Car? Holiday? Respect? I can give you more respect than you'll know what to do with Jack the Lad.'

'And what do I have to do?' Jack asked. They stopped dead centre in the playground.

'That's the best bit.' The creature turned and stood in front of Jack. He grabbed Jack by the shoulders. 'Nothing. You just let me take over during the day. People will say things and I'll answer for you. It's synergy Jack, and nothing stops synergy. We'll be invincible.'

The heat made the distance hazy, Jack and the creature stood alone. The drone danced around them, low and unthreatening. He could do it. Share his mind with this creature and become successful in all the ways that seemed to matter. Jack's life flashed before his eyes: the promotions, the meetings and mid-range cars. The holidays in Europe, a stock portfolio and retiring to a charming village steeped in history and casual racism. It would all be so easy.

'Well?' the creature said.

Jack said nothing and the pontificator smiled.

The drone grew loud.

The drone was Jack and Jack was the drone.

He submitted to the noise and let it wash over him.

. . .

Jack stood in a very flash London flat. Open plan and on the north side of the Thames, it was filled with uncomfortable and serious furniture. It screamed refined city living. His clothes were different too, he wore the same sharp green suit he had seen the pontificator in moments ago. He caught himself in a mirror. He looked good: grown up and successful — like he knew what he was doing. At the edge of Jack's hearing, the drone continued.

A door opened behind him and he turned to see another Jack enter. This Jack was dressed in a silk blouse and high heels. It carried two tasteful canvas tote bags full to the brim with bottles of wine and fresh vegetables poking out the top.

'There you are darling,' the second Jack said. 'You were meant to be home hours ago. You promised you would get out of work early to help set up before the Robinsons got here.'

'Sorry,' Jack said, more out of reflex than understanding.

The other Jack dropped the shopping on a marble-topped kitchen island before giving Jack a squeeze and a kiss. 'You're forgiven. Now, can you start on dinner while I get ready? I told them seven, but you know they're always early.'

Jack was left alone in the combined kitchen, living room and dining room. There was even a balcony. Everything was white, but a real white, not the off-white he lived in now. The flat was just as cold and empty as his real flat but it seemed intentional here. Whereas Jack's flat was bland this place was tranquil. *Not bad at all.*

Floor-to-ceiling windows were filled with London in the late afternoon. The city looked so small and benign from up here. This far up, away from the noise and chaos, London seemed manageable.

Is this what Muriel had tried to protect him from in the lift shaft? Air conditioning and tasteful decoration? Maybe he was better off leaving her to The Dragon and Mimi. She clearly didn't want any help and Jack was no hero.

'I can't hear any dinner being made,' the other Jack's voice chimed from the bedroom.

'Right, yes, just getting started,' Jack replied. He fumbled through the kitchen cupboards and drawers looking for chopping boards and other cooking implements. The knives were Japanese and the pans French, unfortunately, the drawers were British and didn't shut properly without a good push. The hob was a thing of beauty. Racing car red and twice as fast, it had six burners and a bread-proving drawer. The pinnacle of German engineering. Jack had spent many an exam invigilation reading the specs on his phone imaging his life with the hob. This was that life.

The tote bags were full of the makings for a salad, a mix of red and white wine and a vat of olives. *Damn, he couldn't fire up the hob.*

When the Robinsons arrived they were copies of Jack too. One wore an almost identical suit to Jack but in navy and the other an expensive but laidback dress from one of those shops with only a few items on each rack and a team of staff so relaxed and carefree it is intimidating.

The four of them sat and ate and drank. Everyone had heavy opinions about light things and light opinions about heavy things. They talked of muted tiles and coloured grout. Farmhouse sinks and Carrara marble. And it was all so wonderful and easy. Jack sat without a worry, he had wine and food, he had a designer kitchen with a view. Excusing himself earlier in the night, he had given himself the once over in the bathroom mirror and discovered he had the time and inclination to go to the gym. He had it all. This could be his life if he only gave up a little of himself.

Hours passed and the sun began to set, turning the walls of the flat a hellish red, and still the talking continued. The conversations turned to interest rates and the silly names they give paint now. Jack sat in silence, he had no opinions on paint. Their voices were smooth and confident like the wine they drank. They sparred and laughed like friends should. On and on it went deep into the night.

If that day in the lab had gone differently this is the life he could have had. He would sit with Sophie in their beautiful home and have friends over. Last he had heard she was living in Battersea, he should give her a call, just to see how she is.

Friends, luxury, opinions, Jack could have it all if he submitted to the pontificator. A life of untested virtue and principles — that was the secret to happiness, not hunting dragons and caring about things. The key was nice food, nicer wine and friends just like you. Talk moved on to work and careers. Jack stood instinctively and started to clear the plates.

In the kitchen, he approached a chrome-tinted coffee machine. It was a completely manual one that relied on gears and skill. Levels and dials covered the machine and actually did things depending on how much pressure you applied and in what order. Complete control for the real aficionado.

Jack opened a cupboard, found a cafetière, and began to fill a kettle.

'My boss was screaming for blood at this point,' one of the Robinsons said. 'I thought — this is it. I'm gone. Fired. I'll never work in cross-platform digital marketing with a speciality in older teens and young adults again.'

'He was terribly stressed,'his wife added, stroking his cheek with one hand and holding a glass of wine with the other.

'So what did you do?' Jack's Jack asked.

'I blamed the cleaners of course. Said one of them must have stolen it.'

'Very clever.'

'Yes, I thought so. The boss got the whole cleaning team fired which is a bit unfortunate but I lived to fight another day. Besides, cleaners are in such demand I figured they'd be fine.' He turned to his wife. 'You remember all the trouble your sister had trying to find a cleaner after her first one pinched that laptop.'

'Sorry,' Jack said, turning to face the other Jacks. He had listened from the kitchen in stunned silence. Water flowed over the top of the kettle into the sink. 'You got a cleaner fired to get out of trouble at work?'

The three Jacks at the table stared at Jack, unable to process what he had asked.

Jack stared back.

The staring contest ended with a belch. The sink began spewing thick black water from the plughole. A vicious smell joined the water and hit Jack like a punch to the gut. The water quickly filled the sink and snaked along the counter and onto the floor.

Jack stepped back and looked at the Jacks expectantly.

The other Jacks had turned away from him and continued their talk of holidays and great little places to get coffee, oblivious to the scene raging next to them.

Jack grabbed a tea towel and tried to plug the hole and stem the flow. It seemed to work for a second before the black liquid returned with a vengeance and burst through the plughole, ripping the sink from the counter and sending Jack crashing to the floor. The water was ankle deep and rising quickly.

The Jacks at the table continued to chatter and ignore the pungent water filling the room. They all talked at once and over each other until it became a riotous mess.

The lights flickered on and off in time to their own whims.

Jack looked at the beautiful versions of himself, the tasteful crockery and exquisite interior design. He didn't want any of it. Well, he did. He wanted all the nice things he had seen and the security and peace that comes with giving yourself over to the pontificator. He wanted to be able to ignore the rising tide.

But he wanted more too.

The trouble was he knew none of it mattered, not the racing car red hob or even the beautiful flat with views of London.

A city built on the shoulders of a giant. Generations working to create things that were taller than before, spurred on by the pressure to make everything better. Was this better or was it just more? After a thousand generations, it was becoming too much for most people, the gaze of all of human history bearing down on you causing the need for bigger and more. What could you achieve that would outlast the century to come? Maybe nothing. Perhaps all Jack had to do was choose to try. To try and stop Mimi. That's what he wanted. 'No,' he said.

The water stopped. The other Jacks froze. The lights still flickered.

The pontificator appeared and stood in front of Jack. It still looked like Jack. 'Pardon?' it said.

'Thank you but no. I don't want this. I'm going to be a hero. I'm going to find Muriel and Nisha and we're going to stop Mimi.'

The pontificator winced. 'That's not the plan though, is it?'

'Stopping Mimi is important. Even if no one ever knows what we did, it will be worth it.'

'We? There is no we, only you. Your own life and your own success. That's what's important. That's what I can give you,' the pontificator said and gestured to the room drenched in sewage water with sporadic lighting.

Jack pushed past the pontificator and tried to open the front door. He rattled the handle but it was locked.

'There's no way out, but why leave? It's so pleasant here,' the pontificator said.

Cursing, Jack waded through the water onto the balcony.

'There's nothing for you out there,' the pontificator called from the kitchen island. It was making itself a macchiato.

Jack stood on the balcony, clueless over what to do next. The water had made its way outside and soaked through his trousers.

The pontificator joined him and leaned against the door-frame, coffee in hand. 'Come back inside. We can forget this ever happened and get you back to your friends.' He gestured with a tilt of his head to the still-frozen Jacks sitting around the dinner table.

Jack paced on the balcony, trying to figure out how to leave but the drone buffeted his thoughts.

'Well?' the pontificator asked.

'I'm leaving,' Jack said. He looked over the balcony, desperate for an escape route. *I think.* He turned to face the pontificator. 'I'm leaving and I'm going to stop Mimi. I'm going to live a good life. Not this fake one or the one I had before but one I want to live.'

The pontificator threw back its head in frustration before shattering the coffee cup against the wall.

With two quick steps, the pontificator was in front of Jack. The creature's arm shot out and tried to grab Jack by the throat. Jack ducked and ran back into the flat.

The pontificator seized him from behind and pulled him onto the floor. Fingers pressed into Jack's windpipe and robbed him of air. 'I don't believe you,' the creature said. 'I believe you think that you're going to live a life filled with pride and achievement but you are wrong. You are going to go and live the little life I have planned for us instead and it will be glorious. You will lose yourself in it. You will become someone else. A new Jack. He will be charming and outgoing and hold people in my thrall in meetings. I will feed off you and everyone close to you until you forget who you are. You will be a husk of a person but my god you will have a beautiful kitchen. Don't you want a beautiful kitchen?'

Jack clawed at the hands at his throat and couldn't help but think of the kitchen. He imagined the meals he would make in it and the wine he would keep in his wine fridge. He thought of the people he wanted at his table and thought only of Muriel and Nisha. *Muriel and Nisha.* Strength welled in him. He roared and threw the pontificator to one side then staggered to his feet. 'I don't want a beautiful kitchen!' *A white lie.*

He ran to the other side of the kitchen island and picked up a bar stool, swinging it hard at the racing car red cooker.

The pontificator screamed. 'What are you doing?! It's got six burners and—'

'—and a bread-proving drawer!' Jack swung again sending the gas rings flying. A hiss joined the drone. 'It even has an app you can download to your phone!' He hit the cooker again. The bar stool broke in two. The pipework inside the cooker was exposed. Singing a low hiss as it filled the room with gas.

The pontificator's face filled with a rage that matched the

cooker. Jack had never seen himself so angry. Snatching a fork from a frozen Jack still sat at the table, the pontificator dove at Jack. Jack stepped back and opened a drawer, causing the pontificator to trip and crash to the floor.

Jack coughed and spluttered on gas. There, sat in the newly opened drawer was a small blowtorch, perfect for crème brûlée. He grabbed it and held it like a gun at the creature.

The pontificator, seeing this new threat, dropped the fork and slowly got to his feet with his hands raised in surrender. 'Don't do anything stupid. You'll die.'

'Staying here is death,' Jack said.

The pontificator's eyes became hard. 'Maybe, maybe not. You'd exist at least. Just existing is what you're best at. Isn't it better to exist with me than to die?'

Jack's finger danced over the button on the side of the blow torch.

The flat was gone.

The pontificator was gone.

Jack lay spread-eagled on the playground. The hot tarmac receding under his weight. The world was silent, the birds and wind both hid from the sun. The scent of gas lingered for a moment but was gone before Jack could be sure.

'You ok mate?'

Jack lifted his head off the ground. It was Michael, one of the PE teachers. 'Hi Mike. I'm good. Just having a think.'

Michael played with his whistle around his neck. 'Say no more. It's a good spot. You could also try around the back of the swimming pool, the drone of the pump is very relaxing. Takes you out of yourself.'

'I think I've had enough of that type of thing for today, but thanks.' Jack stood. 'Anyway, I need to go meet someone.' Jack headed for the school gates and to find Muriel and Nisha.

FIFTEEN

Theo stood with Reece and The Elf in The Paisley Suit in the courtyard outside the lab. They watched in silence while Mimi inspected his boat. It was a snug fit in the courtyard since Theo's boat had come back with them after their little incursion to the ocean. The stern had pinned one of the shipping container's doors shut which didn't help matters. Reece had been unable to come up with a solution on how to move it, much to Theo's annoyance. You don't expect much from the hoi polloi but moving a boat should be straightforward.

Mimi's hands traced the barnacles and limpets. Her face changed, it wasn't a smile but her face shifted to say she was pleased, or at least not angry. The Elf in The Paisley Suit relaxed and put her hands in her jacket pockets. Theo stepped forward to speak and was met with a raised finger.

'And this is your boat?' Mimi said.

'Yes, in more ways than one,' Theo said. 'I phoned Mum and Dad to see if the one in Jersey was still there, it isn't by the way, this is it. But they *think* it's my boat, they remember, or think they remember, giving it to me when I was eighteen. I wished I had the boat and I did. Anything could be changed around my thought or wish, including memories. Their mind was changed by it.'

'So you consumed the liver and...' Mimi waved her hand above her head, 'wished it here?'

Theo's face became pained. He found it hard to talk at this level. 'Yes, and changed the memories of anyone that matters. I checked just before you got here, they still think it's mine. And I know how to do it again.'

Mimi pursed her lips. 'And you didn't think to open with that?'

Theo, who had been raised to always treat boats as the priority in any conversation, wasn't sure how to answer. 'In order for you to understand I thought it best—'

Screeching metal interrupted Theo. Reece pulled open the other lab door and gestured for everyone to enter. 'Yes, good idea Reece. Let's show them what I found.'

Blue light poured over the group filling them with calm as they entered the lab. On the table, a pile of luminous blue crystals sat on a petri dish, only a tablespoonful or two but every surface and object in the room took on a cobalt hue. There was no need for lights. Theo stood next to the crystals and faced his audience. 'I don't entirely know how these work or what they are but I do know these are what we're after.'

Mimi pushed Theo out of the way and grabbed the petri dish. Holding it up to her face, the blue glow overpowered her features until she was just teeth and eyes.

The Paisley Elf made a feeble excuse and edged close to Reece. She squeezed next to him in the corner, their arms touching.

'What's interesting is the crystals we found in the liver should be in the heart.'

'What?' Mimi said without taking her eyes off the dish.

Theo internalised a sigh. He'd have to get used to these kinds of questions once he started the lecture circuit. 'The crystals are attached to small pieces of heart muscle.' He paused and tried again. 'Most animals have three types of muscle: smooth, skeletal and cardiac. Smooth and skeletal are found all over the place but cardiac, as you may have guessed by the name, is only found in the heart. It's heart muscle that the crystals seem to grow on.' Theo feared he was losing them, even Reece seemed distracted. This was his chance to achieve something. 'Possibly due to the decomposition process or illness or how the creature is put together, I don't know. But it has ended up with bits of cardiac muscle in its liver and probably everywhere else for that matter. Now, going forward I would like to have some time to study this but I know that's not why you're paying me.'

Mimi placed a small crystal in her mouth and swallowed. She closed her eyes and muttered something under her breath. Her skin shifted and hardened as if dipped in wax.

'But if we want the source of the crystals you need to find the heart,' Theo said.

Mimi turned to face him. 'Very good, and your next project sounds very interesting. However, I'm afraid I'm going to have to let you go.'

Theo stood, mouth open. *They had an agreement.*

The Paisley Elf tensed and clicked her knuckles.

'Someone has been sneaking bits of meat out and people have been going around asking questions. Parts started going missing about the time you came on board.' Mimi turned on her heels to face Reece. 'And you. People have been telling me you've been taking trips out of the city to meet redheaded ladies in country pubs. Now, it's none of my business how you keep yourself entertained but when they don't even get a peck on the cheek I do wonder what the meeting was really about.'

Theo took a step back. He had so much still to do, so many plans.

'So you're both surplus to requirements I'm afraid.'

'Both?' the Paisley Elf asked.

'Yes,' Mimi said, her eyes firm on the matter. 'Both. And when you're done here get everyone underground. We've got a heart to cut out.' She pocketed the crystals and the room went dark.

As Jack was shown to his seat by the restaurant manager, he wondered about the odds of there being CCTV in the alley to catch curry thieves or in the kitchen to catch people who set fire to the deep-fat fryer. The kitchen was more likely but he doubted any restaurant wanted video evidence of how the sausage, or curry, was made.

'Have you eaten here before?' the manager asked, pulling out a chair for Jack.

'No, but it looked good from the outside.'

'Excellent, your waitress will be along shortly with the lunch menu. We're having the kitchen decorated, so some things may not be available I'm afraid.'

'That's ok,' Jack said, trying to sound like he had no idea why the kitchen might need a new coat of paint.

'Can I get you a drink?'

'Pint?'

The manager nodded and left.

The restaurant was decorated like all Indian restaurants of a certain age: symbols of past glories stuck to the walls and benign photos of diplomats' wives posing with local children. Comforting in an odd sort of way.

Nisha appeared with a beer and a menu. She checked the manager was busy and whipped the menu at Jack when she was a few feet from the table. 'What do you want?'

'I want to help and I think you do too.'

'The chef recommends the Prawn Jalfrezi but you seem like a Chicken Korma man if I ever saw one.' Nisha produced a pen and order pad from her apron.

Jack reeled in his seat. 'Wow, there's no need for that.'

'What else would you recommend to a man who doesn't want to save the world with his friends? One who leaves at the slightest push?'

'It's not the world, it's just the country,' Jack said, pretending to point at something on the menu whenever the manager glanced over. She had said friend, maybe she wanted to sit around his kitchen table and drink wine too? They had only known each other for a few days but they had been long days. Is this why adults find it hard to make friends? They don't do anything dangerous. They join jogging clubs and meet for coffee but you can't bond while running in a park or knocking back flat whites. Children do dangerous things: They stand up to bullies and win the world cup. They fight demons and save the universe. If his run-in with the pontificator had taught him anything it was that he needed friends.

Nisha drew circles on her order pad. Her left forearm was wrapped in bandages and she had a small cut on her cheek. Jack wanted to ask what had happened but wasn't sure this was the time.

'The country? What are you talking about? The Dragon won't stick to borders,' she said.

'It was just a nerve. We only have to deal with Mimi.'

Nisha flicked her pen at Jack.

'What? There's nothing to say The Dragon is waking up.'

'Why are you so sure?'

Jack wasn't sure. He wasn't sure about most things but they didn't matter; it mattered if The Dragon was alive or not. If it was alive it meant the end of everything. The city would be destroyed, not because The Dragon meant it harm — it would just yawn and London would be gone. He wasn't sure. He just wanted The Dragon to be dead. Everything is easier if you can pretend The Dragon is dead. 'I just am. Do you want to stop Mimi? Because I do, and I want to do it with you and Muriel.'

'Of course,' Nisha said, 'but in case you forgot she abandoned me — us — because you mucked up.'

'So let's go find Muriel, make her take us back, stop Mimi and then if there is time we can make sure The Dragon is dead.'

Nisha stared out the window for a moment in thought. She took a deep breath. 'Meet me out front in ten minutes. I've got something I need to do first.'

'Thank you,' Jack said with a smile.

'Whatever.' She went to leave.

'Wait,' Jack said. He scanned the menu. It was full of the bland and the mild. Jack needed the food of a hero, a hero who was going to save the world with his friends. He also didn't want anything too spicy as it was bound to be a busy day so he ordered a Chicken Korma to take away.

Jack stuck his fingers through the allotment fence and attempted to pull himself up. His feet flat against the fence he hung a foot from the ground. The allotment seemed deserted, no one had come or gone in an hour.

'Get down, you'll get us in trouble.' Nisha threw Muriel's duck boots in the air one by one. They disappeared at the equilibrium and flashed into her hand.

'Stop showing off. Are you sure she hasn't been and gone?'

Nisha carried on. 'No, and until she answers her phone I don't have a better idea. Do you?'

Jack leaned against the fence and looked at the houses surrounding the allotment. The owners had seemed to have entered a death spiral of one-upmanship: tastefully appointed firewood in the newly built porch, ivy, or for the really ambitious, wisteria, growing up the side, loft conversion dormers stuck on the roof like oversized dovecots. Mutually assured decoration.

Nisha sat on the kerb. 'Do you know where I could get a lot of stomach acid from?'

Jack gave the question some serious thought. 'Human?'

'Ideally, but not essential.'

'Why do you want it?'

'Art,' she said in a way that implied she had given a full and comprehensive answer.

'Maybe a vet?'

She nodded politely as if she hadn't already thought of that.

Jack joined her on the kerb. 'Shall we go?'

'No. Let's give it a bit longer.' Nisha stuck a finger under her bandages and tried to scratch.

'What did you do to your arm?' Jack asked.

She continued to scratch. 'I thought I would have a go at greatness.''

'Went well?'

'No one died,' she said. 'Question for you.'

'Go on.'

'What are we doing?'

'Waiting for Muriel,' Jack said.

'No I mean, how are we going to stop Mimi? We know where she lives but she isn't living there at the moment because it's a building site. We can't steal or hide The Dragon from her, it's too big. What are we doing?'

'You know what she looks like, you served her in the restaurant. We could use that.'

'Kind of, all rich people look the same to me if I'm honest,' Nisha said. 'But I'm sure I'll know her when I see her.'

'We know where she might live and what she might look like. We do know that at some point she'll probably turn up underground.'

Nisha seemed unconvinced. 'Do we though? I mean, oil barons don't hang around on oil rigs do they?'

Jack checked his watch. 'Another five minutes?'

'No, let's go.' Nisha stood. 'She's not here and her phone is going straight to voicemail. She might not want our help.'

They headed back towards the station.

'She's just busy,' Jack said. 'We could always try and head her off at the entrance to the cavern.'

'Nisha!'

Jack turned and jumped out of his skin when a blur of a body grabbed Nisha and tackled her to the ground. Muriel straddled Nisha and kissed her. It was a kiss like the tide. It wasn't good or bad, it was just inevitable.

'Hello,' Nisha said. Her eyes fixed on Muriel and only Muriel.

'You're the best, most unexpected thing to happen to me,' Muriel said. 'And I'm glad you're here. You make me brave.'

Muriel clambered to her feet and gave Jack a nod. Nisha followed and gave Jack a second nod. Everyone smiled and Jack felt for the first time in a long time that he was in the right place.

Muriel had made the bold choice to pair a very flattering skirt and blouse with a dirty green jacket. She had something wrapped in an old rag in her pocket. Nisha took her in for the first time.

'What?' Muriel asked.

'Nothing, you look hot,' Nisha said picking up Muriel's boots and passing them back to their rightful owner.

'You're very kind. What are we talking about?' Muriel asked.

'Now we've found you, how to save the world,' Nisha said.

'Kill The Dragon or stop Mimi?' Muriel asked.

'The second but maybe the first if it comes up,' Nisha said interrupting Jack before he could speak.

'If it comes up,' Jack agreed, it wasn't the time to bring up if The Dragon was waking or not. 'And we want to do it your way, follow orders and not get carried away.'

'Well, the good news is we won't need to kill it.' Muriel pulled a large syringe from her jacket pocket. 'And I don't believe you two could follow orders if your lives depended on it.'

Nisha and Jack took a step back. 'What is that?' they said in unison.

Muriel admired the cruel needle gleaming in the sun. 'The short answer? Dragon tranquilliser.'

'Can you give us the long answer?' Jack asked.

Muriel wrapped the syringe back up in the rag and started walking away from the allotments. 'The Dragon's been leaking magic for centuries and that's what allowed a bunch of damp hinterlanders to punch above their weight and do the whole empire thing.'

Nisha raised an eyebrow at this abridged version of history.

Muriel continued. 'Less magic has been released in the last hundred years or so because The Dragon's been dying. Only now The Laurels reckon it might release more as it seems to be on the mend and we can go do great stuff again.'

Nisha stopped. 'Sorry, you mean bring back empire?'

Muriel rolled her eyes much to Nisha's annoyance. 'Of course not, the magic will seep into whatever is there. Four hundred years ago it filtered into a bunch of rich blokes with mild lead poisoning but now it will seep into universities and people who can read. We'll get flying cars out of it.' Muriel rocked on the balls of her feet.

'Won't it also seep into tabloid newspapers and hedge funds?' Jack said.

'Maybe, but there's more good than bad out there, isn't there?'

Nisha sucked on her teeth.

'It's letting it seep into everyone or we can let Mimi have it all and do whatever it is people do when they have absolute power,' Muriel said.

Nisha walked ahead. 'Fine, but if we start a second British Empire I won't let you live it down.'

'We won't, it will be world peace and warp drive, I promise.'

Jack pictured the pickaxe-wielding goblins carving chunks out of the creature. 'And how exactly are we meant to get down there and put a dragon to sleep?'

'We just need to go back down into the cavern and find somewhere to stick this,' Muriel said, patting the syringe.

'And Mimi?' Jack asked.

Muriel smiled. 'We just follow the lead of our lead-lined ancestors.'

Nisha and Jack looked at each other.

'What does that mean?' Jack asked.

Muriel's shoulders slumped. 'We kill her.'

The plan was agreed. They would get the train into town and then find the sewer they had used to escape to the surface. After that, it all got a bit vague.

The sun gloated over the train station platform. It burned concrete and skin alike. It frayed tempers and, if the announcements were to be believed, vital infrastructure. Track further down the line had buckled and warped in the heat causing delays all over the network. People simmered waiting for their trains.

Nisha and Muriel had joined a queue to get coffee while Jack tried to carve out a spot for them to stand.

On their walk to the station, Jack's phone sent him a news alert that Copernicus 6, the satellite in orbit around Saturn, wasn't responding. It had failed to send back any images and was ignoring any attempts to communicate with it. Jack wondered if this was all part of Mimi's plan. The kids at school were excited about Copernicus 6 and the images it would bring back. It was a big story, not just on the news, but for humanity, a big joint enterprise and a sign of what people could do but instead, it had failed. Jack gazed up at the sky and imagined the satellite, now just a piece of metal floating up in space, useless and without purpose. *Every week a new crisis.* Was Copernicus 6 even real or just an implanted memory? Maybe the news it had failed was Mimi. It wasn't a disaster and no one had died but Jack thought of everyone who would be disappointed. It could be the start of a flood of false memories to make everyone sad and angry, demanding change but accepting a rehashed same. His memories didn't normally have an internal monologue but this wouldn't be a normal memory, maybe these strange thoughts were part of it. Was he a magically implanted memory that had become self-aware, forever damned to live the day Mimi seized power over and over again as nothing more than a glint in the eye of an unambitious little man?

Nisha and Muriel returned from the booth with a coffee for Jack. 'If you were Mimi, what would you do with The Dragon?' Nisha asked.

This didn't seem like the type of thing Mimi would put in a false memory, he relaxed.

'I'd fix everything,' Muriel said without a moment's thought.

'What does that mean?' Jack asked.

Muriel took a sip of her coffee. 'What it says, I'd make everything ok.'

'This isn't Miss World, you can't wave a magic wand and make everything better,' Jack said, taking his coffee from Nisha.

'I think that's *exactly* what I can do,' Muriel said.

'But what specifically would you do? So, you can't end war but you can get rid of all the guns.' He drank his coffee and everything felt ok for a fleeting moment. Talking nonsense hypotheticals with friends, he felt his body become ten years younger and his brain forget what was to come.

'That's no good,' Muriel said. 'People would just make more. Can I get rid of the knowledge of how to make guns?'

Jack nodded. 'Yeah. Why not.'

'That's no good either,' Nisha said. 'If people can remember guns and know they're possible, they'll reinvent them. It's how most technology spreads. The Phoenicians didn't sit everyone down and teach them the alphabet. People saw it and went, "oh that's clever" and invented their own.'

Muriel grew tired of the game and went and stood on the edge of the platform. She looked out of town to see if she could see a train. 'So can I get rid of the very idea of guns then?'

'How does the magic work? Will it go back through time and remove every gun from existence or just change everyone's memory?' Nisha asked.

'The way Jones and Jones were talking, it can do memories and small changes. They needed to add images to the BBC,' Jack said.

'So, even if I got rid of the idea of guns they would still be warehouses full of them for people to find? I couldn't get rid of all the guns?' Muriel asked, returning to the conversation and wrapping an arm around Nisha.

A train heading out of town pulled into the opposite plat-form. Exhausted faces peer out of the carriage.

'I'd make everyone believe in evil Mole People,' Nisha said.

Jack had so many questions he didn't know where to start but Muriel gave him a look that said Nisha wasn't done.

'They'd be so evil that people would be petrified of them, I mean poop their pants scared. To the point it's considered normal to be scared and no one tries to cure it. That way, the idea of drilling into the earth to get oil becomes unthinkable in case we anger the Mole People. If we can't make people respect the planet then they should fear it.'

'It's a bit mean,' Muriel said.

'Give it a few years and people will be fearing Mother Earth anyway so I'm just skipping a few steps and adding Mole People.'

An announcement cut through the chatter, a train was on

its way but people were asked not to travel unless they had to. This caused a murmur of disagreement along the platform, even the British Stiff Upper Lip was sagging in the heat.

'Who rules over the Mole People?' Muriel asked.

'A queen, she's immortal and fell in love with a human aeons ago but he wasn't having any of it so, long story short, the Mole people now hate humans.'

Muriel laughed.

'What about you Jack?' Nisha asked.

What would he do? He probably wouldn't have the follow-through to even find The Dragon let alone figure out how to channel its magic. He would sit on it and do nothing if he was honest. He'd be sure he'd have a brilliant idea one day so would do nothing until he had that idea. Years would pass and The Dragon would sit gathering dust. Jack would come up with ideas but then think better of it and carry on working and living his life until one day he'd realise it was too late and any idea thirty years ago is better than a brilliant idea that never arrived.

'Jack?' Muriel said.

The train limped into the station. Each carriage that passed looked hotter than the last.

'I'd make everyone happy,' Jack said.

Nisha and Muriel both booed his answer as the doors opened and they pushed their way onto the train. A silence descended on them as they found a place to stand in the crowded carriage. The train was an older model and the tiny windows did nothing more than funnel warm air into the carriage. Despite the sweat and polyester, the air was scentless. When everyone smells no one smells.

Jack stood by the far set of carriage doors looking out onto the other platform. A stream of people made their way up onto the platform causing everyone to stand much closer to each other than they would like to in this heat.

A man wearing a sandwich board that read: *Cease employ-ment! The end is nigh!* walked onto the platform, his hair dishevelled and suit splitting at the seams. He stood next to a woman at the end of the platform and her tether.

Jack couldn't make out what he said but she didn't take it well.

Words were exchanged.

She pushed him.

He pushed her back. More words, loud ones. Foreheads glistered in the sunlight under blankets of sweat.

Jack's train pulled away and the figures began to shrink into the distance. The train took a bend and the last thing Jack saw was the man falling onto the track.

The train headed into town and Jack watched miles of suburban London pass by, millions of lives that had no idea what might happen if the plan failed. If they were lucky Mimi might plan to rule as a benevolent tyrant and maybe things would continue much the same. People would go to school and then work and then die. If you didn't kick up a fuss you would be fine. Nothing would change but things were meant to change, that was the point of all this, to go forward. Freezing everything was nice — Jack knew that more than most — it was comforting, a security blanket against the world, decisions made for you and safety for the silent. This was the future they were facing. The worrying thing was how low the stakes seemed, Jack had led a quiet life before and he could again. Perhaps this was how injustices carried on, why serfdom lasted a thousand years, or why most of the twentieth century was allowed to happen.

The universal desire to be left alone. Humanity isn't evil, it's just indifferent to things far away.

The train doors opened at Clapham Junction and silence fled to be replaced by madness. A mass of people pushed onto the train and Jack, Nisha and Muriel were squeezed up against the side of the carriage.

'Why are we saving these people again?' Nisha asked, her face pressed against the chest of a man who decided a packed train on a hot day was the best time to eat a Cornish pasty.

'Because we're good people,' Jack said, as he watched the gravy teeter on the edge of the pasty inches from Nisha's head. 'I think.'

Nisha maneuvered herself and got the man's attention. 'If any of that touches me I will perform a magic trick on you that will keep you guessing for days. What you will be guessing is where it went. And "it" won't be the pasty. Do you understand?'

The man understood and performed his own magic trick by finding room to stand on the other side of the carriage far from Nisha.

Muriel stared at Nisha.

'What?'

'Nothing, you look hot.'

'I know.'

The train left Clapham Junction and passed through Vauxhall station before heading for Waterloo, its final stop.

'Do we need to prepare anything?' Jack asked.

'Like what?' Muriel said.

'Weapons?' he said in a low voice.

'Masks wouldn't be a terrible idea,' Nisha said. 'At least for the sewer.'

'Do you know how to use a weapon?' Muriel said to Jack.

Jack mumbled something to himself.

'Besides, we don't have time,' Muriel said. 'I'll deal with all the violent bits.'

'Whatdo we do?' Nisha said.

Muriel smiled. 'Cause utter chaos that works out in the end.'

'That, we can do,' Nisha said.

The train bellowed in pain and jolted to a stop. Everyone was thrown forward. People fell and crushed each other. The Cornish pasty flew out of the man's hand and slammed against the window with a thud. The carriage sat at a strange angle, tilting to the left in a way trains shouldn't.

Nisha peered out the window. 'We've come loose.'

'Trains don't come loose, they derail,' Jack said.

'Fine, we've derailed.'

The train's tinpot speaker system burst into life: 'Ladies and —— risk —— tracks –uck — in — heat —— W——loo—— train ——ed Plea—wait —— rescue—'

'We don't have time for this,' Muriel said. 'Help me open the door.'

'I think we're meant to wait for someone to come rescue us,' a passenger said.

Muriel got her fingers between the doors. Jack started to pull on one door while Nisha did the same with the second.

'You can wait, I'm rescuing myself,' Muriel said to the crowd.

The doors relented and the three of them jumped down onto the tracks and headed back to Vauxhall Station. Jack glanced behind and saw the passengers following them. A patch of grey spread upwards into the sky and checked his stride.

At first, Jack thought it was a welcome cloud but it drifted with malice. Smoke rose from behind the flats that lined the tracks, great plumes climbed into the sky. The patterns and movements on the smoke's surface told Jack that the fire was far away.

Nisha and Muriel returned and stood next to Jack.

'Where do you think it is?' Jack asked.

'Nowhere near, which is good I guess,' Muriel said.

'It must be a forest fire,' Nisha said. 'There isn't enough wood in all of East London for a fire that size.'

'Epping, maybe?'

Nisha nodded. 'Maybe.'

With the train network barely holding together and the city on the verge of catching fire, they decided to walk to Wapping and the manhole cover that would take them back to the cavern. At Muriel's insistence, they crossed to the north bank at the first opportunity. They walked through Westminster and along The Strand. The normal throngs of tourists were gone. The occasional figure looked down on them from an air-conditioned office but London seemed to be hiding from the heat.

Muriel and Nisha removed the manhole cover and slid it out the way. An almighty smell exploded from the sewer and Jack took a step back. 'Are we sure we need to do this? Maybe it will all sort itself out.'

'Nope,' Muriel said, peering down into the hole, 'if you want to save the world you need to wade through the waste.'

Jack took one last look at the city. It may have been his imagination but he could smell smoke. This was the end of the world, he thought. Whatever happened next it would be something new. Jack, like most people, believed he would survive the end of the world. Not in an action hero rounding up survivors way but, more that it would just pass him by. The soil would die and the sky would boil but he would carry on. He'd go to work, shop in a well-stocked supermarket and visit his parents every fifth weekend. After all, he had survived up till now and came from a long line of survivors so why wouldn't he survive the end of the world too? Not only would Jack survive but he imagined everyone he knew would too. Hell is for other people.

'Jack, you coming?' Muriel said, half poking out of the manhole.

The sewer was the terrible ordeal Jack knew it was going to be. They wadded through ankle-high waste and swam through polluted air. No one spoke to save having to open their mouths. Like a shining beacon of hope, they found the collapsed section of wall and scrambled into the cavern. Jack took great gasping breaths and remembered this was only the beginning.

They followed the stream to the cavern floor slower than the last time they were here and Jack realised how alive the forest was. Every surface vibrated with life, ants paraded along branches, birds silently dive-bombed midges and the trees were covered in tiny flowers releasing so much pollen it drifted like smoke into the vast cavern above.

They stopped for a break and sat on a fallen tree trunk. The air smelt sweet and fresh. This wasn't country air which country folk liked to tell you was clean, as if there was anywhere left that wasn't contaminated by civilisation. The air here was ancient and wild, when it entered your lungs your muscles shimmered.

They watched in silence as a crow landed a few feet from where they sat. The bird met Jack's gaze and he saw a curiosity behind the bird's eyes that only an animal could possess. It wasn't caught in the past or future, it didn't care for ethics or stress about rent. It lived free from the baggage of human existence. It was the curiosity of a creature that took each moment as it came. The Dragon may have lived the same way, coming across mankind and attempting to meet its gaze only to find fear and steel.

The eye, however, was still terrifying. They stood before the yellow iris like early man before the sun. Wonder seemed to settle on them. The creature defied both God and Darwin. Jacks's eyes wandered over The Dragon and his mind became clear, his brain shut down, his heart slowed and his breathing steady.

By some unspoken signal, they decided it was time to move on.

They found the campsite used by Moth Whisper and his friends. The fire contained only dying embers and there were no signs of life. Muriel suggested they play it safe and wait to see if anyone came out of the wound in the side of The Dragon.

Minutes passed lying on the red sandstone outcrop for a sign of Mimi or her people.

'There's something I didn't tell you,' Muriel said shifting position amongst the undergrowth. 'You know how you can stick a vaccine anywhere in someone and it will work, as in, it could be their arm or leg and the effect will be the same?'

Nisha continued to focus on the cave's entrance. 'Yeah.'

'And something like adrenaline needs to go in a particular place like the heart.'

They both turned to look at Muriel.

'Well, this is more of an adrenaline job than a vaccine job.'

'Where does it need to go?' Nisha asked.

Muriel turned back to the cave, giving it all her attention. 'The heart.'

Nisha blinked hard and slow before punching Muriel in the arm. 'The heart?'

'The heart,' Muriel said rubbing her arm.

Jack said nothing. *The heart.*

'How are we even...' Nisha voice trailed off. 'I mean Jesus, Muriel.'

Muriel sat up, her dress damp from the cool ground. 'We should be able to walk around in there, it might be a squeeze at times but we just need to follow the blood.'

Jack's eyes widened. 'Follow the blood?'

'Not literally, or maybe it is literally, I'm not sure. We need to find a vein and follow it.'

'How do we know it won't be an artery and going away from the heart?' Nisha asked, her arms folded.

'Well,' Muriel said attempting confidence, 'we'll just deal with that if it happens.' She slid down from the outcrop and headed into the wound.

Sixteen

Jack scanned the lip of the wound with his phone light. Jagged cuts and tears had been made in the beast with saws and blades. A few tiny scales were scattered on the ground, like branches after a storm. A giant toothless mouth. The beam of light from Jack's phone torch reflected each scale back at him a different colour. In any other situation, it would have been beautiful.

Blood-soaked carts, shopping trolleys and every conceivable device designed to make pushing heavy loads easier littered the opening. Work had increased in the last few days, there had been no signs of industry before, just four guys with hacksaws. Mimi's project had picked up pace.

Jack stepped into The Dragon. Last time, he had stepped into a damp cave searching for The Dragon but now he knew what he was doing. And with one step he was inside a beast, a god, a cadaver and a tool to bring untold misery to millions.

Jack reached for the nearest wall and placed his palm on the damp surface. A hum of vibration, he put his ear against the muscle to check he wasn't imagining it. He didn't know if he was hearing it or feeling it or both but it was like a trickster spirit had packed the ocean behind the wall. Jack shut his eyes. 'It's alive.'

'Yeah,' Muriel said.

Jack opened his eyes and rolled them. 'I mean it's really alive. I can feel blood flowing back there.'

Nisha gave him a concerned look. 'Jack, you saw it blink.'

'Yeah, but this means it's got a pulse. I mean that might still have been a nerve but...' he held his hand up to the wall, '...I'm touching it. It's alive.'

Muriel touched the wall as well, and a flash of reverence fell across her face. 'Ok, you've realised what we've all known for days now. What of it?'

'You were right. We do need to put it to sleep.'

'I know I was right and,' she paused, her voice becoming softer, 'I'm glad we're on the same page. Let's go save the world.'

Mimi's gang had been thorough in butchering The Dragon, they had carved wide boulevards through the muscle of the creature. The ground was taut beneath Jack's feet and the air fresh and tinged with vanilla. Seams of alabaster fat ran like rivers in the divots and gullies of The Dragon's muscle. Tunnels darted off from the main thoroughfare, jutting out at regular intervals, some tunnels stopping after a few feet, the decision made that there was nothing worth exploring, no rich veins of fat or bone, no signs of organs or arteries to be tapped like maple trees, while other tunnels disappeared deep into The Dragon. Despite being cocooned in the shell of a dragon and far from trains and airports and city life there was still noise. Low and small but just as constant, it was the sound of a million moving parts, of oxygen being pumped around a mountain. It was the sound of life itself.

They continued further into The Dragon until they came across the hub of Mimi's operation. Scattered around the main tunnel were generators, tents, and even makeshift kitchens. A frontier town with dragon fever. The only thing the town needed was people.

The tents were a mix of styles: gazebos from garden centres, large camping tents and some made from khaki canvas you get from those strange shops selling old military equipment. They walked down the rows of empty tents until they heard whistling. They stopped.

Nisha pulled out a bloodied potato peeler and held it at the ready.

'Where did you get that from?' Jack asked in a low whisper.

'The restaurant.'

'Why's there blood on it?'

Nisha inspected the end of the utensil. 'Because I don't work there anymore.'

Muriel put a finger to her lips and they crept toward the tent flap hiding the whistler. It was the absentminded whistle of someone engaged in a mindless task. Jack and Nisha approached from the other side like the world's worst SWAT team. Nisha held the potato peeler above her head, ready to strike. Muriel counted down.

One.

Jack filled his lungs. *Move the atoms*

Two.

His bladder tightened. *Don't move the can.*

Three.

Muriel bent low and threw back the zip. Jack didn't

remember what happened next but he woke bound and in the dark.

The darkness was complete and covered every inch of Jack's world. His arms and wrists had been tied behind his back with rope. Not that it mattered, but the rope had been wrapped around his palms and fingers stopping any chance of magic.

The body is capable of much more than the five senses we give it credit for and Jack's were telling him he was still far underground in a place that had never seen sunlight. The over-powering stench of offal was another clue. He rolled onto his back and felt his body sink slightly into the soft embrace of dragon tissue. 'Muriel? Nisha?'

'Jack?'

'Nisha?'

'Jack!'

'Where's Muriel?'

'I don't know. Where are you? Where am I?'

Jack stumbled to his feet and walked towards where he hoped Nisha's voice was coming from. 'We're in The Dragon.' Jack could almost see her eye roll despite the darkness.

'I can always count on you to make me feel better about myself.'

Her voice was close. 'Keep talking, I think you're near.'

'What do you want me to say?'

Jack stumbled on the uneven ground. 'I don't know, sing if you have to.'

Out of the darkness came one of the worst renditions of *Puff the Magic Dragon* that Jack had ever heard. Nisha's voice scraped against his soul and willed him to find her sooner.

The song ended and Jack was still alone. 'I hate to say this but you need to sing something else.'

'But I don't know any more songs about dragons.'

Jack stopped dead. 'What?'

'I just heard it,' Nisha said and started up again with *What's New Pussycat?*

Jack carried on up the slope and her voice became more painful with each step. He sensed a presence in front of him and leant in with his shoulder and felt another form. 'Nisha?'

'Yes, are you ok?'

He could feel her breath but she was a bodiless voice in the dark. 'I think so, are you tied up too?' Jack asked.

'Yes, and they've taken my peeler. But if we went back to back I might be able to untie you.' After many apologies and some obligatory jokes about people buying other people dinner first, they realised they were too tightly bound to free each other.

'Now what?' Jack asked.

Nisha exhaled. 'We try and find Muriel? Where are we anyway?'

'We-'

'Don't say in The Dragon.'

'I wasn't going to. I was going to say we might be in an organ.'

'Like its liver?'

'I don't know but the ground is soft, much softer than before.' Jack jumped up and down on the balls of feet to prove his point. It was dark and Nisha didn't see, but the point stood.

'Is it?'

'Yes, this isn't muscle like before, it's something else.'

'Why would they put us in a liver?'

'I never said liver and I don't know. Besides, it's more likely we're *on* the liver. It's out the way and no one is going to find us,' Jack said. 'Maybe the plan is to leave us down here to starve.'

'Sod that, follow me.' Nisha grabbed hold of Jack's arm as best she could and started walking.

'Where are you going? You could be going the wrong way.'

'I'm in a dragon, there isn't a wrong way. Muriel!'

Jack felt it first. His hair shifted and stroked his forehead and ears. A perfectly normal sensation out of place nowhere except inside a dragon deep underground. A breeze. It built to a gust before becoming a gale. It cut across them and Jack needed to plant both feet into the ground to stop himself from falling over.

'What's happening?' Nisha asked.

'I don't know.'

The wind became relentless, a wall of pressure depriving them of breath. Jack turned into the wind and took deep lungfuls of air. *Of course.* 'Lungs!'

Jack lurched forward causing Nisha to break into a run.

There was no movement in the dark. No dark greys or patches of purple to give a sense of time or space. They could be running on the spot, about to fall off the edge of a precipice or moments from salvation. It was a lot like being back at work.

An organic rumble crept out of the darkness like a glacier moving at speed. It grew louder until it filled the darkness. The lungs were expanding towards them. *Giving The Dragon life and taking theirs.* They were going to be crushed against the rib cage. 'We need to be quicker.' Jack pulled on his reserves of energy and pushed Nisha forward. The air grew thick as molecules raced ahead of the ever-expanding lungs. The pressure grew and grew until Jack's mouth filled with the taste of iron, his temples burned and his breath became short.

The noise became overpowering but the expanding mass was still hidden in the dark. Jack knew it was close. An invisible death moments away.

Nisha cried out.

Jack saw it too. A light, an artificial man-made light. He held his breath and launched them towards it.

The light led Jack and Nisha to a tunnel that had nowhere to hide.

The tunnel twisted regularly like the diggers were in no rush to get to their location. Lamps had been placed on the floor illuminating every inch of every surface so the muscle walls were washed out and exposed. Jack and Nisha's shadows spun around them as they passed each light. The shadow leapt out in front, ten times their size, before shrinking back. Their hands still tied they ran how Jack imagined sock puppets to run if they had legs, the image caused a tiny giggle to escape his lips.

'What?' Nisha said. 'What is it?'

'Nothing,' Jack said behind a smile.

The smile caught on and Nisha wanted in on the joke. 'No, go on what?'

'It's just,' he said. 'It's just we're running like sock puppets. How they bob up and down as you move them along, that's what we're doing.' He ran in a wide circle bobbing up and down.

'That's not how sock puppets run, they run like this.' She

added a swing to her bob so she went left to right as well as up and down.

'That seems more like a string—' there was talking, ahead and out of sight. They both froze. Jack thawed first and herded Nisha against the wall with his shoulder. The tunnel veered left and hid the owner of the voice. *It was a stupid place to discuss puppetry.* Someone responded to the voice. *Two on two, they were equally matched.*

A laugh, it belonged to a third voice. *They were outnumbered and as good as dead.*

'What do we do?' Jack said in a whisper.

'Follow me.' Nisha crept forward, keeping low to the wall. The soft tissue surrounding them muffled the voices and Jack hoped it did the same for them. Inch by inch Jack skirted around the corner. Ahead, he could make out three figures sitting in a natural recess ten feet wide. A work lamp shone directly out of the recess into the tunnel, there was no way they could cross without being seen. Risking another step forward, Jack listened to the voices.

'And then the vicar went: I've got no trousers on!' a man said.

'That didn't really happen, did it?' a female voice said.

'No you idiot, it was a joke,' the man said with disdain.

'I know, I was joking too.'

'Do you think the lungs have got them yet?' a third voice, also male, said.

'Give it another ten minutes, I'm in no rush to get back to work. Are you?'

'What if we get caught?' the female voice said.

The question was repeated in mocking tones by the first man who Jack had decided was in charge.

'Hey, would you rather be crushed by a lung or drowned in stomach acid?' the third voice said.

Nisha turned to Jack. 'How do we get around?'

If they were smart enough to skive off work they might be smart enough to be reasoned with. 'Why don't we talk to them and explain our side of things and see if they'll help us?'

Nisha stared at Jack.

'What do you want to do then?'

She said nothing for a moment. 'Ok fine, but you go first.'

The thought of stepping in front of a group of gangsters, his hands tied, and asking them to see reason didn't scare Jack. He was worried but not scared, worried he would fail and let Muriel down but not scared of what might happen to him. Finding Muriel and stopping Mimi was more important than any risk to Jack's life. He felt less ok about realising that but maybe this is how real heroes feel. He took a deep breath, stepped out and put faces to the voices: two very gruff looking men and a female goblin. All three were fingering very big knives and sitting on upturned crates, the whole recess was being used as a storage area for tools and other equipment. 'Hello. I'm Jack. I think we've met before but I don't remember at the time as I had taken a blow to the head. This is Nisha. We wanted to check if you were entirely happy with your employment and the ethical ramifications of what your boss is planning. If not, why not untie us and help save the world.'

One of the men turned to the other. 'That didn't really happen, did it?'

'No, you idiot, it was a joke,' came the reply. The three stood, knives in hand.

Muriel would have known that three people who skive off work wouldn't take other parts of their job seriously, including how to fight and stab people. Jack didn't know this so when he lunged and ducked between swipes of blades, he couldn't figure out how he wasn't dead. In the midst of all the weaving and spinning, he came face to face with the female goblin and head-butted her without a moment's thought. He apologised.

She grabbed her bloodied nose and dropped the knife. Jack turned to see a different blade coming for him. He ducked and the knife slid into the gut of the goblin. Everyone froze. The goblin grabbed the blade from her gut and drove it deep into her colleague's neck showering Jack in blood.

The first to react to this turn of events, and with her hands still tied behind her back, was Nisha, who dropkicked their final quarry. She landed on the floor hard. The final man staggered back but stayed standing. He raised his knife to end Nisha. Jack jumped through the air, shoulder first and threw the killing blow off balance. The knife came down and became lodged in the tissue wall. Jack barged into the gruff man again. The gruff man swayed, he reached out and grabbed at Jack's arm to try and steady himself. Jack lost his balance and they both went down, Jack landing on top of the man with a thud.

'Keep him there!' Nisha called out. She had positioned a knife between her feet and began cutting through her binding.

Jack squirmed on top of the man but with his hands still tied, the man began to overpower him. Jack crawled so they were face to face and bit him on the nose. The sound of cartilage snapping vibrated up into Jack's skull.

'Move!' Nisha, now standing, yelled. Jack rolled. Her blade landed straight and true in the man's chest.

Jack wanted to scream, to weep, he wanted to run, not from fear of death but fear that that wasn't the worst thirty seconds of his life. He had fought and survived, and he might be able to do it again.

Nisha grabbed Jack's hands and freed him. She handed him

the knife and used a spell to make the knife in the wall appear in her palm.

'We did that,' Jack said, looking at the three corpses.

'We did, but we tried talking first. Come on we need to find Muriel,' Nisha said, heading off down the tunnel.

'You dropkicked that guy,' Jack said, still standing over the scene.

Nisha ran back and grabbed Jack. 'I did, it was awesome. We can talk about it later. We need to find Muriel. I won't lose her again.'

They set off down the tunnel at pace following the cables that ran between the work lamps.

'Muriel is ok. She wasn't in the lung because she escaped when they ambushed us and she got away,' Nisha said, taking the lead down yet another side tunnel. 'She's waging a one-woman guerrilla war on Mimi as we speak.'

Jack didn't say anything, he ran and wanted Nisha to be right.

'And we're armed now.' Nisha waved the knife. 'So we can help. Let's try and find the heart, I think that's where Muriel will be aiming for. We can meet her there, be her cavalry.'

'It's a good plan,' Jack said and offered a weak smile.

They ran through The Dragon and didn't meet another soul. They followed the cabling for the lights. Tunnels became passages which became corridors which became shafts and on and on it went. Nisha refused to slow in her search for Muriel.

Jack's muscles turned against him and refused to go on. 'We need to stop,' he said, leaning against the tunnel.

'No. We keep going.'

'This is pointless, we're lost. This thing is too big.'

Nisha paced with her hands on her hips. 'She's out there fighting on her own. We need to find her.'

Jack sat on the floor and put his head between his legs. 'Let me just sit for a bit.'

Nisha tutted but joined him anyway, her breathing deep and fast and her eyes filled with worry. The tunnel ahead veered to the left and out of sight. 'You know,' Jack said. 'I bet it's just around that corner. We'll stand and the heart, Muriel, all of it will be just round the bend. Like magic, I promise.'

Nisha let out a groan. 'Of course, I'm an idiot. The cavern provides!'

'What?'

'Magic Jack, we just need to do magic. Like Foresight.'

Jack's face said it all.

'We need to make the heart chamber appear around that corner using magic.'

'That's not how it works, it's just the one spell and it's for moving baked bean cans, not the internal organs of a dragon.'

'It's the same principle. Think of the hippies with their fire and food or Foresight. How does he know where you are? There might only be one spell but there's magic too.' Nisha stood again and Jack felt compelled to join her in case she ran off. She had the same glint in her eye that Jack's nan had had towards the end.

'Right, hang on. No,' she said. 'I've got it. The hippies had that awful chant "the cavern provides" or whatever and Foresight had his playing cards. We need something like that.' She held her knife up and smiled. 'I got it. You stand against that wall and I'll throw the knife just above your head and think really hard and then it will work.'

Jack's face said it all.

'Ok no, right, hang on,' she said.

'How about this?' Jack tried with a smile. He didn't believe what Nisha was suggesting would work but hope is a powerful thing. So is having five minutes to catch your breath. 'The chanting and playing cards are both rituals of sorts, maybe that's how they work. They clear the mind by doing one simple thing and we need to do the same. I admit, you throwing a knife at me would bring clarity of thought but perhaps we just need to sit.'

'To sit?'

'Sitting can be a ritual. Just for a few minutes and think about what we want. When we stand, Muriel will be just around that corner,' Jack said, lying on the ground in more ways than one.

Nisha seemed sceptical. 'Fine.'

They sat and rested and said nothing.

Muriel thought of the dinosaur she was chewing on and what kind of life it had had. Did it stalk the plains of Pangea and consume the flesh of weaker dinosaurs, or maybe, it was a nice one that ate leaves and had its flesh consumed? Either way, she doubted it could comprehend dying and its corpse being crushed by so much dirt it became a liquid. Then, for that liquid to be taken out of the ground millions of years later by mostly hairless monkeys who would turn it into nylon rope. Not all of it, of course, some of its body would float high in the atmosphere and look down on the planet it had once lived on like a crap reptilian nirvana.

She was making good progress gnawing at the rope that bound her hands and wrists, they had tied her palms together as if in prayer. Spitting out frayed pieces of plastic she cursed herself for falling for an ambush. She cursed herself more for bringing Jack and Nisha into this. They weren't here at least but that wasn't much comfort. There was nowhere good they could be, above or below ground, right now.

The tent she was held in was spartan even for a shanty town with just a rug and two chairs, one of which Muriel was tied to by her ankles, the syringe discarded on the floor. Her attackers hadn't realised its importance which was a blessing. Only a few more strands and she would be free.

'That's not very good for your teeth.' The Elf in The Paisley Suit stood at the opening of the tent. The Elf pulled a gleaming knife from her breast pocket and Muriel doubled her efforts with the rope.

The Elf grabbed Muriel's forearm and slid the knife through what remained of the rope. 'Better?'

Their eyes locked, two dinosaurs trying to figure out if the other wanted to eat leaves. Muriel's palm shot out and attempted to remove a fistful of The Elf's skull. She was quick but The Elf was quicker and sidestepped the spell. Still tied by her ankles, Muriel stood and swung her fist the old-fashioned way, but The Elf caught the blow. Pain shot up Muriel's arm as The Elf squeezed her nails into Muriel's closed fist and drew blood.

'Now you have two options,' the Elf said pushing Muriel back into the chair without letting go. 'You can keep fighting and it happens slowly or,' she dug her nails in further, 'you answer a few questions and maybe, just maybe, depending on your answers, you don't die and neither do your friends.'

Muriel drew back a glob of spit ready to give her answer and then a small voice tapped on her shoulder and reminded her that Nisha, and to a lesser degree Jack, were somewhere nearby at the mercy of this beautifully dressed psychopath. She swallowed.

'I thought so,' the Elf said. She used her free hand to pull up the other chair and sit opposite Muriel. 'Question one: Reece.'

Muriel's face shut down like a cheese shop in a recession. A mistake.

'As I suspected, did he always work for you, or did you turn him?'

Muriel hadn't heard from Reece since the pub but The Paisley Elf might be bluffing. The Elf squeezed and Muriel clenched her jaw to muffle a scream.

'Well?'

'Works for us! He's always worked for us and how are you doing that?' Muriel said, taking deep breaths to control the pain.

The Elf smiled. 'Steel-tipped false nails, my own invention. Do you like them?'

'No!'

'And what do you know because of him? What did he give you?'

She was being tortured for information and the very fate of the city rested on her resolve and strength. Muriel had imagined this exact situation a million times right down to the nylon rope. She had read about all the techniques, picturing yourself somewhere else, understanding the pain will pass, and reminding yourself you are a small cog in a mighty machine that you must serve. *She wasn't though. It was just her.* In all these situations, not once did she imagine there was a chance the pain would be happening to Nisha next.

'I don't know.'

The Elf went to squeeze.

Fear escaped Muriel's throat and took words with it. 'I

swear, he reports directly to The Laurels, not me. He said something about boxes.'

'There's more, I can tell.' The Elf applied some pressure.

'And notes! The Laurels mentioned some notes. He may have made copies of some notes and snuck out to them.'

The Elf loosened her grip. Cautiously, Muriel pulled her hand back and out of danger. She flexed her fingers and was relieved when everything seemed in working order.

'He was playing a role the whole time,' the Elf said to herself. Her eyes seemed to fade.

'Sorry, is this about a man?' Muriel said, taken aback. 'Is this about *Reece*?'

'No, of course not.' The Elf sat up and avoided eye contact.

'Reece? Reece who wears a straw hat. Look at my hand.' Muriel shoved her hand under The Elf's nose. 'You may have caused me permanent nerve damage over Reece. Reece who insists on My Fair Lady code names. Reece who irons his socks.'

'His socks?' This seemed to snap The Elf out of it.

Muriel dropped her hands to her sides and as close to her bound ankles as she dared. 'If you don't mind me saying I think you've lost your way a bit.' One by one Muriel summoned the rope fibres into her palms. 'You are one of the scariest people I've ever met. When you came in here I thought I was dead. Not a chance in hell dead. But if you keep running around doing things like this people are going to talk. Trust me, image is everything in this line of work.' She tried to pull her ankles away from the chair. Still too tight.

'I know that.' The Elf stood and started to worry the rug.

Muriel closed her fists to hide her plan.

The Elf turned to face her. 'But don't you ever get tired of playing the role?'

'Of course,' Muriel said. 'I'm not saying you can't have a

private life, if anything I've learnt you need one otherwise you'll go mad. You just can't let anyone at work know you have a pen or that you want to dip it in ink.' She would have to risk it. Muriel opened her fists a fraction and continued working on the rope.

'But where do you find ink that isn't company ink?' The Elf started to pace again.

'That is tricky, I'll admit, but have you considered pencils or highlighters?'

The Elf stopped in her tracks. 'I think we've stretched this metaphor as far as we can.'

Muriel stood and threw a fist full of rope fibres into the air in one smooth motion. The Elf followed the fibres expectantly and didn't see Muriel's left hook until it was too late.

Muriel watched The Elf in The Paisley Suit for a moment to make sure she was out cold. *God, it was a good suit. Did she have time to check the label and see where it was from?* She shook her head, ran over to the syringe and slipped it into her jacket pocket. She picked up the rest of the nylon rope, looked at both chairs and then at The Paisley Elf.

Muriel tightened the last knot and gave The Paisley Elf a little slap. She was still out cold. Muriel stood and left the tent. There stood a woman who had to be Mimi Kensington-Jones. She stood like a fixed point in space and time. Around her were half a dozen minions, armed with knives and axes. 'I was just coming to see you,' Mimi said.

Muriel's hand shot out and aimed for Mimi's throat. Muriel's arm spasmed and stiffened, her palm empty and Mimi unhurt.

Pain shot through Muriel's head like lightning. She fell to

her knees. A goblin came into view holding a pipe smeared with Muriel's blood.

'Very good,' Mimi said. 'Get me my crowbar and hammer.'

'What about her?' someone said. Mimi walked over to the tent and saw what The Elf in The Paisley Suit had got herself into. She tutted at what she saw. 'Leave her.'

Muriel's arms were grabbed and bound again.

SEVENTEEN

Nisha stood in an infinite abyss and prepared herself for the ritual. She didn't have time to worry about how she got here. Jack had told her to rest but he was wrong. She had to do something. She needed a ritual and there was one ritual she was born to do. Nisha's father had done it. Her grandfather had done it before him. She had heard rumours of an uncle up north who had done it with such aplomb that it had landed him a girl-friend. Nisha's aunt wasn't best pleased when she found out. And now, it was Nisha's turn. This day was inevitable really — a family rite of passage — one she had been avoiding but if it meant she found Muriel then Nisha would do it. She would do it until her feet bled and her muscles ached. She would do it with all her heart as it was the only way it could be done. She jingled up to her dance partner and pulled a bright white hankie from her pocket. It was just her and The Dragon. She didn't know if she was big or if it was small but it didn't matter. The Dragon nodded, signalling it was ready. The dance began.

EIGHTEEN

Much to his annoyance, Jack was shaken awake by Nisha. Detective Campbell was finally going to show him why she was Clyde Valley's foremost law enforcer.

'Jack,' Nisha said. She stood over him, out of breath and pleased with herself.

'I wasn't asleep.'

'Sure, but I've done it.'

'Done what?'

'A ritual,' Nisha said. 'I decided you were half right but sitting down was stupid so I did something else.'

'Dare I ask?' They were still in the tunnel. It could have been minutes or hours.

'I thought that it needs to be a proper ritual like chanting or tarot cards so I thought: Morris dancing.'

'Morris dancing?'

'Yep, ancient, bit weird: ritual.'

'I'm sorry I missed that.'

'Me too, but come on.' She pulled him up. 'When we go round this corner we'll find Muriel. You ready?'

Jack picked up his knife and gave it a shake to signal he was ready.

He took a deep breath, and tried to think what he would say when they went around the corner and found more endless tunnel. Jack shut his eyes to delay the inevitable disappointment. He heard Nisha gasp.

'It's ok, we'll keep looking.' He opened his eyes to find the tunnel had ended. Ahead, was a room bathed in blue light.

The tunnel gave way to a vast chamber filled with a natural blue light emitting from the centre. Pillars that looked manmade jutted out from the wall and it took Jack a beat to realise they were ribs. The bones flew upwards and arched overhead as if someone had made a temple to, and out of, a leviathan. Hanging in the middle was a rolling mass of muscle, claret red and latticed with veins of fluorescent blue light that were bright enough to make other light sources unnecessary. It was designed for one purpose: to be the engine of a living mountain. And it was beating. Flooding tissue, organs and capillaries with blood. Muscles tightening and organs waking from dormancy to power a creature larger than a city. A creature that knew the impossibility of flight, had seen civilisations expand and gorge themselves to death. And it was stirring. If it woke it would destroy everything.

Jack took the lead and they crept forward, sticking as close to the ribs as they could.

Mimi's gang moved with a chaotic energy. Bosses barked orders at subordinates who carried out their tasks with care and due diligence until they were out of sight and earshot of their superiors. There seemed to be three main tasks being carried out: first, a group of five or six figures stood on top of hastily built scaffolding that reached up to the heart. They worked in small groups to scrape off whatever was causing the blue light. This was passed to a second group who collected it in buckets and, once full, passed them down the scaffolding to a waiting chain gang of thirty or forty that dumped it in a pile in front of a wooden table where it was grabbed by the fistful and pounded in pestle and mortars. Finally, a last group stood around the table doing very little. Everyone seemed armed with the type of weapon you could get in any DIY shop: hammers, crowbars, there were even some garden forks. Moving closer still, Jack saw someone, a woman, sitting at the table with her back to him. 'That's her,' Nisha said with a grin. 'That's Mimi. She *is* wearing the same red suit as the other day. Muriel's going to be furious.'

She didn't look like a would-be dictator. She looked like someone on the train home staring at her phone with a furious glint in her eye, trying to stop the world from ending one out-of-hours email at a time. She was Atlas with a portable phone charger.

The heart began to swell and twist in on itself.

A wary panic spread through the workers on the scaffolding. They grabbed their tools and buckets and headed down to the ground.

The heart's movements reached their zenith and began to contract.

All work stopped.

A beat. A pulsing living beat. A blinding blue light filled the space and a wave of pressure rushed out. The force was so great Jack had to brace himself. The light began to fade. In front of Mimi, bathed in a dying blue light and blood lay a body. A mass of red hair pulled back into a bun and an A-line skirt crumpled around it.

Nisha lurched toward Muriel. Jack grabbed her and pulled

her back. 'We'll get her, we'll save her, just not yet. She would want us to stop Mimi.'

'I don't care about Mimi, I care about Muriel.' Nisha tried to fight out of Jack's grip.

'I do too, but if you run out there you'll die,' he said.

Nisha's shoulders slumped in resignation. Jack let go. 'What's the plan then?' she said without taking her eyes off Muriel.

'Do you think Muriel's still got the syringe on her? They'd be unlikely to find it and think "This must be dragon tranquilliser", right?'

Nisha's eyes were fixed on Muriel and she didn't answer.

Mimi's men had returned to work, and great sweeping movements filled the space. Not a person or moment was wasted. Jack had nothing, no idea of what to do next. It was an impregnable mass, there was no way they could get to Mimi or Muriel but he would try anyway. 'Wait for my signal. Get the syringe, kill Mimi.'

'What's the signal?' Nisha asked. But he was gone. 'What's the signal?'

When The Elf in The Paisley Suit got back to the surface she would check if the Germans had a word for it. They had a word for everything. It wouldn't be Schadenfreude, more Mich-Schaden or maybe MichSchadenfreude: to take pleasure in harm done to oneself. The Germans had to have a word for it. The Paisley Elf stopped biting at the knots that bound her wrists to admire the work and rest her jaw. Tying the chairs to her instead of the other way around. It was brilliant and something she'd be doing going forward. You think you've seen everything, a master of your art, and then someone ties one chair to your chest with your arms outstretched so you're hugging it and bound at the wrists and then ties another chair between your legs with the back riding high to stop you sitting. You could still waddle, which was somehow worse than being stuck to the spot. You could go and get help but then someone would see you like this. Keeping someone captive with their own ego. She blinked to stop the tears of joy and started working the knot again with her teeth.

Jack walked with confidence and pretended he belonged, his old work persona was back from the dead. Slipping the knife into the top of his trousers, he headed for the middle of the chain gang at a point that seemed unsupervised by upper management. He scanned the workers until he saw what he was after, a squat elf sweating under the strain of passing buckets. Jack grabbed the elf's bucket and spoke before they had a chance to react. 'The boss wants to see you.' Jack stepped into the chain gang like it was the most normal thing in the world.

'Did he say what he wanted?' the squat elf said with a hint of panic in his voice.

Jack shrugged and continued passing buckets along the line.

'Did he seem mad?'

'No more than normal.'

The elf stood rooted to the spot, his eyes darted from left to right replaying everything he'd done that day.

Jack put his bucket down causing traffic to build up. 'He probably isn't mad but if you keep him waiting he will be.'

The elf nodded and walked off at speed leaving Jack to roll

his eyes at his neighbour who waited expectantly with the next bucket.

Once the backlog had gone Jack took a chance to peer into the buckets as they passed. They were full of tiny blue crystals, thousands of them in each bucket. Jack was new to the world of magic but guessed that these were the crux of Mimi's plan. Now he just needed a signal and a plan of his own otherwise this might be the second train crash he was involved in today. *Which might not be the worst thing.* He grabbed the bucket off his neighbour, turned and shoved the bucket to the next person in the line with a smirk that threw down the gauntlet. The neighbour took the challenge and sped up.

The Paisley Elf jumped out of the last loop of rope keeping her tied to the chair. She ran out of the tent and down the carved boulevard towards the heart. She pulled a piece of paper, folded into a neat square, from her pocket. Handwritten on cheap lined paper, it contained a list of events that had shaped the last fifty years. Times when the country had worked together, to solve problems, to fund solutions, times when the underdog had won, times when people had seen the big picture and times when they hadn't listened to that little voice that was so full of doubt and fear. She closed her eyes. She could still remember these times which meant Mimi hadn't succeeded yet.

Sweat dripped down into Jack's eyes as he worked faster and faster. Shunting buckets to his left and taking them from the right. *Shunt take.* Crystals were passed from worker to worker filling the chamber with a rhythmic beat. *Shunt take.* Jack's arms became burdens, his muscles spent from bucket after bucket. *Shunt take.* The supervisors seemed pleased at the burst of energy. *Shunt take.* They yelled at the workers to go faster still. *Shunt take.* The workers scraping the crystals worked harder and harder to meet demand. *Shunt take.* Jack risked a glance behind him. *Shunt take.* Muriel hadn't moved. Her skin was pale and her eyes closed. Jack saw the source of the blood: two holes — crude circles — had been punctured through her palms. *Shunt take.* The buckets were only half full now. *Shunt take.* The workers had become one. *Shunt take.* They moved without thinking. It was time. *Shunt take.* Jack took a bucket and dropped it. His neighbour bent down to pick it up. Jack did the same. The next worker in the chain didn't notice and passed another bucket to no one. It fell to the ground with a clang. The machine faltered at every point. Springs burst and tempers frayed. A shout led to a shove which led to blows being exchanged further down the line. Chaplin would be proud.

The Paisley Elf left the shanty town behind. The lighting became sporadic as she neared the heart chamber. When they had realised the size of the beast they had rationed the lamps until their only use was to guide you through the darkness. She ran through the darkness and headed for the light. The telltale blue glow of the heart crept over the walls of the tunnel. Yelling and the all too familiar sound of fist on flesh drifted down the tunnel. She clicked her knuckles and pushed herself on.

The blue light was intense and she stopped at the entrance to the chamber to let her eyes adjust. A riot had broken out under the heart, a mass of brawling figures swung at each other, crushing crystals underfoot. The whole enterprise, Mimi's grand plans, reduced to a bar fight.

Mimi's face glowed red, her rage overpowering the blue light. The Elf watched the fighting and thought of flour and eggs and butter. She thought of rose water and the human drive for sugar and fat and wondered if the lump of fat and pile of sugar had gotten too big. Sugar and fat made everything possible and nothing seem impossible. She thought about turning down her OBE and wondered when she stopped wanting to not have things. It was time.

Mimi stood and rested her fingertips on the table. 'Stop.'

And they did.

She walked around to the front of the table. The sound of spilt crystals crunching underfoot was the only noise. The room turned to face her and waited.

Jack, who, moments ago was watching a fist hurtle towards his face, took two steps towards a man a foot shorter than him in case the fighting started up again. Mimi's eyes darted to the movement. She pointed at Jack. The room turned to him. *Oh well.* He went to bolt but a multitude of arms grabbed him and dragged in front of Mimi.

A noise like all the meat being stripped from a roast chicken in one smooth motion surrounded Jack. Jack's guards fell to the ground, chunks missing from limbs and torsos. The chamber coiled ready to face an unseen threat. More of Mimi's men fell before a goblin spotted Nisha running towards the heart, with one hand she cast spell after spell, and the other held the syringe taken from Muriel's pocket. The room sprung at her.

Nisha reached the scaffolding, pushing her way past henchmen, she neared the top.

'Slice the poles, you idiots!' Mimi shouted. Several of Mimi's men stepped forward and fired spell after spell at key supports, reducing them to scrap metal and bringing down a section of the tower down in a flurry of havoc and fury. Nisha fell.

The world held its breath, waiting to see if anyone would emerge from the pile of broken metal. Jack tried to run forward. His wrist kept him in place; Mimi held him in a czar-like grip. She pulled him close until they were face to face, twisting his wrist and sending searing pain along his arm. His knees buckled as she leered over him. She smiled and held out her other hand expectantly. A moment of stillness passed before Jack felt a cold sting where the tips of his fingers should be. His nails split and fractured. Dismembered lumps of Jack's hand landed gently in Mimi's palm. Finger bones cracked and splintered sending pain down into his palm and forearm.

Jack turned to see Muriel's lifeless body. He saw the pile of metal that entombed Nisha. He reached into the top of his trousers and pulled out the knife. Swinging hard, he swung the blade at Mimi's neck. The blade bent, bouncing off her skin, and jumped out of his hand.

She laughed at his futile attempt. Jack had heard the laugh before, it was the laugh of someone who had never failed, the laugh of someone who mistook opportunity for talent, the laugh of someone who thinks advantage is work ethic.

'I was only going to take your fingers but for that, I'll keep going.'

His knuckle bones popped out of his palm one by one.

Jack swung again at Mimi and again she laughed. Her smug red mouth filled Jack's vision. Against her pale plastic skin, her mouth seemed grotesque like a pimple waiting to be popped. He opened his palm. *Don't move the can. Muriel's lifeless body. Slice the space.* The pimple was gone, replaced with a void.

Jack floated, still held in the air by Mimi's lagging arm.

Everything was in balance and perfect.

Gravity returned and Mimi's arm let him go. He fell to the ground, still holding the innards of her skull and the roof of her mouth

The ground didn't shake, it moved. It tilted. The buckets, forgotten in the fight, began to tumble from one end of the chamber to another. Slowly at first, they gained speed, dancing and bouncing past Jack. The scaffold poles rattled and clanged as they chased after the buckets. Next came the realisation of what was happening, it jumped from brain to brain keeping pace with the buckets and poles. Mimi's remaining men ran back to the tunnel, back through the shanty town and out to the cavern.

The ground slid upwards nearly throwing Jack off balance. He ran over to the cairn of metal that contained Nisha. He tugged and pulled, he threw in anger. Her face bloodied and her eyes closed. Jack cursed and offered prayers to any god that would listen. Nisha coughed and spluttered, her eyes opened. Relief swelled in Jack and he threw up.

'Jesus, Jack,' Nisha said.

'Sorry.'

With help from Jack's good hand, Nisha pulled herself out of the rumble. Blood ran down her head from cuts and gashes but she he thought she would be okay. 'Where's Muriel?'

Muriel.

Under the blue light, Muriel seemed almost angelic, Jack had got to know Muriel quite well in the last few days and knew it was just a trick of the light. Nisha went to hold Muriel's hand, saw the wounds and hesitated. She grabbed her shoulders instead and shook.

The ground moved again. The Dragon was waking up and it was all Jack's fault, all of it. He had climbed into its eye and woke it. But he could stop it too. Jack left Nisha to her grief and searched amongst the debris for the syringe. *There.*

He scrambled up the scaffolding, loose planks of wood sliding under his feet. The heart began to swell, the blue light grew stronger. He took a running jump over the gap where Nisha had fallen and landed badly. He lost his grip on the syringe as he tried to stop himself from falling. The syringe rolled out of his hand towards the edge of the platform. 'Nice try,' he said, grabbing it. Heart muscles contracted ready to unleash another beat.

The metal casing felt cool in Jack's palm. The gold serum danced behind the glass window. He stood in front of The Dragon's heart. It filled his vision. Blue light and red muscle. The Dragon was all. It was everything.

The needle pierced the skin with ease. Jack's hand rested on the plunger, ready to push and save the day. He turned to see Nisha sitting next to Muriel, neither of them moving. The corpses of Mimi's gang littered the ground around them. Jack tried to hold The Dragon in his mind, but he couldn't. This great unknown creature, alive under London was too big. Stripped and mined so some petty human could feel powerful. Even now they had stopped Mimi, Jack knew it wouldn't be the end of it. Someone else would find it and continue Mimi's work, they might not have the same plan but humans are limitless in their desire for greatness. Jack now realised the problem wasn't The Dragon or even Mimi, it was the power that The Dragon could give you. People are fine, they're not great but they try to not get in each other's way. Give them a whiff of power and they go insane. The Dragon was pure physical lunacy. Maybe Jack was different? He now knew the answer to the question they had posed to him at the train station. He would sneak back down and carve out a chunk for himself. He wouldn't do anything evil with it, just bend reality to win a few horse races or magic up a big pile of untraceable fifty-pound notes. The creature could support one person's small dreams. Jack didn't want a dream, he wanted a life, one with purpose.

Jack took his hand off the plunger, pulled the syringe out of the heart and dropped it from the platform onto the ground below, the glass shattered, spilling the solution.

It was over, The Dragon would wake.

'Jack!' It was Nisha. 'She's alive!'

On cue, the heart pumped a beat and filled the chamber with a gale of pressure. Jack was thrown backwards, off the scaffolding and into the air. He didn't know if it was the idea of The Dragon waking or Muriel being alive but a lightness flooded through him as he fell. There was no time to feel pain, he got to his feet and ran to Muriel.

Her eyes fluttered.

'We don't have long. It's waking up,' Jack said. He picked up Muriel's arm and wrapped it around his neck. Nisha, without a word, grabbed Muriel's other arm and Jack led them away from the heart.

Muriel coughed and Nisha let out a joyous laugh.

· · ·

They followed a tunnel leading out of the heart chamber that ran straight and wide to the shanty town. It was downhill the whole way as the dragon slowly stood. *The Dragon was standing up.*

Muriel drifted in and out of concussions. She garbled orders before passing out again. Jack didn't have time to think about what Muriel would do, he would have to act. He would get them out alive.

The wound they had entered through came into view. The cavern outside shifted downward as The Dragon ascended. The last of Mimi's henchmen jumped the few feet to the cavern floor and were gone.

Jack and Nisha approached the edge of the wound. It was ten feet drop to the ground and rising fast. The canopy of the forest floated past as they climbed ever higher. Jack slipped Muriel into Nisha's arms.

'What are you doing?' Nisha asked.

'I'm not sure.' He took a few steps back from the edge to get a run-up.

For one glorious moment, Jack flew. For the rest, he hurtled towards the ground screaming.

A branch broke his fall and likely a rib.

He landed hard on the soft moss-covered ground. Eyes closed, he waited to see if he was dead.

'Jack!' Nisha called out.

'I'm not dead. I think.'

'I don't care. I mean I do. I'm happy for you but we need to leave.'

Nisha and Muriel must have been twenty or thirty feet from the ground now. 'Jump!'

'Are you insane? I'll die and if I don't, I'll break every bone in my body.'

'I'll catch you.'

'What!'

'Nisha, do you trust me?'

Forty feet. It would reach the cavern roof soon. It would burst through and it would all end. 'Well? Do you?' Jack called out.

'Yes,' Nisha said. 'Get ready.' Carrying Muriel, she had no room for a run-up and they dropped like a stone.

Don't move the can. Muriel's lifeless body. It was always there. Jack held out his arms. Nisha and Muriel disappeared. They were simply gone; only to appear in Jack's waiting arms. They fell into a heap with Jack acting as little more than a crash mat.

Jack crawled out from under his friends and checked on Muriel. She was bleeding heavily from her palms. Jack was never great at counting pints — things always got blurry after the third — but she must be down to six or seven.

They picked Muriel up and carried her towards the sewer tunnel and aimed for the surface. In the dark, The Dragon's form blocked out the lights above. Chaos enveloped them. Half-remembered landmarks were their only guide. The roof began to fall in and the sound of the world changing filled Jack's head. The city would follow. A great gush of wind whipped past them. Air filled the space left by The Dragon as it stood, blood rushing to ancient limbs. Endless muscles moving skyscraper bones. They turned a corner and came face to face with it.

They stood and waited. The Dragon's great eyes burned with life.

'What do we do?' Nisha whispered.

The Dragon's gaze held them in place. It took them in and tried to understand them. It wasn't a mountain or a monster. It

was a thing. A strange unknowing thing but no more or less strange and unknowing than anyone else. *"You can't go around thinking something is out to get you just because it looks odd."*
'Nothing, we let it go,' he said.

'I know that! How do we not die?'

'We run like hell.'

They emerged into the open air to find the sun setting, turning the city a brilliant purple. The dried blood and dust that coated their clothes had congealed to a mucky mauve, allowing them to hide amongst the fading light. They had missed most of the chaos. The cavern that had hidden The Dragon for centuries now stood like a gaping maw at the centre of the city.

Sunlight filled the cavern. Even with The Dragon gone, trees filled every inch of the land under London. The ancient forest ran through and under the city for miles in every direction. London had been built on a living thing, the city had taken without asking or thinking, and now life had escaped as it always did.

The Thames, the river that once cut the city in two and gave it life, spilt uselessly onto the ancient forest below. The once great geological spectacle of the capital reduced to a water feature. Flocks of birds flew out of the cavern. They danced on unseen winds.

Cut off from its source, the riverbed on this side of the cavern was already drying out. Flowers shot through the mud, tiny yellow and purple things, no bigger than pound coins. The buildings that had escaped the initial calamity succumbed and collapsed. The sky began to cloud over and a light drizzle fell. Jack realised he hadn't felt rain in months and it felt good.

With tectonic wings, The Dragon passed overhead and

blocked out the fading light. Finally free after centuries, it soared over the city, immeasurable in size, it mocked every known law that humans had to understand the world.

There were dragons in the world again.

There were dragons in the world again but also magic and a city that floated above a forest.

The Dragon passed twice more before heading north followed by a billowing cloud of life as moss, trees and soil fell from its body.

Muriel was awake and asked to sit. They climbed down onto the dried riverbed and walked to the edge of the hole. Jack lowered Muriel to the ground and sat next to her.

'I think I did the right thing,' Jack said.

Muriel's eyes focused and took in the scene in front of her. Her head swung to Jack, her gaze deep with unsaid things.

'I do too,' Nisha said, without looking away from the remains of the city. 'The Dragon was always going to escape in some form, it's too big. With Mimi's plan or someone else's, or just like this. The city as we knew it disappeared the moment Mimi found it. This was inevitable.'

The drizzle became fully-fledged rain.

The maw was still. It would grow no more, content with consuming the city's core.

Muriel took a deep breath. 'I think—'

Jack looked out over the destruction he had wrought, at the travesty he had perpetrated, and knew what Muriel was going to say. That a city that was a haven for all was gone and could never be replaced, but she was wrong. London had been many things before and would be many things again. It would adapt and come up with new ways of doing things. Jack didn't know how these new things would play out or what they would look like but, sitting there, with miles of trees stretching in every direction, he did know there would be a forest at its heart.

'We should get out of the rain,' Muriel said at last.

'Typical isn't?' Nisha said, helping Muriel stand up. 'I finally get a day off and it rains.'

NINETEEN

The mixer on the kitchen countertop juddered around like an uncle at a wedding reception. Suze took a step back and tried to see if there was a way to unplug it without getting closer. 'Jenny, can you get in here? This contraption of yours is possessed.'

Jenny stared out of the front door and watched a murmuration of starlings fly over the houses on the other side of the street. It had been a week since The Dragon had woken from its slumber and destroyed Central London. In a similar fashion, a beech tree had burst through the pavement, fully formed, and now towered over the house, casting a cooling shade. Trees, owls and starlings as well as countless other forms of life that Jenny couldn't name had returned to the city. It had rained a lot as well, which the residents of Epping were particularly grateful for. 'Hmm?'

'I said, come and turn this ridiculous device off before I throw it out the window.'

Jenny took one last look at the starlings before returning to the kitchen. She stopped in the hallway to stroke a decrepit dog she had found under London. Suze had named it Flapjack. It slobbered over her hand with its toothless jaws. It gnawed as best it could but gave no chase when she stood to find out what was wrong with the mixer.

Suze was attempting to turn the mixer off at the wall by lunging at the switch with a broom.

'It's fine, you just had it set too high, see.' With a flick of a switch, the mixer calmed and slowly plodded in a circle like a different uncle at the same wedding. She removed the bowl and presented the well-mixed batter to Suze who pursed her lips in begrudging respect.

'We'll see...' Suze said.

The radio was full of chatter about sightings of The Dragon as it headed north. There had been a roiling sea of experts on as well, talking about everything that had happened. They said we would need to come up with different ways of living now that the city was covered in trees. The only other news story was that the death toll from the destruction wrought by The Dragon was much lower than first thought — it seems that when the world is ending, people don't go to work.

'Oh, I almost forgot,' Jenny said, putting the bowl down. She began rooting around in her bag. 'I was reading about the Winchester Standard Measurements and realised they would have been used when the pound cake was invented instead of Imperial Measurements, which means we've been making pound cake with the wrong amounts this whole time.' Finding what she was after, she pulled a cast iron weight from her bag and held it proudly for Suze to inspect. 'It's a Winchester Pound. With this, we can try pound cake as intended.'

Suze considered this. 'There's a logic to it. Let's make a batch and see what comes out. Grab your apron.'

Jenny looped her apron over her head and tied a knot with the string. She flattened the Paisley material, made from a suit she wore at an old job, and got to work.

ACKNOWLEDGMENTS

I would like to thank Emma for encouraging me from day one. Damien Mosley, Kate Pasola, and the whole team at Indie Novella thank you for spotting the potential in this story and making it a hundred times better. To Victoria Heath Silk for the excellent cover. Bill, Hilke, Steve and Matt for their advice and feedback. Olivia, for the Latin — please direct all complaints about that bit of Greek to her. Mum, Dad and Kara too. To my friend Jack, who isn't the inspiration for the fictional Jack, thank you for being cool and letting me use your name in my book.

THE ROCK 'N' ROLL OF INDIE PUBLISHING

We're Indie Novella and we were founded by a group of friends with one mission, to make publishing more accessible to everyone.

We love literary fiction, but we don't love the snobbery that gets associated with it. Great literary fiction comprises of stories that capture our imagination and resonate with us. Stories that shed light on modern issues, which use relatable and understandable language, which are about characters who speak for the communities we live in.

That's why we're publishing novels which make literary fiction less elitist and get readers as passionate about books as we are. We're also revolutionising publishing by doing something so few others are. Levelling the playing field. Our writing course is funded by the Arts Council and has been designed in collaboration with leading literary agencies such as Watson Little, David Godwin Associates and Georgina Capel and is completely free.

When it comes to writing and storytelling we believe there are so many voices that go unheard. Therefore we made a vow: We won't sit down. We won't shut up. We will commit to being our authentic selves. Just like our authors.

Stories of identity, community, belonging, and being proud of who we are. Our authors write the stories that represent what they stand for, in a truly authentic voice.

If that's not Rock 'n' Roll, I don't know what is.

indie
NOVELLA